# THE GIRL WITH THE RED RIBBON

CARLY SCHABOWSKI

Boldwood

First published in Great Britain in 2024 by Boldwood Books Ltd.

Copyright © Carly Schabowski, 2024

Cover Design by JD Smith Design Ltd.

Cover Photography: Shutterstock

Interior images designed by JD Smith Design Ltd.

The moral right of Carly Schabowski to be identified as the author of this work has been asserted in accordance with the Copyright, Designs and Patents Act 1988.

Every effort has been made to obtain the necessary permissions with reference to copyright material, both illustrative and quoted. We apologise for any omissions in this respect and will be pleased to make the appropriate acknowledgements in any future edition.

A CIP catalogue record for this book is available from the British Library.

Paperback ISBN 978-1-83603-497-1

Large Print ISBN 978-1-83603-498-8

Hardback ISBN 978-1-83603-496-4

Ebook ISBN 978-1-83603-499-5

Kindle ISBN 978-1-83603-500-8

Audio CD ISBN 978-1-83603-491-9

MP3 CD ISBN 978-1-83603-492-6

Digital audio download ISBN 978-1-83603-494-0

This book is printed on certified sustainable paper. Boldwood Books is dedicated to putting sustainability at the heart of our business. For more information please visit https://www.boldwoodbooks.com/about-us/sustainability/

Boldwood Books Ltd, 23 Bowerdean Street, London, SW6 3TN

www.boldwoodbooks.com

*To my niece Emily, whose youthful, teenage exuberance is a delight to behold. Also, it makes me feel old. So thanks for that.*

There is no great genius without a touch of madness.

— ARISTOTLE

# INTRODUCTION

In 1968, Benjamin Herschell read that an author, Cilka Shaw Crosby, was writing a history that perhaps he was a part of. She had set out in a newspaper article that she was looking for people native to Lublin, who understood the forests, and what happened and when. She wanted, she said, to investigate those stories and memories that were laced with trauma. She wanted to know what the horror they had witnessed had done to them and how it had shaped their history.

He wasn't an intellectual fellow and could not quite grasp the historical facts that this author had set forth. There were names of forests that he did not know; battles he was sure had happened, but was unsure of whether he had witnessed them or not; people he was sure he had met, but their faces and even names were a blur to him. The facts that the author spoke of didn't seem to fit with the picture in his mind. He could not meld the two together – the apparent historical truth and his reality.

He had never been one to know much. Names of places had

never been able to lodge themselves in his brain for long, memories merged together, and even days of the week and months were sometimes hard to track. It wasn't that he didn't try to, it was just that he couldn't. And, in the days when events seemed to fold themselves one on top of the other, moulding themselves into a revolting sculpture, it became harder and harder to know what was real and what was not, what had happened when, and whether in fact he had even been there at all.

There was one person, though, that he remembered. And remembered still. Ania Sobolewska. He wondered whether this author would write about her – a woman who looked like a girl, a genius and yet one who was also affected by a form of madness. She was still spoken about, he supposed. She had become a story that parents told their children, her exploits becoming more and more exaggerated upon each time her story was told. In the bars, men would talk about her too, again making her more and more mythical so that when Benjamin would return home, he would have to remind himself that those stories were not true – that he was the only one who'd known anything of who she had been.

He hoped that the author would not try to write all these fantastical stories. He hoped that they would not pick apart the woman he once knew and change the history that he had shared with her – the only thing that had stayed in his mind all these years.

Benjamin was left, then, with no other option but to try to piece together a history of his own, one that was fragmented, yet one that might just be more real than any fact could aspire to present.

There was just one problem. There was someone he needed to speak to.

Ania.
But Ania was dead.

# 1

Benjamin Herschell was old. He was nearing eighty, and his hands no longer worked as they should – swollen at the joints, bent and weak; he could barely open a jar. His legs too had become harder to drag as he walked – and indeed he did drag them.

The old man made his way through the Parczew forest, a hand on each tree as he passed it to steady himself, the bark damp under his fingertips after that morning's rain. In his other hand he held a sepia photograph, one he had taken himself so many years ago. It was creased in the middle and the left corner was torn, but the photograph was the only one he had of her – as macabre as it was.

As he walked, he could hear the sounds of a church bell ring out to the faithful. It was Sunday and the Catholics would be going to Mass, all dressed up and scrubbed as if God was worried about how clean you were – like that could absolve you of some sin. He shook his head. God didn't care about that – at least he hoped not.

He stopped for a moment in a small clearing. The dead leaves underfoot had lost their autumnal crunch and had started to rot, turning into a mulch underfoot and letting off a heady scent that he realised he quite liked.

There was a flutter of wings high up above him and it made him think of the day he had first met Ania. In a barn where pigeons roosted, where their coos and constant pitter patter of their feet gave him comfort in the quieter hours.

The bells had stopped. They were inside now, all of them praying and listening to their priest. Would they be absolved of their sins this Sunday? Would they be free from the ache of guilt they carried?

He began to walk again, and now and then his eyes caught a glimpse of the photograph in his hand. Black. White. A face. Eyes closed. Hands clasped. Not moving, not seeing.

A few more steps got him to a large oak, the biggest in the woods, he knew. He rested his forehead for a second on its trunk and whispered a prayer.

Then he sat, leaning against the bark, and cleared away some leaves from the ground until he could see fresh soil. He placed the photograph down and stared at it.

Here she was. Dressed in white, her face white too. Eyes closed. Hair black, that ribbon tied around her wrist – black too, in this photograph, but he knew the ribbon to be blood red. She looked as if she were asleep, but he knew she hadn't been. He had stood here, long ago, and taken the photograph of her in her makeshift coffin with Levi's camera – one thing he had brought with him when he had fled his home, a camera that he treasured, it seemed, more than a thick winter coat. Levi had shown Benjamin how to use it, and he stood close beside him whilst he took the photograph before she was lowered into the ground, then snatched the camera back from his hands and held it to his chest like a small child. It had been only after the war had ended that Benjamin had received the photograph of her from Levi, who had made the journey to Nałęczów before he left for America.

'I always thought it odd that you did this,' Levi had said as he handed him the picture. 'But you said it was a tradition, yes?'

Benjamin had nodded. Yes, it was a tradition of hers, and other families, to take photos of the dead. He wasn't sure he liked it, and yet now as he sat, knowing she was underneath him, looking at the picture of her, he was glad he had done it. Glad that he had something to look at when he came here – it made him remember her, made him realise that she was truly gone.

'I'm here again,' he told the photograph. 'Same time, every year. I told you I would come.'

He waited for a response even though he knew none would be forthcoming.

'There won't be many more years that I can come. I'm getting old, you know,' he said, chuckling.

He could hear her voice now, telling him, as she had nearly thirty years ago, 'Benj, you're not old, not yet.'

'I know, I know, you always say that, but this time, I am old. Not like before.'

There was a whisper of a breeze that scuttled a few still-dry leaves past him. 'You'd hate this time of year. Good job you're not here. Cold, damp. All those autumnal colours are gone. It's just grey now, Ania. Just grey.'

Then, he realised it wasn't all grey and felt about in his pocket. He drew out the scarlet ribbon she had given him, a little faded now, turned reddish-brown from years of being worn and collecting years' worth of dirt and grime. She wore its twin, tied to her wrist, even in death.

He shivered as another breeze blew, this time a little stronger, making the ends of the ribbon quiver. 'I can't stay long,' he told the photograph. 'I just came to say thank you. As I do every year. That, and of course that I am sorry too.'

The wind picked up and lifted the edge of the photo, carrying it just a foot or so away. His heart leapt with fear. He got on all fours and placed his hand square on top of it to stop it from blowing away. He could hear his breathing coming fast. He had almost lost her.

'All right,' he said, moving back to sit down. He placed the photo in his pocket for safe keeping but the ribbon he held on to. 'I'll stay a while longer. You win.'

He sat for some time, imagining her talking to him and what she would say – how it was so different from the others, how she would say what was on her mind, with no awareness that sometimes what she would say would offend. She spoke often, as a child did too. Full of rambling sentences, sometimes inappropriate questions, of thoughts that tumbled out of her mouth, one on top of the other, her eyes wildly scanning the face in front of her, waiting to see if they understood what she meant or not. He chuckled at the image of her, a tiny mite, a woman who looked no more than a fourteen-year-old child, who would stand in front of men, men with guns, men who had seen hardened battle, and argue with them. There was never any fear on her face because she simply did not feel it – did not know what fear was.

'You feel the fear for the both of us.' That's what she would say to him. 'You will *feel* things and I will *think* things. That way, no one can stop us.'

He had believed her. He had thought that both of them would have survived.

'Don't get all sentimental now, Benj.'

He fancied then that he could hear her voice, as he sat in the woods. A voice low for such a small woman, and that slight hold on her s's as if she had trouble letting go of the sound. So he allowed her to speak to him.

'I see you still have the ribbon. Did I tell you about the day I got it? Did I ever tell you how I killed my mother?'

## 2

## THE GIRL WHO KILLED HER MOTHER

*Łąki, Lublin Voivodeship, Poland*
*Ania*

I came into the world on a spring wind that rattled windows and whispered to be let in. I came on the wind borne from the east, carrying scents along its way of smoking chimneys, thick pine trees and the damp earth. This wind played with everything in its path, taking delight in startling the horses so that they bolted from the barn and would not rest until I had arrived and until someone else had departed.

I was small – too small, my skin the colour of pork belly, my mouth open as if I were crying, and yet no sound came out, my toes angrily curled, my hands balled into fists. My father said it was as though I didn't want to be there – like I knew it was too soon.

The storm blew smoke down the chimneys, creating a fug of soot and burnt ash, so much so that all the windows had to be opened, letting in the coarse words that storms speak. My father did not listen to my mother, who begged him to close the windows – she told him that something was wrong, that the wind was whispering to her, that it was going to take her and me away.

He tried to soothe her, placing a damp cloth on her head, as my sister, Basia, at two years old, stood in the doorway and cried.

I came though. Pushed out into the world as the wind whipped up its stories and nightmares, whilst my sister cried, as my father tied red ribbons to my crib to ward off evil spirits.

My mother held me in arms that were too tired to hold me. She tried to tell my father once more that something was wrong, that the windows should be closed, but he did not listen.

When he turned to look at his darling wife and show her his handiwork, he saw that she had slumped in bed, her eyes open, her mouth wide, seeing nothing, saying nothing.

As soon as she had died, the wind died too. My father told me once that he had gone to the window to check – to see if he were imagining things. Surely a wind could not disappear so quickly. But outside, all was still, the horses that had bolted stood, oddly at peace in the field below. He turned once more to my mother, then picked up the tiny bundle, placing me in his arms, telling me that the storm was over – a lie. Because the storm never ended.

Over the years, my father would say that he should have tied the red ribbons to my mother's bed that night, and I agreed he should have. After all, I was the one that killed her with my poorly timed arrival; giving her my red ribbons was the least I could have done. We gave her one in death though it was too late.

Before my arrival, my father had not been a godly man. He

was a farmer – potatoes mostly, and toiled at the earth. He ate with his wife and daughter – my older sister, Basia – and would, occasionally, step over the threshold into a church, but only when it was Easter or Christmas. He believed in hard work, in selling potatoes and in creating a family that could help him with such endeavours. But after my early arrival and my mother's subsequent death, he turned into a man of superstition, of God, and, apparently, to anyone or anything he thought could cure his strange younger daughter.

Because I *was* strange. I was not like the other children. Not only had I had the audacity to kill my mother, I was odd. Basia, would call me *szalony*. Mad. I'm not sure that was a fair assessment of me – mad – but I was certainly different and I knew it too.

I don't recall my first memory of being a child. Rather, those very early years – those years when I suppose children are exploring the world, making friends and playing with toys – are all intermingled into one blur of being taken to one doctor after another. To a priest, to Isaac, a local Rabbi in the nearby spa town of Nałęczów even though we were not Jewish, all in search of a name to put to my strangeness.

'She's small for her age,' Isaac had told my father. 'And those eyes of hers – dark – almost without colour,' he'd mused, his face leaning close into mine. 'She doesn't smile much.'

My father, wringing his hands in despair, had tried to explain my predicament. 'I know! I see all these things, but there is more. She understands things in books that even I do not understand; she looks at the night sky for hours and then the following day will tell me where all the planets are. I ask you, is that normal for a child of six?'

Isaac smiled. 'She's just intelligent. There's nothing wrong with that.'

'No. No.' My father started to pace the room. 'There are fits of temper, throwing herself onto the floor and screaming and tearing at her hair. And then she stands up, wipes her face as if nothing has happened and takes herself to bed. Sometimes she won't eat. Then sometimes she will eat the same thing every day for a month. She talks to herself. She mutters and sings in the middle of the street and everyone stares at her. Then suddenly she will laugh at something but when I ask her what was funny, she says she doesn't know. She hits too. She hits her sister who is two years older than her – smacks her right across the face and then cannot understand why Basia is crying! And then there were the damned chickens and the shoes! I mean, she can read, write, understand things in books, but she cannot understand why someone is upset, nor does she understand laughter, happiness. It is as though...' He trailed off.

'As though what?' Isaac prompted.

'As though... as though there's something missing. A piece missing.'

Isaac did not say anything, and I remember looking to my father, wondering what he meant about a piece missing. I had two arms, two legs, a head; what was possibly missing from me?

'She came early, you know,' my father rambled, trying to fill a silence that made Isaac sit back in his chair and look at me with a strange smile on his face. 'Too early, and I wonder if that's what did it – she wasn't ready to be born and so part of her wasn't formed?'

'Ania,' Isaac said, addressing me directly, 'do you like books?'

I thought it was a stupid question to ask but I nodded anyway.

'Shall I give you some to read?'

'No! No more of that!' my father pleaded with him. 'Just fix her – you know the bit that isn't working. She's a girl, she doesn't need to learn anything more.'

Isaac's face had turned red. He'd stood, gone to his bookshelf and handed me a few books and asked me to wait in the hall. As soon as I was out of the room, I'd heard Isaac's voice, low, different. Anger. He was angry with my father, I knew that, but I just didn't understand why.

From that day on, I read whatever I was able to, from either Isaac or books that Father would sometimes bring me from town. Although, he would always bring childish fairy tales which did not satisfy my cravings for long. So it was to Isaac that I looked for guidance. I found that fiction was not something I liked to read. I understood the words, but their placement irritated me. I didn't have much use for the words I learned either – there was no one to understand them anyway.

Languages, geography and philosophy interested me greatly. I found languages easy to learn and as soon as I would learn one, I would ask Isaac for a book about the country – its history, geography – so that I was able to dream at night that I was there, wandering around the Colosseum in ancient Rome or stood by the Eiffel Tower in Paris, talking in that mellifluous language to anyone who would speak to me.

I learned about my own country too, about its history and politics, its topography, its culture. Even though I had never travelled far from home – the furthest was to my uncle's home in Czerniejów just outside Lublin – from my learnings I could imagine the country and all that it had to offer, and I would desperately beg Father to one day take me to Kraków, to Warsaw and to Gdańsk. I wanted to see how Poland had become what it had – I wanted to see why so many other countries were constantly wanting to take it for themselves and how we had only recently, since the end of the war, become truly independent again – truly Polish. He would nod and smile at me and say, 'One day,' or 'We'll see,' and we both knew what that meant.

As books were sometimes hard to come by, whenever I was bored I would take things apart, desperate to see their innards. Nothing was safe from my roving hands: a radio was disassembled – a radio that Tata loved, and he hit me with his belt for breaking it. I told him I could fix it and he didn't believe me, yet the next morning he woke to his radio, functioning properly. I was seven at the time.

Other objects disappeared in the house – Basia's dolly was taken so I could mark with charcoal on her body where all her organs were; a carriage clock did not fare well – I tried to take it apart and fix it as I had done the radio, but the tiny cogs and springs would not stay in my lumpy fingers and ran for freedom from me, underneath a cupboard and my bed. In the more tedious hours, I would pester Basia to challenge me with the names of countries, capital cities, towns even, but Basia soon ran out of steam with this game and I was left doing it myself.

As I grew, or rather aged, my father did not stop in his endeavours to find someone to fix me, or to find that elusive piece of me that was missing. It wasn't to be found in the mental hospital that he took me to – one that I escaped from within a day. It wasn't to be found in the tarot lady's cards in that incense-filled house; it was not in the healing spa waters of Nałęczów; it was not in church; it was not in a synagogue.

'We'll find someone to help us, Ania,' he would say, holding my hand and squeezing it a bit too tightly. 'Don't worry. We'll find someone.'

'I'm not worried,' I would say, and I'd watch as his brow crinkled as he would let go of my hand and ferret about in his pocket for his cigarettes, light one, clamp it between his lips then grab my hand again.

'We'll find someone,' he'd mutter between puffs. 'We can find someone.'

I watched, over the years, my father age and wear. His once black hair that shone almost blue in the sunlight was replaced by white strands that were so thin I could see the pink of his scalp. His face had become crinkled like the dried plums we would eat in the winter, and his hands, his long fingers that had spent so many years touching the soil, finding food to bring home, had become bent and knobbly. Basia would say I had aged him, making his hair white with all the worry I caused. She told me I should feel bad about it, or sad. But I did not feel anything other than anger – that was something I felt almost on a daily basis, and sometimes I knew why and sometimes I did not.

I wanted to feel sad for what Basia said I had done to him. Of course I did. I just couldn't and as I grew up I came to understand how my lack of emotion perturbed my sister and father so I would try to mimic them, laugh when they laughed, cry when I pricked my finger. But rather than assuaging their fears, it seemed to make their concerns worse. I saw the looks they gave me, the parting of their lips, ready to say the word. *Szalony.*

I am not saying that I did not do some, well, questionable things that might have also made them want to call me *Szalony.* I mean, there was the incident with the chickens...

One winter morning, I woke and decided that I had had enough of the empty room in our house. It jutted off the hall-way, supposedly a room for the child after me who would never arrive, and I decided that it must be filled.

I was not sure why the empty room bothered me so. It was just one of those things that did – like how if a door was ajar, I

had to get up and open it wide or close it, or how once I hid all
of the shoes in the house as I thought that by having bare feet,
like I did all the time, then my sister and father would feel the
earth underneath them and see that it was all connected – we
were all connected. The hiding of shoes just made Father angry.
The hiding of shoes made Basia hit me. But I did not regret it.
They just didn't understand and I could not get mad about that.
I was mad enough.

That morning I went outside, smashed the ice off the chickens' water bowls and knew instantly what I was going to fill the
empty room with. Chickens.

Logically, it was sound. It was freezing, the chickens were
cold, and we had a room inside that would suit them nicely.

And so I carried each one of the feathered friends of mine
into the house, and for once they did not squawk when I picked
them up, and within minutes I ferried them into the room and
closed the door.

Amazingly, no one noticed the chickens in the house until
late that evening when somehow one escaped and casually
walked down the hallway and stood in front of my father, who
was sat in his chair in front of the fire, picking bits of soil out
from under his nails with a sliver of wood.

For a moment, he carried on picking away at his nails, his
eyes on the chicken, no doubt his mind whirring as to how the
chicken had managed to get into the house. It was only when
Basia began to scream, and a flurry of feathers entered the
room, that he properly registered what was happening as the
rest of the chickens ran about, screaming at us as if we had
invaded their home.

I did not help catch the birds and place them outside again. I
sat instead, in front of the fire, watching the flames lick at the

logs, and thought about how the chickens had managed to open a door.

'Ania.' My father's voice was cutting.

I turned and looked at him. 'It was cold out,' I said, then added, 'We have an empty room.' I shrugged and turned back to look at the flames, only registering my father again when he slapped me on the back of my head, causing my teeth to knock into each other.

I didn't cry from the pain, nor from the action. It was simply something my father did when he was angry with me, and I could see the logic in that too. And I didn't try to further explain my actions to him – he wouldn't, couldn't, see my reasoning. The chickens were cold, the empty room was making my palms itch and the two of them together had solved a problem for me. I could, of course, see his point of view too. Chickens were meant to live outside; they defecate all over the floor and that's not really something you want in a house. That was reasonable, I suppose. I could see that, but I could not see how they could fail to be aware of my genius problem solving – an empty room, cold chickens, *et voila!*

After the chicken incident and perhaps the fourth time that I had hidden his shoes, my father rarely took me into town any more – not that we went often anyway, confined as we were to the countryside with the nearest neighbour over two miles away – nor did I go to school. He treated me, that day forward, as an unruly child and did not care that I was desperate for books, for guidance. In his and Basia's minds, I would never be an adult – there was no life for me out of the confines of our farm, picking potatoes. I would have no desires to marry, to have children, so they kept me, their tiny living doll all those years, allowing me brief visits to Isaac and shaking their heads at me when I spoke.

I am not sure if they loved me or not. I think they did. But they just did not know what to do with me. So as the years went by, with no one to speak to, no dreams of my own, I continued to act at times like a child, and I spoke like one too – rambling sentences, all my thoughts intermingled and falling out of my mouth without a second thought. Isaac had at times tried to show me how to pace my thoughts, how I did not need to act as a child would. But I had no real comparison and really no need to act any differently because, what was the point.

I often wondered if Matka had survived my coming into this world whether things would have been different. That's why one day, I took the red ribbons that had been on my crib and then my bed, untying them from their moorings and wrapping them around my wrists.

'What'd you do that for?' Basia asked me the day she first saw me with the scarlet ribbons half covering my forearms.

'Tata said it wards off evil. Maybe if I wear them he won't need to go looking for someone to fix me any more. Maybe I can fix myself.'

Basia said one word – '*Szalony*' – and went back to baking bread.

I was never lonely in those years. I ought to have been, I suppose as it was only Isaac who I could perhaps count as some form of a friend, even though I did not see him that often and he was older than Tata. But books were my comfort – my escape into a world that was so much bigger than the one I was born into. The knowledge would sit and fill my brain, making me feel satisfied like Father was when we ate pork and potatoes. He would lean back in his chair and sigh, rub his belly, light a cigarette and pick bits of food from his teeth. That's how I felt with books. But, like food, it never lasted. Within days I was starving again, roaming around the house, throwing already read books onto the floor and screaming in frustration that there was nothing to satiate my appetite.

But as the war began, my visits to Isaac stopped so my source of books dissipated. To say that it irked me was an understatement, yet I knew then I could not be selfish, could not throw my usual tantrums whenever I liked. Because there were people dying everywhere, all day, every day, and only one person had one of my red ribbons to protect them.

# 3

## ISAAC'S GOODBYE

*Summer, 1939*
*Nałęczów, Lublin Voivodeship, Poland*
*Ania*

The summer heat of 1939 was oppressive, turning my father's skin from pinky white to a chestnut brown, turning Basia into a quieter version of herself – one that would mope about the house, placing cool cloths on her forehead and send her lying under windows for a hint of a breeze. That summer sun did not brown me as it had Father, nor send me into some sort of ailing ladyship like Basia; instead it ignited a hunger in me for something to do – something to read – something to occupy my thoughts when conversation inevitably turned to Germany, Hitler and what Father had learned from talking to other men in the town.

Whenever I pressed Father for information, he would tell me it was not a woman's business to know such things, least of all a child. I would remind him that I was sixteen, not a child any more, but he would swat away my comments like an annoying fattened fly.

So, on a particular day when Basia lay under her bedroom window, dozing in the slight breeze that flicked at her curtains, and when Father was busy in the field, looking at the dry soil, hand on hips, his skin turning darker by the second, I decided that a trip to see Isaac was called for.

The walk took just over an hour, leading me through golden fields of corn that swayed and whispered in the breeze then through the fields of rape, the pungent scent making me sneeze as I walked the tracks between the yellow flowers. Above me, only crows flew in this heat, cawing to each other then dive-bombing into the fields when they spotted something to eat.

Isaac's house stood at the edge of the town of Nałęczów – a town that prided itself on its healing waters, drawing people from all over the country to stay in their sanatoriums. His home, a few yards from the road, was devoid of neighbours and looked a strange sight when arriving – almost as if the house had magically appeared one day and settled itself.

I opened the green painted door as I always did, and immediately I knew things were not quite right. Leah, Isaac's wife, would normally be in the kitchen – banging pots and pans about as she cooked, humming a tune, the smells of roasting chicken, or sweet honeyed pastries, floating to me. The house this day was stale. There was no noise.

I stood for a moment, unsure of myself. Was this Isaac's house? Had I made some error?

But no. There to my left was a wooden cabinet, atop which always sat three vases, one large, white, painted with blue flowers, the smaller two to its side painted blue with white flowers. Leah loved these vases, said they had come from her grandmother, and she always filled them with flowers from the garden

– roses, honeysuckle, tulips. There was only the large vase left. The two smaller ones sat next to an empty space, a perfect circle of its base left on the dusty wood. This wasn't right. Leah never left dust on any surface.

'Isaac?' I called out, my voice rattling off the walls.

I walked to his study – our study – a place I normally could not wait to get to. But something niggled at me – the vases, the dust, the quiet. I didn't want to be there all of a sudden.

Upon opening the door, I found Isaac stood at the window, his hands clasped behind his back, his greying hair mussed as if he had just got out of bed. Leah was not in the room – the blue sofa, a sofa which I loved to lounge on as I read, was piled high with books, trinkets, even clothing. His desk, normally a neat affair, was scattered with papers, and a cup sat in the middle of them, weighing them down.

'Isaac,' I said again.

He turned to look at me and for a moment it was as if he did not recognise me. His eyebrows scrunched together, making the crease in his forehead deeper. Then, 'Ania,' he said.

'Where's Leah?' I asked.

'Lublin. She had to go and see to some matters.' He stepped towards me and placed one hand on the desk, his eyes no longer on my face but on the scattered papers. 'We have been trying to sort through some things,' he said, giving a small laugh. He picked up one piece of paper, looked at it and laid it back down.

'What matters?'

'Just some things,' he said. 'Now, what can I do for you?'

I found this strange. Isaac had never asked me why I was there before. He would allow me to come over at any time, and we'd race into the study and he'd start handing me books or would set the globe in front of me and test me on finding the countries.

'It's hot,' I told him. 'And I am bored.'

This made him smile, but at the same time he drew a hand over his face and gently shook his head. 'I am not sure I am in much of a mind for lessons today.'

Despite the bubble of frustration that was beginning to froth in my stomach at being told 'no', I asked if I could come tomorrow or the day after instead.

'Oh Ania!' He went to his desk chair and flopped into it. 'That's not a good idea. I don't think that we can be friends any more.'

'Why?'

'Because.' He waved a hand at the window as if the answer lay in his garden.

I went to the sofa and moved a few things away to give me space to perch on the edge. I thought for a moment with just the sound of Isaac's breathing and the ticking of a clock to interrupt the quiet as to what was going on around me and what was not being said. I thought that this was perhaps a lesson of his, of Isaac's, teaching me to read people, to pick up on the obvious, but he knew as did I that I did not fare well at this – I needed people to tell me what they meant, what they felt.

'Can you just tell me?' I implored, Isaac. 'I don't understand.'

'You're so impatient,' Isaac said. 'You want to know everything, right now. Sometimes people cannot give you what you need so you have to read between the lines. Look at how someone looks that day – are they tired, sad? Look at their face, their expressions. Look at the many, many clues that surround you. For God's sake Ania, you're a genius, you can piece it together. You need to stop being so impatient and train yourself to do it.'

'And what is a genius?' I challenged him.

'You mean, what does the word mean?' he asked.

'No. You know I know this, from the Latin *gignere*: "beget – the attendant spirit present from one's birth, innate ability or inclination",' I recited for him dryly. 'I mean, what do you think it means? You say I am, but Basia says I'm mad. So are they intertwined? Can you not be a genius unless you are *szalony*? Are all those who are *szalony* secretly geniuses?'

'Ania.' He sighed. 'Stop being obstinate. You're trying to change the course of this discussion. I said you were impatient and you do not want to address what I said.'

'I am impatient because why not just say what you feel? Why must I decipher it?'

'Because that is human nature. That is how we express ourselves. Think of it like a puzzle. Think of all the clues you have seen since you arrived in the house a few minutes ago. Now think, then tell me why I may be upset, or if I am in fact upset at all.'

I thought of the pieces of the puzzle that were straight in front of me. No Leah. The quiet house. The missing vase, the dust, the belongings, the papers on Isaac's desk, his mussed-up hair, Leah in Lublin. Isaac saying we could not be friends any more.

'The war,' I started. 'The one everyone is talking about. You're scared it will happen?'

He tore his eyes away from the window. 'And why am I so scared, Ania?'

'Because you're Jewish. Because in Germany things are happening to the Jews. Because if the Germans come here, you think the same thing will happen.'

He nodded. 'Very good. Now why is Leah in Lublin?'

Ah! So this was a game. A test.

I thought hard. The vase had something to do with it, I was sure. It was worth money – she had told me that before.

'She's selling the vase?' I suggested.

He nodded again. 'She is getting us as much money as possible and is visiting Eva and her husband in the city.'

'Why do you need so much money?' I asked. I could not hazard a guess at what that was about.

'To leave, my dear. To leave as soon as possible.'

'And where will you go?'

He shrugged. 'Anywhere as long as it is not here.'

He sat quietly again and allowed me to process what he had said. He would leave and take Eva, his married daughter, and her husband with him and Leah. How did it make me feel?

'How does that make you feel?' he asked, matching my thoughts. 'Sad?'

I shook my head. 'Angry,' I said.

He smiled. 'That's fair. Are you angry at me?'

I searched the anger. Where was it directed? I wasn't sure. All I knew was that I did not want Isaac to leave. I did not want to be alone.

'Can I come with you?' I blurted. 'Father and Basia don't want me here anyway. I could come with you.'

'I'm afraid not, my dear.'

'But you said you were my friend. You said that I could come here any time I liked and read and you would teach me things,' I rambled. The anger was stirring. 'You said' – I stood, my hands curled into fists at my side – 'you said—'

'I said a lot of things, Ania. And at the time I meant them. You need to control those feelings that all ball themselves up inside you and rush forth as anger. I wish I could stay. And I still might. But things are happening that are not in my control. Not in yours either.'

'If you stay then I will still be your friend, Isaac,' I said.

'I am sure you think so now, Ania.' He smiled. 'But things are already changing. People are already calling us names, telling us to leave.'

'Which people?' I demanded.

'In the villages, in the towns. Some of them want Germany to come. Some of them like the things that Hitler is saying. Some people who I thought were friends are agreeing with him.'

'Tell me who!'

He laughed. 'Oh, Ania. And what will you do, eh? You cannot change their minds.'

I thought of how when Basia said something mean to me I would punch her, kick her until she said sorry. I was sure I could do that to other people too.

'Now. Calm down and come and sit here and I will get the globe. You can help me decide where to go – should we leave.'

Despite the anger, the swirl of voices going about my head, asking me to think, to say something else, to understand Isaac, had touched upon my Achilles' heel. Grumpily, I went to the desk and sat in the chair that he vacated for me, and once the globe was placed in front of me, I could feel something shift, and suddenly I felt calmer.

He turned the globe slowly and asked me the name of each country in turn, making some remark now and then of what it might be like for him and his family to live there.

Australia. I liked that country. It was an interesting word – the sound of it, and the look of the country that resembled, to me at least, a barking dog.

England I wasn't so sure of. The word, that is. It didn't sound right when I said it: 'Enga land.'

Usually Isaac would correct my pronunciation, but not today. 'Now in German,' he said once I had named them all in Polish.

German. A language I certainly did not like in my mouth, but it was one that Isaac had forced me to learn, saying that one day it might come in handy.

Once the countries had been listed in German, English and Russian, next were Spanish and French.

Spanish and French I adored. The sounds, the stress on the vowels and the s's. I could speak them all day, every day, if I had someone to speak them to. Russian was like German. Clipped. Harsh, almost bitter to the taste. I had not learned much Russian so far, always asking to learn something else, but please God, no more Russian!

After we had finished, he handed me a few books. One on philosophy, another obscure book about fauna and flora.

'Plants and animals?' I asked him as I opened it. 'I'm not interested in that.'

'You should be,' he said. 'They're all around you. You should know about what is right in front of your face.'

I shrugged. He knew I would read it regardless.

'You should go now, Ania,' he said, looking at the clock. 'I need to think quietly a while.'

'I can stay and be quiet,' I suggested.

He went to the study door and waited.

Picking up the books, I went to the door.

'This is for you,' he said and pulled out from his pocket a compass – one that he had carried with him since he was a boy. On the reverse of it was an inscription from his father – 'So you never lose your way in this life.'

'But it is yours,' I said, hearing Basia's voice in my head to never take things that are not ours – like her bear and her doll.

'And I am giving it to you. A gift. So that it becomes yours.'

A gift. I had not ever received an avital gift before. Not even on my birthday. Perhaps Tata would bring us fruit or sweets and clothes that we needed, but never an actual gift that was not meant to be eaten or worn.

I reached out and took the compass in my hand, feeling the cool weight of the metal against my skin.

'You shall not lose your way now, Ania,' he said, and he kissed my forehead. 'Remember everything you have learned. Not just from the books, but from me – how every answer is right there in front of you – you just need to be patient and think!'

'Thank you, Isaac,' I said and walked to the front door. Before I even reached it, I heard the study door close shut. I was sure that Isaac wouldn't really leave, not even if there was to be a war. I was sure he was wrong that he thought I could not be his friend.

But, just in case it did happen, I placed the compass and books on the floor and unwound one of my ribbons from my wrists and settled it in the circle left by the missing vase. If what Isaac said was true then, maybe, just maybe, he would need one of my ribbons to protect him.

# 4

## THE MAN WITH HALF A SMILE

*1 December 1942*
*Łąki, Lublin Voivodeship, Poland*
*Ania*

His face was remarkable. When he smiled, the left side rose and the right stayed put, leaving a sort of grimace. Not that he smiled much. The right cheek was red, mottled, puckered, like it had melted then reset itself. A scar too reached from his right eyebrow up to his forehead, disappearing underneath his hair line. As I sat and watched him, I imagined that the silvery scar was a piece of thread, and once pulled it would raise that lopsided face of his.

He knew I was here, his watcher. And I knew that he knew, but we both pretended otherwise.

His name was Benjamin, a Jew who had been brought here by Bartok, my father's friend. He was not the first, but I didn't know when I met him that he would certainly be the last to take refuge in our farm.

Since early spring, all the Jews in Nałęczów had been

rounded up and taken away. I saw it with my own eyes, when Father and I had gone into the town hoping to sell a few sacks of potatoes. We stood on the pavement as soldiers with guns bashed down doors, yelled at the occupants to get one bag each, one suitcase only and leave their homes. Tata had held my hand tight in his, a muscle in his jaw jumping as he watched the scene unfold.

There were others that watched too. All of us saying and doing nothing as it unravelled before our eyes. We watched as the jeweller and his family were marched out of their house, followed by the old couple who used to run the bakery. We stood and we did nothing.

I itched to let go of Tata's hand, to run up to the soldiers with their guns, to yell at them, tell them to let people alone. But I didn't because I wasn't stupid. I knew what the outcome would be. A quick shot and that would be that. I had seen it before, when Tomasz, a young boy, had tried to shoot an officer with a gun he had stolen from his father's shed. He had missed, the gun a hunting rifle too big for a small boy to handle, had sent him flying onto his back. The officer had laughed at first and offered Tomasz an outstretched hand, pulling him to his feet. But, seconds later, he drew his pistol from his holster and shot Tomasz quickly and neatly in the forehead.

It had not frightened me seeing that; more so, I felt what I always did: that strange bubble of something in my stomach that soon fermented into anger and when we had reached home that afternoon, I had punched my bedroom door, barely causing a crack to appear, but bruising my knuckles badly.

Isaac was safe, however. He had been right about everything and had left the town soon after our last meeting in 1939, going to Warsaw to stay with his brother. I was glad that I had not had to see him dragged away like the others because I knew that

Father's grip on my hand would not have been strong enough to hold me back from running after him.

Father allowing Jews to stay in the barn pleased me. He had had enough, he had said. This was something he could do – an act of rebellion, I suppose – but I often wondered if it was less about rebellion and more that he felt guilty that we had watched the others be dragged away and done nothing.

News of what was happening elsewhere in Poland, and even the world, was sparse, and Father, whatever he knew, would not tell me or Basia anything. And where Basia liked the not knowing, for me, it was torturous. So when the Jews came to stay, it meant that I could maybe find some form of satisfactory answers to what was happening and perhaps what was to come. Yet, they were all quiet, worried even, looking at me as if I were not to be trusted. I had tried to reassure them, of course I had.

'But you're just a child,' one of them had said to me. 'You could tell people who we are and not even mean to.'

Indignant, I had told them that I was almost twenty years old, and they would smile and nod their heads as if we were playing some childish game. I was aware that I did not look my age and that confused them. I still had the large expressionless eyes that worried my father so, the almost black hair that I refused to cut so that Basia had to plait it each night into a thick braid, and I had not grown tall – not even as tall as Basia, who was petite. I had stood once next to one of the horses and tried to measure my height, transferring it from hands into feet and inches. I just about made five feet.

So when Benjamin came, with his half a smile, I decided that I would not pester him as I had done the others. I would wait, watch, and when the time was right, I would find a way to get him to tell me everything I was desperate to know about.

That's how we first got to know each other – by sitting in a warm, hay-filled barn, dust motes dancing in the air, neither of us talking, both of us thinking. I never thought you could get to know someone without speaking, but there was a way about him, something I couldn't put my finger on that made me want to stay quiet and simply watch him. Perhaps it was the way that he would sit on a bale of hay and stare at his feet for hours at a time that told me something about him. Or perhaps it was how he would hum a tune, so lonesome that it made me think I knew exactly who he was. Sometimes, I would mirror his slight actions, both of us picking at a piece of hay or straw and playing with it. He would twist and turn his into nothingness. Me, I would try to stretch the hay until it snapped, feeling some joy when it did, then I would look to him to see if he had seen what I had done – to see if he was getting to know me too.

On the third day I left my hiding spot, clambered down the ladder and stood in front of this man with half a smile. It was time for him to speak.

He did not look at me and kept his eyes on the straw-littered floor, perhaps waiting for me to make the first move.

'I'm Ania,' I said.

Still he did not look at me.

'Father said you're staying awhile. Where will you go next?'

My direct question made him raise his head slightly. But still he would not speak.

Sighing, I sat down opposite him on a bale of straw, the dried prongs scratchy even beneath my clothes. 'There have been others, you know. They wouldn't talk to me. You're different, aren't you, though? This' – I pointed to the side of my face – 'it makes you different.'

I knew that if Basia could hear me, she would chastise me for being rude, for asking too many questions like a child. But there was no other way for me to talk to people. It was this or stay silent, and God knew I had been silent in my own home for long enough. Sick of the stares, the worry, the name calling from Basia, I wanted to speak, and for some reason, the man with half a smile was who I wanted to talk to.

He looked at me. His sky-blue irises were surrounded by red spidery veins, obscuring the white. 'How old are you?' he asked. His speech was a little slurred and he had to keep licking his lips. 'Should you be here? I think your *tata* said I should not talk to anyone. That's what he said. Your *tata* said it.' His voice was a childlike singsong. I decided I liked it.

'Nineteen. How old are you?'

'Fifty-four,' he said.

'Old then.'

'Yes. I think so. I think I'm old,' he said in such a way that I could tell he wasn't sure.

'Tata is older than you, but not by much. Did you know that the average lifespan of a man is sixty-five? But that depends on where you live, your health and the country you are in. It differs, you see, country to country and region to region.'

'I suppose I don't have long left then,' he said with a sigh.

'I suppose not,' I agreed.

Quiet descended on us once more with just the roosting pigeons in the eaves making their night-time coos and flutter of wings that scattered downy feathers on the ground.

'I don't like pigeons much,' I said and looked above me.

'I quite like them.'

'Why?'

He shrugged. 'Bit of noise, I suppose. Means I'm not alone.'

'Where are your family?' I asked.

'Not here,' he replied, licking at some spittle that had gobbed on the right side of his lip.

'Does it hurt, the scar?' I itched to reach out and touch his face now that I was closer and trace the crevices and ravines of his skin and find out what it felt like underneath my fingertips. But I didn't as Basia had told me that I couldn't just touch people whenever I was curious. It was rude, apparently.

'Not any more. It used to.'

There was quiet again for a minute. Then, I couldn't help myself. 'Can I touch it?'

For some reason, my request made him laugh, a proper laugh that made his face contort in such a way that for a moment you couldn't see his deformity.

I didn't like that he laughed. I felt I had gone about the whole thing in the right way – polite conversation, introductions and shown an interest in how he looked. That's what Basia had said was proper and right, so why was he laughing at me?

'I'm sorry,' he said, shaking his head, recognising perhaps the screwed-up face I got when I was annoyed. 'I didn't mean to laugh. It doesn't frighten you? The scar? You're not disgusted by it?'

'Why would I be disgusted? It's just your face. Most people's faces look all the same to me, and at least you have an interesting face. Sort of like there's a story you are showing on it but not telling anyone – a secret that you can see but never know.'

He scrunched up his nose. 'I'm not sure I understand that,' he said.

'That's all right,' I replied. 'I don't understand a lot of things. Like feelings and why people get so upset. I don't understand those a lot of the time, but I'm learning to watch people, to see what they mean when they say nothing. But I do understand other things – like maps, and books, and languages.'

'Those are good things to know,' he said.

I nodded in agreement. 'But it makes me different from them all. I can see the stars and understand what is in the sky,

and look at trees and name them all. I can recite the history of
Poland to you; Italy too. I prefer Italy's history – so much more
elegant than ours.' I sighed wistfully, thinking of Italy, its
culture, its language, desperate to see it for myself and knowing
that I never would. 'But when Tata gets angry I don't know what
that means, or why he should be so angry that his dinner was
burned. It is just food. Just nothing. It doesn't matter.'

Benjamin shrugged in his slouched way. 'It matters to some.'

'I suppose,' I said. 'I can invent things too – make things. I
once made a trap for Tata to catch rabbits and it was the only
time that he said that I was clever, that he was proud of me. I
ruined it the next day though because I took apart his rake, a
brush and some other things to make something else. He got
pretty cross at me.'

'I am sure he did,' Benjamin said.

'Do you understand those feelings?'

'I do,' he said. 'I feel everything. All of it. Sometimes for me
the feelings are too much. But that's all I understand. I'm not so
clever in other ways. Stupid, that's what my teachers called me,
sometimes my family too. I know I can't read well or speak that
well, but I know what I know and I feel what I feel, and I think
that should be enough.'

I did not answer straight away but tried to understand him.
Then, I suppose a feeling overcame me. A warmth. 'Then we
complement each other,' I said. 'You feel things I cannot, and I
know things you do not.'

'Perhaps we do,' he answered.

Then, he looked at the red ribbons on my wrist. I had two of
them left.

'They were supposed to be for my mother,' I told him.

'She doesn't want them?'

'She doesn't need them. She's dead. I killed her by coming too early.'

He scrunched his face again and I could see that he didn't understand, but before I could properly explain myself he said, 'My mother is dead too.'

'How did she die?' I asked.

'She was taken away. My mother and my father. They were old and they told me to run because I could and they could not.'

'If they were taken that doesn't mean they are dead,' I said.

'No. They're dead. That's what it means. That's what they told me it means. If they come to take you away, it means you're going to die.'

Suddenly, my father's voice rang out, calling me in for dinner.

'You should go,' he said.

'But you'll be alone.'

He shrugged.

I stood and walked to the barn door, then turned around to see his shoulders slumped. He was staring at his shoes again, which I knew would probably go on for hours.

I turned and removed one of the ribbons from my wrist and placed it on the bale of straw next to him. Then without a word, I made my way to the house, feeling somewhat satisfied with my encounter. I almost thought that perhaps I had made a new friend – a new Isaac.

# 5

## THE DOWNFALL OF A FAMILY

*1 December 1942*
*Łąki, Lublin Voivodeship, Poland*
*Ania*

Our downfall was that we did not look German enough, and Father said they were finally coming for us. 'Not German enough,' he said then frowned at my black hair, as if he could turn it lighter with just one look.

I paused in raising my spoon to my mouth, the soup spilling back into the bowl. I could hear Benjamin's voice in my head: '*If you are taken away it means you are going to die.*'

'So we have to leave?' Basia asked, her voice quieter than usual.

My father nodded. 'Volksdeutsche will come and take our farm. We have to leave before they come, that's what Bartok said. We have to go before they make us go. He said to burn the farm and leave. Not to let anyone else take it from us.'

'When was Bartok here?' I asked. I hadn't seen him arrive, nor depart. He had joined the Polish Armia Krajowa – the AK –

the underground state and resistance, and had been instrumental in bringing Jews to the farm.

I liked Bartok, gruff as he was. He was also the only man I knew who had a full beard – mostly ginger with flecks of yellow and grey intertwined. Whenever he ate with us, crumbs would get caught in the thickness, and when I would tell him he would just say, 'I'm saving some food for later.'

At first I had taken him at his literal word and thought that he would sit later in the evening, picking out bits of food from his beard. Basia soon told me he had been joking, but I still liked to think of him ferreting about in that coarse hair for a tasty scrap.

He had once worked for the council, not that I knew exactly what he did. But when the Germans came, he was told he no longer had a job, and within months he had disappeared with some others from the nearby towns to create a resistance. I liked the sound of the resistance – the word, I mean – and wanted to know more, so I was annoyed that Bartok had come and gone without so much as a greeting.

'I saw him earlier,' Father said. 'He came to warn us – he's warning everyone with farms or land. He said, and I quote, "They'll come and take it from you. Deport you to a work camp. Burn the damned place to the ground and leave so they can never have it."'

'But where is there to go?' Basia asked. 'If we leave before they come, where will we go? And if we stay and they come and take us, where will they take us? Can we not sign the list? Maybe we can sign and be Volksdeutsche?'

Her questions came quicker and quicker, her eyes roving about the tiny kitchen, as if some hidden answer lay in the bare cupboards.

I placed my spoon back in the bowl and watched my father

as he went to the stove, then back to the table, rushing between the two as he spoke.

'We tried that, Basia. We couldn't sign. No German ancestry. God, we don't even speak the language other than Ania! We're just Poles to them – not worthy of living in our own country.'

'Tata,' Basia started, but he spoke over her, his thoughts rambling out of his mouth, quite similar in the way that I would talk and be chastised for.

'I mean, we could leave, I think. I don't know. Basia's right; where would we go? And maybe Bartok was wrong; maybe they'll let us stay instead of bringing a German family to run the farm? Maybe we will be fine.'

He talked to himself, mostly, and now and then would look to Basia, who nodded her head along with him, her eyes filling with tears.

Then he stopped in the middle of the kitchen. It was as though all the energy had suddenly seeped out of his body. 'I... I...' he started, but could not find an end to the sentence.

I did not speak. I knew that if I did, it would annoy them both. I had the same questions as Basia but if I asked them, in my way, it wouldn't come out right.

'We can leave,' Father said, almost a question but not quite, and looked at us both. Basia nodded. I stared at him.

But it was not only us three. 'What about Benjamin?'

My father too seemed to have forgotten about the Jew in our barn, and his eyes widened. 'He won't be able to come with us.'

'Why not?' I asked. 'If we are in danger anyway, what does it matter if he comes with us?'

'His face,' Father said.

'My face doesn't look German enough either – that's what you said.'

'No, no. I mean his face.' Father traced a finger down his cheek. 'He stands out too much.'

Suddenly, Basia burst into tears. Father went to her and wrapped his arms around her shoulders and whispered in her ear. I didn't cry; I wasn't sure what I felt. Did I want to leave? Perhaps I did. Perhaps if we left I would have a different kind of life; perhaps I would be able to read, to learn. But what about Benjamin? Surely we couldn't leave him behind.

'Tata,' I said, drawing myself up in my chair as much as I could. 'I think Benjamin should come with us. It isn't fair to leave him. He won't know where to go.'

'We don't even know where to go,' Father replied.

'I know, but—'

'But nothing, Ania,' Father snapped. 'Don't you think I have enough to worry about without worrying for him too? Don't you think that taking you somewhere else might make us stand out too?'

'Me? Why?' I asked. My face was fine.

'Because you're *szalony*!' Basia yelled. 'You do things and say things and you're always getting into trouble. I'm twenty-two, Ania! Twenty-two! And yet here I am taking care of you, when I should have been married by now – I should have a life of my own!'

Her recriminations continued and I sat and listened to each one of them. The story of the chickens came up again, then the fact that I hardly ever wore shoes, how I would randomly say something that made no sense, how I couldn't even cook dinner, and how I whined when we had to pick the potatoes. It seemed I was good at nothing, and all I had done so far was to be a thorn in their sides.

'Enough, Basia,' Father said gently. 'She's your sister and we are family. We have to stick together.'

Basia nodded and Father kissed the top of her head, then, oddly for him, he kissed the top of mine too, then sat down, his elbows on the table, cradling his face in his hands. 'I need to think,' he said. 'Go to bed now. Let me think where we can go.'

Basia and I left him in the kitchen and went to our rooms. Before Basia went into her own, she turned to me.

'I'm sorry about what I said, Ania.'

'It's all right,' I replied.

'It's just that sometimes, it feels like I don't know you – like we are so different – like we are speaking different languages. I do love you. It's just hard to love you sometimes.'

My hand was on the doorknob, ready to push open the door and lie on my bed and think. Instead, I copied Father. I went to my sister, her face all red and splotchy from her tears, and on tiptoe, I kissed her forehead and whispered that I loved her, even though I wasn't entirely sure what love was.

She smiled at me, a smile that reached her eyes and creased her skin. 'Goodnight, sister,' she said.

I watched her go into her room and went to my own and dressed in a nightgown. But I knew I wouldn't be able to sleep. I knew that my mind would whirr so fast that it would make me angry and even perhaps make me do something stupid that would annoy Basia and Tata, and I couldn't do that to them – not tonight.

But there was something I could do – someone I could talk to who could maybe calm my brain.

\* \* \*

Benjamin was still sitting on his bale of hay and I was sure that he had not moved an inch since a few hours before.

The red ribbon that I had left beside him was gone but I could not see that it was tied to his wrist.

I sat opposite him and waited for him to look up from his shoes, but he didn't. Instead he talked at them.

'I heard your sister,' he said.

'You did?'

He nodded. 'I went outside to look at the sky and walked a little and I heard your father and then your sister. She said some mean things.'

'She did. But it's fine. She says things all the time,' I reassured him.

'It doesn't upset you when people say that you are mad?'

'Not really.' My fingers found the ribbon on my wrist and I began to stroke it.

'It upsets me when people say I am stupid. Or ugly. I don't like it when they say things like that.'

'Does it make you cry?' I asked.

'Sometimes,' he said. 'My mother, she was very good at making me feel better. She would tell me how she loved me and how perfect I was when I was born.'

'So your face – I mean, you weren't born with it?' I asked.

'No. It was an accident when I was four or five. I don't remember. Something fell from the stove. I think I might have grabbed it – I don't know. But it was hot and it burned and then we couldn't get to a doctor right away, and then I slept a lot and when I woke up, my mother said that the skin had died or something and my face was all a mess.'

'You don't remember it happening?' I asked.

'I don't remember a lot of things. Things won't stay in my mind where they are supposed to. But I remember when people have been mean to me. I can remember those things.'

'They're not good things to have in your mind,' I told him. 'I just ignore it when Basia yells at me. She yells nearly every day at something I have said or done. If I held on to each thing she had ever said, I wouldn't have any room left in my head to think of other things.'

'Maybe you have other things to think about. I don't have many things to think about,' he said. We sat quietly for a few minutes, then he said, 'You said that you came too early, that it killed your mother.'

'I did.'

'That's why you wear the ribbons, to think of her?'

I shrugged. 'I don't know why I wear them.'

'I think sometimes it would be better if I had not been born. Do you ever think that too?'

I didn't answer straight away. I thought on it. Had I ever thought about it? 'No,' I told him. 'That kind of thinking is pointless because I am alive and so are you. We can't change that so there is no purpose to be gained from wondering what if.'

Finally, he looked up. I didn't know whether it was because he was tired or upset, but his face seemed to have drooped more, his right eye hidden under a heavy lid. 'I heard your father,' he said.

'We have to leave.'

'Do you know where you will go?'

'Father is thinking about it now. But he said that you couldn't come with us. Do you know where you will go?' I asked hopefully.

He shook his head. 'Bartok, he was good. I ran and he found me and he brought me here and he said that other people had stayed a while, but it wasn't safe to stay long, so I would have to go somewhere soon. He said I had to think too. I had to think about where I could go. But there isn't anywhere for me to go.'

'Maybe you should find Bartok too,' I suggested. 'Maybe he can help you again.'

'He's in the woods. That's what he said. He's in the woods and the forests with other people – all sorts of people, he said. All sorts of people hiding and fighting. But he said that it might not be the best place for me.'

'Why?'

'I don't like the dark,' he said. 'And Bartok said it would be dark a lot and that I would have to sleep under the ground and that I would have to learn to fight. I don't like guns either. I don't think I would make a good fighter.'

'What if all of us went with you to the woods!' Suddenly I knew exactly what we should do, and I would tell Tata about it. 'What if I was there with you? Would you still be afraid?'

He wiped at his mouth, taking away some spittle that had dripped onto his chin. 'Maybe not,' he said.

'Then I will tell Father. That's what we'll do.'

A small smile lifted half of his face. 'Do you know which woods we will find Bartok in?' he asked.

I thought for a moment of the maps I had studied of Poland. I could name most of the towns, areas of historical significance, and I knew that thick forests were more common to the east of Lublin, around forty-five miles away. I knew that Bartok would not be too far away as he came often enough to see us on his way to Lublin, to the ghetto, then back out into the countryside again. I remembered that when he had brought Benjamin here, he had spoken to Tata about being so close to the Russians and how he had gone to Zamość to check on his sister. He was in the east, I was sure of it.

'I would think he is in the east,' I told him.

'Are you sure?' Benjamin asked.

'There's only one way to find out,' I said.

The small oil lamp that sat beside Benjamin's feet began to flicker – the fuel was running out.

I saw him look at it and his smile disappeared.

'If you don't like the dark, how have you managed in here at night?' I asked.

'I don't really sleep,' he said. 'I walk about and try to find stars in the sky – some light.'

'But if you close your eyes, it is dark anyway, so what does it matter?'

'I don't know,' he said. 'I just know that I am afraid.'

'I'll stay here tonight,' I told him. I stood, patted him on the arm and made my way to the ladder and climbed into the hayloft. 'I'll stay here and think, and you stay there and sleep, and know that I am here – just up here,' I called down.

He didn't answer. I heard him turn the squeaking knob to turn out the lamp, a rustle as he made himself comfortable and then the sound of his ragged, whistling breathing through his lopsided mouth.

* * *

The gunshots woke me. Not the voices nor the cars. It was the shots.

I opened my eyes then felt a hand covering my mouth. I tried to talk but the hand clamped down tighter.

'Shhh,' Benjamin said. It was Benjamin's hand. No need to be afraid. It was Benjamin.

I nodded and he removed his hand. 'Follow me,' he whispered.

In the dark, he was but a darker shadow, yet I could see him well enough, feel the heat of his body to follow him on all fours over the wooden slats of the hayloft towards a bale of straw that was lodged at the rear of the barn, up against the wall.

I heard him move it aside a little. 'Get in,' he said.

I didn't ask questions because he had told me not to talk, but I had no idea what he meant so I didn't move.

'Like this,' he whispered. Then, like magic, he disappeared.

'Benjamin?' I whispered.

'In here,' he said, his voice coming from the straw.

I crawled forward, the coarse straw biting into my palms, disturbing the hay dust that tickled my nostrils. Then I sat back on my haunches and felt the bale of straw. Where had he gone?

There – there it was. A hole, and inside it my hand found Benjamin's trouser leg. I crawled in next to him, the space so tight that I was sure we would run out of air.

'Hush, Ania,' Benjamin whispered. 'You have to be quiet now. Not one noise. Not one.'

I nodded. Not one noise. Not one.

# 6

## THE VOICES

2 *December 1942*
*Łąki, Lublin Voivodeship, Poland*
*Ania*

There was no sound other than Benjamin's laboured breathing. He smacked his lips together, trying to breathe as quietly through his nose as he could, yet it came out as a whistle.

I did not know why we were hiding or who from. It could be that Father had decided to shoot something – a rabbit maybe, but that didn't make sense. There were no more shots other than the ones that had woken me. There was nothing.

Then it all made sense. It hadn't been Father. Of course it hadn't. Benjamin was scared. There were guns. There were Germans here – for him.

It felt like we waited for hours, but it couldn't have been that long before I heard the crunch of feet; two pairs, I thought. They were loud when they walked, like they wanted everyone to be aware of their arrival. I could smell cigarette smoke.

Then the voices.

'No one here,' the first voice said. German. No, not quite – the accent was a little off, almost like a Pole trying to speak it. The voice sounded familiar to me. His voice was deep – deeper than Father's.

'We should check,' said the second voice. Lighter. Younger perhaps. More eager than the first.

'You think so? If we go now, we could get back to Lublin in an hour. We could go see those women again – you liked those women,' the first voice said, and he laughed. That laugh. I knew it too. It was Krzysztof, the chief of police. A man who Father had always laughed *at* – indeed everyone had. A man whose wife told him what to do and what to say. A man, small, weak, with black hair that he slicked back with pig fat, a man who we all knew was happy to take a bribe. Now it seemed he had sided with our occupiers.

'They said there was a Jew here.' The second voice. Getting nearer. Smell of cigarette stronger. Standing under the haybarn. Shining a light. Kicking at a bucket.

'Doubt it. You saw them in there – terrified. Marek said no one was here, even after you put a gun to his daughter's head – he still said there was no one here. You really think a father would not save his own daughter for a Jew?' Krzysztof. Further away.

The light shone upwards. I could see the light through the gaps in the slats. Benjamin seemed to have stopped breathing.

'You're such a lazy pig, Krzysztof.' Second voice. 'We get paid well for each Jew we find and up to now you were happy to keep looking. Why all of a sudden are you being such a lazy pig?' Light dipped away from us. A foot kicked at the bucket again.

Krzysztof's voice was closer now too. I could smell him underneath the hay loft – that cologne he always wore, telling people it came from France to try to impress them, when we all knew it came from a gypsy who sold it on a market stall. It smelled of basil and of what Basia always said was rotting meat. It was foul.

Suddenly, there was a tap tap underneath us. 'I'm just saying that there is no one else here. I know this family. Just Marek and his *one* daughter. We're just wasting our time when we could be with those women again – remember, Rolf, that Helena you met? I couldn't get you out of her bed this morning!' Krzysztof laughed again. Quickly, like a spatter of bullets. Nervous laughter, the same laughter he used when Father stood up to him.

'I'm not sure. Why would they say a Jew was here and there isn't?'

'I don't know. Maybe they got the wrong family.'

The second voice – Rolf – laughed. 'I guess we got the wrong family too – I mean, what a mess inside.'

'You didn't need to do what you did,' Krzysztof said.

'Says who? They could have been lying. Besides, it's not a waste, is it? They were on track to being moved from here anyway. If anything, I saved them the bother of having to leave their home. Now they can stay!' He laughed and Krzysztof was quiet.

'Didn't you get the joke?' Rolf asked.

Suddenly, Krzysztof let out a loud bark. 'I get it. I see now. So, to the women?'

'I suppose.' Rolf sighed. 'Shame there's no Jew.'

Then the voices disappeared. An engine revved outside followed by the whirr of tyres as they bumped and scrunched over the dirt track.

I made to move and Benjamin told me to stop. To wait.

I wanted to get out. I felt I couldn't breathe. I wanted to know what they had meant about the mess inside. I wanted to get to Tata and Basia.

My heart beat so fast I thought that it was going to tear through my skin. I could feel sweat trickling its way down my neck; I could smell the straw, the hay, the dust, the stale sweat of Benjamin, the lingering smoke from the two men. It was too much – too much. I had to get out.

Before Benjamin could stop me, I crawled out and lay flat, breathing in heavily, wanting all those senses to quieten down.

'Are you sure they are gone?' Benjamin asked.

'The car left. I heard the tyres.'

'They could come back,' he said.

Benjamin scuffled out of the straw and sat next to me. 'What did they say, the men? What did they want?' he asked.

I told him what they had said, how they were looking for him.

'They'll come back and find me!' he slurred, his voice higher than a small child's. 'They'll find me, Ania, they will.'

I couldn't assuage his fears right now. I needed to get inside the house. I scrambled down the ladder, slivers of wood embedding themselves into my palms. I ran out of the barn, my bare feet slapping against the cold hard ground outside, my big toenail catching on a stone and pulling painfully away.

Behind me, Benjamin clomped as fast as he could. Breathing in that ragged way of his.

The front door was wide open, letting the warmth and heady smoke from the fire drift outside. Father would not leave the door open.

I stood in the doorway. There was no need to go further. In front of me, my father lay, face down, his arms above his head, his legs splayed. A deep pool of crimson under his head, getting larger and larger as the seconds ticked by.

A foot away, was Basia, face up, her eyes wide open in surprise, her mouth open like she was about to say something.

A neat hole sat in the middle of her forehead, and strangely, there was little blood, just a deep hole, the edges blackened like coal.

I took a step inside. That's when I could see that there was a pool of blood under Basia's head too.

I looked from one to the other. Oddly marvelling at the neatness of the bullet holes in relation to where the blood came from and the sheer amount of it. I had read somewhere, once, how the body contained about one and a half gallons of blood. Yet, what was already on the floor was surely more than that. Where was it all coming from?

I heard Benjamin wail behind me, then a thud as his legs crumpled in on themselves and he fell to the floor. I didn't turn around to help him. I couldn't. I had to look at my father and my sister. I had to stand here until the message finally got to my brain that they were dead and would not suddenly wake up. Because there was a part of me that couldn't believe it. That couldn't comprehend it. I had to look at them. I *had* to make myself understand.

Benjamin told me through his sobs that we had to leave.

I did not answer. I stared at the bodies and tried to look at them as if they were not real. *That is not my father. That is not my sister*, I told myself. Then, I tried to view them as my father would have done if he had seen a dead cow. He would have looked at it and seen the rump, the meat, the blood vessels, the tongue. They were all just parts.

I had the same parts as these bodies in front of me, but Tata had said I was missing a part. I could not take my eyes from them because of this. I wanted to see what part of them existed that I was missing. I imagined what was beneath the thin sheath of skin – the veins, the muscles, the tendons, all connecting, making them whole.

Father had never found the missing piece of me, and I wanted desperately to know if the answer lay in the bodies of my family. If I stared at them for long enough, I was sure I could find it.

Maybe I stood there for a minute, maybe it was an hour. I have no idea. At some point, the bodies of my family finally became *dead* bodies – they were no longer Basia and Tata. I bent down, kneeling in their blood that had intermingled now on the floor, creating one large puddle, and kissed the bullet hole on Basia's forehead. Then I went to my father and kissed the back of his head. Then, for no reason that I can discern, I left Benjamin crying in the corner of the room, the bodies on the floor, and went to my father's room – the room that I had been born in too early, my scarlet ribbon on my wrist flapping against my skin as I walked.

I lay down on my parents' bed, the left side indented from the years of Father's weight, the right still firm from the lack of my mother. I could feel the blood drying on my skin and knew I should wash, change and go back to the bodies and to Benjamin. I wanted to cry. I wished I could. All I could feel was a pounding in my temples, an ache somewhere in my body, yet it was not physical pain. I knew, in theory, what grief was, what sadness was, and I was sure I had felt it before, but I had felt it at the wrong time and for the wrong things – a torn page in a book, for the chickens that got placed back outside.

I should have been like Benjamin – wailing, afraid – and yet there was just the pounding in my head and that ache in my breast that I was sure would never go away. Perhaps I was dying, I thought. Perhaps this was my time too.

I lay there for an hour or so, waiting patiently for the pain in my breast to ease, for my heart to stop beating, but neither happened.

'We have to go, Ania,' Benjamin cried at me. The slur was more pronounced now that he was upset. I looked up to see him standing in the doorway. His face had fallen more – fallen in on itself into an abyss that I was not sure it could come back from.

I didn't want to leave. I wanted to stay on the bed and just wait for my body to stop working.

'Ania.' Benjamin took a step towards me. 'Please. We cannot stay. It's not safe. They might come back.'

They. *Krzysztof. Rolf.*

I could still hear their voices in my head, going round and round like that carousel we saw once in Lublin. Garish. Nightmarish.

'Ania,' Benjamin pleaded. 'Please, Ania.' He began to cry again, and somewhere deep inside of me I felt a pang of something – grief, worry for Benjamin? I didn't know, but the pang was strong enough that it made me get off the bed and leave the room.

As I left, I thought of something. Something odd but that made absolute sense in that moment. Father and Basia were not really gone. It wasn't real. Their bodies were gone but that bit inside them must still be somewhere. They were still *here*, somewhere! Yes! Perhaps hiding in the empty room that I had once filled with chickens.

I ran to the room, and all the time Benjamin screamed at me that we had to leave. I ignored him and pressed on, certain that I would find them. They had gone there to rest – to the quiet. It would be a joke amongst us all – laughing at how I had once hidden chickens in there and now they had hidden themselves too.

I opened the door and it creaked open as it always had. There were still dried stains on the floorboards from the chicken shit that contained those dark berries they ate.

There was no Father, no Basia.

'Ania, we have to leave.' Benjamin was behind me. I could smell his breath, feel the heat of his skin on mine. 'You need to put on shoes and we need to leave.'

I looked to my bare feet that were always bare. I had to wear shoes? I only had to wear shoes when we went to church or into town. What shoes were suitable for a time like this? The fancy ones – all polished and lacquered – hand-me-downs from Basia that I used at Christmas? Or the boots that Father had given me for winter, when he made me wear them in the fields?

What was suitable to wear when your father and sister were dead, you were covered in blood and you had to leave, with no plan, with a man you barely knew, and whose face only half smiled? Who had invented shoes like that? Anyone?

The idea that Basia and Father were still here left me as quickly as it had arrived. I couldn't understand what was going on in my brain. Although ideas always swirled about in there, I could usually control them to some extent, but now, they did as they wished, propelling me forward into notions that were neither logical nor sane.

*Szalony.* I heard Basia's voice. She was right. I certainly was.

We didn't leave straight away. I went to the kitchen and told Benjamin I was hungry. He said he couldn't eat, that it would make him sick. I told him that we had to. I wasn't particularly hungry either but it made sense to sit and eat before leaving – before going out into the night with no idea of where we would end up.

I couldn't cook, and I wasn't much interested in trying now. I found bread, stale though it was, and poured each of us a glass of water.

I sat at the table, and Benjamin did too, staring at me with a flicker of something in his eyes – fear?

He mimicked me. I chewed on the bread; he did the same. I gulped water to soften it; he followed suit.

'Where are we going?' he asked. 'I know I said we have to leave, but I don't know where we should go.'

'To the forest. To hide,' I told him. 'We'll find Bartok. He'll know what to do.'

'You know the way?'

'Yes,' I said. 'They have to be to the east. It's the most logical place.' I could hear myself talking, telling Benjamin about the forests and woodlands of Poland, of the rivers that ran through our country, of how it was chopped up, parts taken by Russia, by Germany. It was my voice, my knowledge, and yet I felt disconnected from it – almost as if I was listening to myself from far, far away.

'You know the way,' Benjamin interrupted me as I began to ramble about the differences between farmlands. 'I trust you. You know the way.'

I stopped and we ate in silence. Every now and then I took a gulp of water to soften the staleness in my mouth and trying not to look a few yards to my left where the bodies of my father and sister lay. The more the silence dragged the more I felt the pounding in my temples, the churning in my stomach. I needed to talk again, about anything, about everything. But before I could begin another speech, Benjamin said, 'You need to change,' then pointed at my nightgown that was more red than white.

I looked down. I did need to change my clothes. 'I'll find something,' I told him and received a sad nod in reply.

That was it. The two of us. In this house, my house, with dead bodies, blood, stale bread and water. We sat there and chewed and pretended like everything was completely normal. That suited me. I was used to pretending. I was used to ignoring things. Even Benjamin had stopped looking at the bodies and was now eating as if it were all normal too. He wanted to play make-believe with me. He let me tell him about the countries of the world and nodded along.

Then, 'Bread's dry,' Benjamin said.

'Yes.'

'We'll take some with us,' he said.

'It'll just get dryer – more stale,' I told him.

'Better than nothing,' he said.

I shrugged. He was right. There were dead bodies not far from me. Empty rooms that I could not fill. We had to leave, and the stale bread would come with us. Sounded logical. Reasonable.

I bit into the bread and chewed. What would Mother think if she could see me now, I wondered. Then I laughed, realising that none of this was logical.

Benjamin stopped eating but did not respond to my outburst.

'Stale bread,' I eventually said once the laughter had died down. Then in English, '*Eating stale bread and everyone's dead. It rhymes, no?*'

# 7

## THE LONG ROAD

*2 December 1942*
*Lublin Voivodeship, Poland*
*Ania*

I made a clumsy attempt to cut my hair before we left, shearing it away with blunt scissors, leaving the long plait in the kitchen sink and strands all over the floor. I could not get it even, and each time I tried it got shorter and shorter until one side sat just under my chin, the other just above. I stopped and asked Benjamin what he thought. He said it was fine then looked at the door and back at me. 'Fine,' he repeated.

We struck out before dawn, into the cold, black stillness, where only a weak glow from the moon gave us any light. It was as though the whole world had descended into darkness – the church that we passed a mere lighter grey, its bricks, mortar and spire all blurred into one as if the night were slowly consuming it. Houses fared no better than the church, all of them ingested into the inkiness making me wonder if we too – this sad pair – would soon be taken into it.

Benjamin had made me wear shoes, but in the end, I had not chosen my own boots – ones I only wore when out in the fields and which were immediately discarded once the work was done, happy to feel the ground under my soles again – I had chosen Father's, wanting to take something of his with me.

They were heavy, with a steel cap that my own toes did not reach but I could feel the heaviness of them regardless. My feet swam in them despite the two pairs of socks I wore, and I tripped more than once and had to learn to walk in them by placing my feet heavily on the ground. Slap, slap. I walked on. Slap, slap. If the situation we found ourselves in were not as nightmarish as this, then it would have been comical to see and hear me walk. A childlike woman slapping down the street wearing oversized boots, and her father's oversized coat that she had rolled up at the sleeves.

I wore a hat too. Again, not mine but Basia's this time. Her favourite one – knitted yellow that she had made herself. The only thing I carried was a small sack that still had the remnants of corn feed stuck within its weave. Inside were the stale bread from earlier, a knife that I had taken from the kitchen drawer, the compass that Isaac had gifted me and a few belongings of Benjamin's – a teddy bear that had one eye missing and a small pouch of money. That's all he wanted to take from his larger bag that we had left in the barn, which contained clothes and shoes. I was glad of the money, not that we were remotely near a village to spend it. The teddy bear I was less fond of; its missing eye and raggedy fur made me think of the one Basia used to have – the one I had performed an operation on years ago, annoyed that the only thing inside was sawdust and not the heart and lungs I had wanted to find. It had upset Basia. It had upset Tata, and he in turn had upset my head by thwacking it so that it throbbed for days.

'You should have worn your own shoes,' Benjamin whispered to me as we walked. 'You'll be uncomfortable.'

I was always uncomfortable but I didn't tell Benjamin that.

'You'll want to see what I have on underneath,' I said. Meaning that I had in fact taken father's trousers, belt, a shirt and jumper – all too big, all rolled up at the cuffs – again a choice that had made perfect sense to me at the time with my family's bodies on the floor, me in a blood-spattered nightgown.

'You shouldn't say that to a man,' Benjamin said.

'Why?'

He didn't answer for a moment. Then said, 'You just shouldn't.'

I didn't understand why what I said was a problem, but then I said things all the time that people said were wrong, so who was I to get upset about this, at this moment, in the dark that was trying to eat us alive?

Soon we were away from any buildings, the shadows lengthened and contorted, and noises began to fill the blank space – the crunch of twigs, the guttural bark of a fox, the lonely call of an owl as it flew seemingly invisible above us.

Now and then Benjamin would grunt as if he were preparing to say something and I would wait, yet no words would come forth. He wanted to fill the silence. Basia had been that way too – not comfortable with her own thoughts. I usually liked the quiet, but this was too much. The quiet meant I could think, could see my thoughts so clearly as if they were a painting in front of me. And I did not want to see those images, I did not want to know my own thoughts any more.

'Benj,' I said.

'Benjamin,' he replied.

'I like Benj though. Did anyone ever call you that? Or maybe some other name? Isaac would sometimes call me *królowo* – queen. I liked that – having a different, special name.'

'You can call me Benj if you want to,' he said. 'Where are we going, Ania?'

Since we had left the farm, Benj had asked this question at least five times. He had gone from hiding me in a bale of straw, confident that this was the right thing to do, to acting like a small child. He bit at his lip; his hands couldn't seem to find comfort – one minute they were shoved deep into his pockets, the next he drew them out and held on to the edge of his coat, worrying at the material. Oddly, though, I liked that he asked me. I liked that he thought I was the one in charge – this had never happened in my life before. It was then that I realised I had to take care of Benj. He may look like a man, even sound like one, but he needed me more than I needed him.

'Keep on this road,' I said authoritatively, and pointed off into the darkness of the countryside, the tip of my finger disappearing into it.

'Are you sure, Ania? Are you sure this is the way?'

'Yes, Benj, I'm sure,' I said, and heard him let out a sigh of relief.

It was about forty-five miles to Parczew, but that was by road. If we stayed off the roads and stuck to the fields I imagined it would be more likely around sixty miles. And then there was the issue of finding Bartok in the forests that were dense with fir trees and lakes. It was possible that we would have to go into Parczew town itself and find a way to ask about the location of the partisans without arousing suspicion – something I was not sure that we could do and yet my feet were still moving, my mind still thinking about what we could find, what it could mean to be a part of the partisan group, how a gun might feel in my hand, how it might feel to stand in front of a soldier, but it was me holding the gun this time. I wondered...

'Ania.' Benj snapped me out of my thoughts. 'Are we still going the right way?'

'Yes, we are,' I told him.

'What were you thinking about just then?' he asked. 'You went all quiet but now and then you whispered things. Are you worried we're going the wrong way? Are you sure about this, Ania?'

'You think someone will find them?' I asked, cutting him off from asking me the same questions over and over. 'You know. Father and Basia. I don't like the thought of leaving them there on the floor. I'm pretty sure that Basia would hate that.'

'Someone will,' Benjamin said.

'You know, we didn't even take a photograph,' I said.

'Of what?'

'Of Tata and Basia. Tata took one of Mother when she died. All in white and in her coffin. He said that a man came all the way from Lublin to take it. We have ones of my grandparents too.'

'But why?' Benj almost cried.

'So we can remember them,' I said. 'You'll take one of me, if I die, won't you?'

'It's macabre, Ania. It's, it's...' He could not find the words. 'No.'

No matter how much I cajoled, he would not speak to me any more and would not agree to take my photograph when I died. But at least he had stopped his relentless questioning of where we were going.

As we walked, I thought of my mother's photograph, of all the other family members too. How I would stare at them when I was young, how I would ask Tata to tell me who each person was and how they died until he took the photographs away from me and locked them in a drawer. It was odd that for years I had not thought of them at all, but now with the image of Tata and Basia seared into my mind, death was all I could think about.

Underfoot, the road began to slope, so my toes suddenly became crammed at the front of Tata's boots with a steel cap. It hurt, especially the toe that was missing half a nail, when I'd stumbled over a rock some hours earlier, as I had raced to the house to find out what all the gunshots had been about.

Was it really only a few hours ago? Surely not?

'What time is it, Benj?' I asked.

He did not answer straight away, still obviously mulling over the thoughts of my family photographs.

He stopped and I stopped too. He turned up the cuff of his brown coat, revealing not a watch but a red ribbon.

'I don't have a watch,' he said, almost surprised. 'I am sure I used to have one. I am sure that my father gave me one. I don't remember taking it off.'

I touched the ribbon on his wrist.

'It kept me safe,' he said. 'Yours kept you safe too.'

He was right. They had. But Basia hadn't had one, nor Tata, nor poor Mother. Why was it that when people needed a red ribbon, it was me that had one and not them? Why was I to be saved?

'Should we keep going?' Benj asked.

The sun was beginning to rise, highlighting the thick morning mist that hung low over fields of green stretched out for miles in front of us. The road ended just a few yards away, where a rotted wooden gate sat half off its hinges, leading the way into all that green.

'We keep going,' I said. 'There are trees over there, look,' I said, pointing. 'We should stay out of sight, off the roads. We can't be seen otherwise they will stop us and ask us for our *Kennkarten*. It will take longer,' I told him. 'Staying off the roads will take an extra day or more to get to Parczew.'

I saw Benj nod. 'If you say so,' he said.

We traipsed on and the world woke up around us. Silence banished itself as sparrows, wood pigeons and crows called out to each other, flitting from bare branch to bare branch, their eyes seeking out food.

'It will snow soon,' Benj said.

He was right. It would. As the sun rose higher, weighted clouds sat low, and that only meant one thing.

'I like the snow,' I said. 'I like that it makes everything look clean – almost new.'

'I don't think you will like it when we have to sleep outside,' Benj said.

'Perhaps not,' I said.

'Ania—' Benj started.

'Yes.'

'Can I ask you something?'

'Yes. But why do people always say that? Why not just ask the question? Tata would do it and so would Basia, even Isaac too. Why ask a question to ask a question? It's always bothered me,' I rambled on.

'Ania.' Benj cut me off. 'Why are you not upset about your father and sister? Why haven't you cried?'

'I told you before. I don't understand a lot of emotions,' I said, yet I felt a prickle of annoyance on my skin.

'I know. But surely this is different. Surely it has upset you.'

'I am upset.' I stopped walking. 'I am.'

Benj stopped too and stared at me.

'It's just – I don't know – it comes out differently. My mind is different now than it was yesterday – nothing is making much sense.'

'Like why you're wearing your father's clothes and boots,' he suggested.

I looked down at the boots, scuffed with dirt, the laces tied tight; not that it made much difference – they were too big. 'Like the boots,' I agreed.

We walked all day to reach the far end of those fields where trees grew – most of them bare limbed, some with a few rusted leaves holding on until a stronger wind would come by and whip them away.

It was not a forest. Nor really could one call it a wood. A clump of trees? A thicket? This was not where we would find Bartok, I knew, but then something in me had hoped just a little that our journey would be a short one – that we would find someone.

I kicked at the mulched ground as we walked through it, Benj's lumbering frame a few steps ahead, reaching out to snap away twigs so he could break them between his bear-like hands.

So far, I was disappointed with Poland outside of the farm.

The fields were like those at home, which in summer were a patchwork of green, contrasted with fields of golden wheat that swayed in the wind. In winter, the scene on the farm became muted – the earth's brown belly churned up into neat rows, the trees skeletal, the hedgerows quiet of any songbirds. It was the same here too. I don't know what I was hoping to see, but I had expected some difference from the farm – just something.

'Look.' Benj stooped and pointed down into a valley. There a church spire reached up into the late afternoon blue, chimneys spouting puffs of smoke. A village.

'We should stay away from it,' I said.

'But we need to find somewhere to sleep, to eat and rest,' Benj countered.

I agreed that we did, but it could not be there. I remembered those scenes of Tomasz being shot, of the Jews being taken away – it was not safe for us. But we could not stop there, and we could not stop here. We had to keep going.

Benj amused himself on the walk by picking at more twigs, sometimes long grass, and holding a blade between his thumb and finger, blowing on it to try to make a sound. He was not very good, so this kept him busy for a while.

A memory suddenly popped into my head as I watched Benj with his sliver of grass, a memory of my father on a day when he had been happy with me and I with him, a day when we left the farm and travelled to Lublin for a fair.

I had been perhaps six or seven years old and had asked questions for days before we left about what would be at this fair, what we would do and who we would see.

Tata had soon got frustrated with my questions, as did Basia, who told me to wait and see.

'It will be like a surprise,' she said.

'I don't like surprises. I like to know,' I replied.

'I think you should stay here,' she retorted. 'Why Tata thinks you'll behave or even like it, I don't know.'

But I liked it. Not at first. Not as we arrived in the city, with buildings crammed in next to each other, carts and small motor cars dashing down the streets. Throngs of people on the pavements, noise, dust, smells of sun-baked roads, soot and something sweet like the rotting vegetables at home.

I held my father's hand willingly that day, getting upset

when he let go of it to light a cigarette or a pipe, grabbing hold of his leg and whimpering like a puppy.

'We shouldn't have brought her,' Basia said.

It was not until we reached the fair that things started to change. Father lifted me up, grunting as he carried me through the mass of people, perhaps wishing he had left me at home. 'Don't talk to anyone,' he warned as we walked. 'None of that screaming and crying. None of that talking about the stars and the moon again. You just keep quiet and keep close to me.'

I nodded but soon, my chubby hands grasping his neck as we walked loosened as I took in the sights around me.

Stalls lined the fairgrounds; the blues, yellows and reds of awnings flapped gently in the summer breeze. The warm air carried with it the aroma of fresh bread, roasted pork, *naleśniki*, sweet crepes and *rogaliki*, almond cookies intermingling with the sawdust and dry trampled grass underfoot.

I let go of my father's neck and pointed at one stall. 'Look, Tata!' I exclaimed, pointing at the shiny red apples that overflowed from baskets, the pears and blackberries.

I heard my father laugh. 'It's just fruit, Ania,' he said. But to me, it wasn't just fruit – it was the colours of them. How the red, greens and purples all jammed themselves together, how they seemed to shine and wink at me invitingly.

I wriggled free from him and he immediately clamped my hand in his. Rules were still rules, no matter how excited I was.

Basia was allowed to run free and disappeared with a group of children who ran between legs, darting here, there and everywhere, whooping with joy when they found the *pączki* stall, eager to place an order for ones filled with warm strawberry jam.

The merry-go-round, with the twinkling lights and music, I did not like, however. It moved too quickly, faces became blurry and my eyes could not follow where Basia was on her allotted horse. Yellows, reds, golds and greens turned and turned so fast, the music seemingly speeding up too so that I told Tata I felt I was going to be sick. He took me to the edge of the scene, sitting down next to me in the dried, spiky grass, and handed me a shiny red apple. I grinned at him and bit into it, happy to find that it tasted differently from the apples at home – it was juicier, crispier.

As the light began to wane, lanterns were lit, and from somewhere deep in the throng came the whistle of a tin flute, the scratch of a bow on a violin.

'It's a nice apple,' I told my father. 'Thank you, Tata.'

In that moment, he had leaned down and kissed the top of my head, then he had lit his pipe and we two had sat in companiable silence as families wove themselves in amongst stalls, as children whooped with joy, their faces smeared with sugar and jam.

'I like the apple,' I'd told Tata.

'Good.'

'It's red,' I'd said. 'I think I like red.'

'Good. That's good, Ania.'

\* \* \*

'Are we ever going to stop?' Benj asked, breaking me free from the memory of the warm summer air and the sweet smell of Tata's pipe smoke.

'We need to keep moving,' I told him, even though the blanket of night was drawing down its curtain. 'We need to keep moving,' I said again.

I went to Benj's side and took his hand in mine, just as Tata had done that day at the fair. I felt him relax and we walked together, matching each other's pace.

As we walked, I could not stop thinking about the apple – that red apple that had enticed me so. That redness that shone. The same hue that was all over the floor of the farmhouse. The same hue that dripped from Tata and Basia. The more I thought of the apple, of the redness, the burning sensation in my chest grew – Krzysztof, Rolf, their nonchalant way in which they took my family from me. The way that others had come before and made Isaac leave, shot that poor boy Tomasz. The more I thought of the apple, the more the rage grew.

I knew then I would never be able to look at an apple in the same way again.

# 8

*Autumn, 1969*
*Parczew Forest, Lublin Voivodeship, Poland*
*Benjamin*

'Ania.' Benjamin interrupted her. 'I don't know what we did next. We walked, didn't we? For such a long while. I don't know whether it was a day or more. I think I remember us sleeping under some leaves – you were close to me, but I don't know when that was.'

'Come on, Benj,' her voice cajoled. 'You have to remember Gosia at least, you must remember her.'

Benjamin nodded. He did remember Gosia – the old woman. Where was it? In that house with the woman who made them leave. Who'd made them take Gosia with them.

'It was a village, wasn't it? There was a house. It had a red door. I remember the door, Ania. I remember telling you that I didn't think I had seen a red door on a house before. And you said that you would have chosen green – like the fields we had just walked through. You said that you liked all the green.'

'I did. I do,' she told him.

'Do you think our story is real, Ania? Sometimes, at night, I try to remember everything and piece it all together, but the pieces all float away from me.' He shook his head.

'It's getting late in the day,' she said. 'We must hurry now. You don't like the dark.'

'No, I still don't.'

He waited for her voice to begin the story again where it mattered. All that walking – that didn't matter, did it? They walked and walked. She got blisters on her feet and they popped out a clear liquid then soon became bloody as her socks rubbed.

He remembered her taking off the boots one day. He wasn't sure when this had occurred – before Gosia or afterwards? But she had, and he had thought that she would be in more pain – her soles scraping against rocks and stones, slicing into her skin. But as soon as the boots had come off, she had become lighter on her feet.

'I like to feel the earth between my toes,' she had said, standing in a potato field, squidging her feet into the damp soil.

'Benj. That was the day we met Gosia. We stood there and I told you about potatoes and you found it interesting. I told you I hated them and you made me eat a raw one. She was sitting in the field. Remember, Benj? Can you see it now, can you hear me?'

'I can hear you,' he said. But he tried not to listen to her for a moment. He thought instead of Gosia, a woman he'd loved yet had resented somewhat for what she did to Ania – how she had put ideas in her head, changing her, making her mind work differently. Ania became different, harder, and something shifted in her – a darkness that he did not care for, and which he was sure was Gosia's doing.

Not that it had been Gosia's fault, not really. She couldn't help herself. She didn't know what she was talking about half of the time. She was old, ragged, with those four teeth – one of them gold-capped, that winked in the sunlight when she smiled.

'She should have stayed in that hospital,' Benjamin said. 'Or we should have found a new one for her to go to.'

'Don't say that, Benj. I went once. Didn't I tell you how one day, Tata took me to a hospital? Didn't I tell you what it was like and how I had run all the way home, even beating Tata to the front door?'

'You did,' he said.

He remembered now, how Ania had told him about the hospital. How it was on the outskirts of a village not far from the farm – how it had held people there, all different ages, away from their families, away in the middle of nowhere so they could not bother anyone.

She had told him of the doctor with the hawked face, how he had made her stand in her underwear as he had measured her height, the circumference of her head. How she had shivered in the cold room, the white walls seemingly closing in on her.

She had told him how her father had left her for a moment in the room whilst he stepped out to talk to the doctor, and how she had dressed herself, opened the door and made a run for it.

And how, when her father had got home, she was found sat on the doorstep, afraid to go inside lest Basia berate her, so she'd simply waited for her *tata* to come home.

'I had expected him to be angry,' her voice chimed in now. 'But he wasn't. He was relieved, he said, that he had found me. He had hugged me and told me that he would never take me back there, and that he wasn't actually going to leave me there. He said he'd heard the screams from the patients on the floor above and was about to tell the doctor that he had made a mistake when I suddenly bolted from the room and then the building.'

'He loved you,' Benjamin told her.

'In his way, yes,' she agreed.

He thought of his own parents how sometimes they would get mad at him for forgetting things or for not understanding simple instructions. But they always cared for him, always stood up for him, always told him he was special.

'Benj!' Ania's voice was demanding. 'We were talking about Gosia. We were talking about what came next. Let me tell it to you so then maybe you'll understand why I changed and what Gosia said. Maybe you'll see her and me a bit differently.'

Benjamin nodded.

'You ready?'

'Yes,' he answered.

'All right then. I'll tell you about our time with Gosia. About Gosia and the potatoes and the reason I changed.'

# 9

## GOSIA AND THE POTATOES

*4 December 1942*
*Lublin Voivodeship, Poland*
*Ania*

I had always hated potatoes. At home, they came with every meal. And the worst part of that was that Basia, Father and I spent days digging them up, placing them in sacks and moving them to the barn. There was no joy in the work. It was back breaking, and more than that, it was incredibly boring. No matter how many games I invented – counting them, multiplying them, figuring out circumference – within an hour I wanted to howl and cry. My fingers ached, dirt wedged itself under my fingernails, sweat dripped into my underwear. There was nothing good about the exercise that left my muscles aching for days afterwards, throbbing well into the night so that I could not sleep. The only thing to be gained with the endeavour was that Father earned money, but I was sure he had missed a trick somewhere. There must have been a better way to earn money than digging for potatoes.

So when our journey brought us to a large potato field where some of the harvested potatoes were still left half in and half out of the ground, I felt as though we had done a huge circle and were back on the farm. In a way, I was glad at first to think that the past few days had been nothing but a nightmare, and I reached down into the soil and scrabbled about for a potato. I brought it out and looked at its skin, which was covered with dirt, eyes on it beginning to sprout.

It wasn't Tata's potato though. These were different. I knew that. Tata grew large, heavy potatoes for boiling and baking. These were smaller and, if Tata had grown these, he would have thrown them out for their size.

I tossed the potato back onto the field then reached down and unlaced my boots, desperate to feel the soil between my toes and to air out my bloodied feet, the raw skin, the heels that were a mass of blisters.

Benj was a few yards away from me, bending over, digging about in the soil. He was hungry. I needed to do more for him, I could see that he was starting to flail. The first day or so, he had willingly followed me, assuming that I knew what to do and where we were going. I, on the other hand, simply walked and talked. I couldn't go home; we had to move on, and we were doing so. That was all I needed to know. We had found streams from which to drink water, but food was another thing entirely, and I had to admit that even though I sometimes went days without food – my appetite was as strange as my mind – even my stomach was starting to moan.

My feet, finally free from their prison, delighted in the cool soil, the texture of that damp earth seeping between each toe. I let out a sigh of relief as I walked to Benj, who was now sat back on his haunches, his back curved, head down, looking at the soil.

As I stood in front of him, he looked first at my feet and then at my face. He didn't talk because his mouth was full of raw, and possibly rotting, potato. He tried to grin at me as he ate, causing some of the potato to spill from the right side of his mouth.

I waited for him to finish chewing then he stood and handed me a potato.

'I'm not eating that,' I told him.

'You have to. We need to eat,' he said.

'It can make you sick when it's not cooked. You might be regretting it later today.'

'I don't care. Ania, please. You need to eat and you need to put your shoes back on.'

'I like the feel of the earth under me,' I said. 'And I'm not eating it.'

A light drizzle of rain fell, the freezing drips sneaking their way under my collar and down my back. It would snow soon.

'Eat the potato, Ania,' Benj said again.

I took it from him and took a small bite so that he was appeased then left him to return to his digging, finding his next meal.

With Benj busy, I walked through the field and chucked the potato back onto the soil. My mouth was still full of the bite I had taken, floury with a hint of sourness. I spat the remains in the dirt.

As I walked, I imagined I could hear Tata whistling a tune. Had he done that, whistled as he had worked? The whistling got louder, a tune I knew but could not place. I shook my head. My mind was doing some new things. I kept my eyes on my feet, watching the soil devour them, listening to the tune in my head, and trying to think what we should do next. The soil stopped and reached a grassed edge. I turned and followed the next rut.

It was then that I looked up from my feet and saw not one, but two hunched figures in the field.

Benj raised his head and looked at the new figure too.

I went to him. 'Who is it?' he asked. 'Where did they come from?'

I could hear the panic in his voice. 'I don't know. There was no one there a moment ago.'

'What's that song, too?' he asked and scrunched up his nose. 'I know that tune.'

'You can hear it?'

'Of course I can,' he said.

So it wasn't Tata whistling. It was this stooped figure, blurred in the drizzle that fell, wearing a red woollen coat. Red again. Red ribbons. Red apple. Red blood. Red coat. I felt that flare in my chest again. *Basia, Tata, Krzysztof, Rolf, Tomasz and all that red.*

I stepped towards them and Benj grabbed my arm, but he was a little too late and I slipped out of his grasp. Within a few seconds I stood next to the figure. A woman, whose grey hair was wetted to her skull, showing blotches of pink scalp.

She continued to whistle, either not realising that I was there or not caring. I reached out and patted her arm, to which she reacted. The whistling stopped. Her face turned and she grinned at me, revealing a mostly empty mouth, save for four teeth, one that was capped in gold.

'You lost, little girl? Or boy, is it?' she asked and cocked her head to the side. Then she stood, wiping her muddied hands on her coat that had no buttons, revealing a thin yellow summer dress, splotched with stains and not at all suitable for the time of year. Her legs were bare of stockings; she wore grey socks, pulled taut across her calves, and old brown leather lace-up shoes, battered and bruised, encased her feet.

I could understand why she thought I was possibly a boy.

My rushed haircut and Basia's yellow hat most likely made me look like one. 'I'm Ania,' I said and stretched out my arm for her to take my hand and shake it – just like Basia had told me to do when introducing myself to someone.

She wiped her hand again on her coat and took my hand in hers and pumped it enigmatically. 'Gosia,' she said. 'Gosia Dabrowska. Came here to find me some potatoes and I see you and your friend have the same idea.' She nodded at Benjamin, who stood a few feet away, his hands by his side, his fingers doing a nervous dance on the top of his thighs.

'What's with the face then?' she asked him, then she cackled with laughter, making her own face crease up into hundreds of small lines. As suddenly as she started to laugh, she stopped. 'Oh, don't mind me. I'm old, see. It was just a joke. Must have hurt something rotten – all those scars,' she said to Benjamin, who just nodded in reply. 'That your *tata*?' she asked me.

'No. My friend,' I said. 'And I'm not lost – not really. No. I mean, I'm not a girl – I'm almost twenty years old,' I said and stood as tall as I could. 'And certainly not a boy.'

'Is that right?' she said. 'Takes all sorts I suppose. Not lost though? So where are you going?'

I knew I could talk to this woman – she was no threat – a woman in a summer dress, no stockings and foraging for potatoes.

'To the forests, woodlands,' I told her. 'In the east.'

'Forest, eh? No big forests around here.'

'I know,' I said, repeating 'in the east,' to her again.

She shrugged. 'No forests here,' she said, as if she hadn't heard me.

Seemingly bored of our conversation, she bent back down to dig once more in the dirt, whistling a new tune. Then she stopped, her hands still in the soil.

'You seen many of them?' Gosia whispered.

'Who?' I asked.

'Shush! They could hear you, you know!'

'Who?' I asked again, quieter now.

'The Germans, of course. Who else do you think I'm talking about? I've seen them. Dealt with them too. But they couldn't catch me – oh no! Couldn't catch old Gosia. They tried, you know, to get me. Tried to bundle me into one of their trucks. All the others went – had no choice, did they? But me, I hid. I'm good at hiding and I knew that hospital like the back of my hand and hid for hours and hours and then they went and I had to leave, but on my own, see.' She turned to look at me. 'Just me. Just Gosia. I had to go on my own.'

'Are you cold?' Benj suddenly asked. Gosia's legs were goose-pimpled, her hands red and cracked. He stepped towards her, took off his coat and handed it to her.

She stood and looked at Benj's large brown coat as if she had never seen one before. 'For me? For Gosia?' she asked.

He nodded.

Then she grinned and showed that gold tooth again. 'Not for me. I like this red one. A nice lady gave it to me. Do you want to meet her? She's nice. She wants me to leave but where can I go? I mean, that's what I say to her every day. "Where would Gosia go?" So I come out here and look for potatoes and keep out of her way until at night she lets me back in the house to sleep. But I think she would like you two. Yes. Yes, she would.' She nodded, then held out her hand for Benj to take.

He took it and looked at me, waiting to see if it was okay. I couldn't see why not. We had slept overnight, curled together under leaves and moss. We needed warmth and we needed food – not raw potatoes.

I nodded at him and he took his coat from Gosia, put it on

and then took the old woman's hand and began to pick their way over the soft, moist earth. I stood back and watched them both for a moment. Benj so big and cumbersome, Gosia small next to him, her red coat flapping open to reveal a flash of the dirty yellow sundress. She walked slowly, carefully, her legs slightly bowed. Benj matched her pace, the pair of them ambling along, seemingly happy to have found each other.

'Ania!' Benj turned his head and yelled for me. 'Come, be quick!'

Trying to ignore the ache, I caught up with the two of them and listened to Gosia's inane chatter that made little sense to me, but seemed to make perfect sense to Benj, who nodded along, giving her one of his lopsided smiles as the day began to slowly turn into night, blanketing the field behind us in shadows.

'I like your hat,' Gosia said. 'Yellow. I like yellow.'

I touched the soft wool, damp from the cold drizzle that fell. 'It was my sister's,' I told her.

'I had a sister once,' she said. 'But she left me in a hospital, so I said to her when she visited me, "Don't you come here again. You're no sister of mine!" So she didn't come back. Will your sister come and look for you? Did she make you come outside in the cold and with all these soldiers everywhere? If she did, you must tell her that she's not your sister any more,' she advised.

'She's not coming back either,' was all I said by way of explanation.

'That's all well and good then. You stick with me, gal, with old Gosia. She'll show you the way.'

It seemed that Gosia's way was fairly honed. She kept away from the roads, dragging us through brambles that caught at my legs as we waded through them, through thickets of trees, across small streams. She was agile for her age and was able to chatter most of the time, whereas I found it hard to catch my breath. More than once I took out Isaac's compass to check the direction in which she was taking us, sure that she was getting us lost.

But no, within the hour, just as the drizzle turned into sleet, we reached a small cottage as the sky spotted itself with stars and a sliver of moon. It sat at the bottom of a rutted, dusty track, surrounded by thick firs and pines that shielded it from any prying eyes. A welcoming glow came from between the cracks in the drawn curtains, the scent of a woodfire filled my nostrils and I suddenly felt a tiredness wash over me.

We reached the front door – painted red, and once more my mind went to the apple, and then the burning in my chest started again with such force that I had to take a deep breath of the ice-cold air.

Gosia had already pushed open the door and Benj was making his way inside.

'Ania,' he said.

'I'm coming,' I replied, but my feet did not move.

'It's cold out here.'

'I know.'

'What is it?' he asked, his voice little more than a whisper.

'The door. It's red,' I said.

He nodded, unsure of what I meant.

'I don't like red any more. It should be green. Green is better. Green always made me feel lighter,' I rambled.

'I don't understand, Ania.'

'No, you wouldn't. It's fine. I don't expect anyone to understand.'

Then I gave a laugh and shook my head. Was I dreaming, was any of this really happening?

'You're tired,' Benj said. 'Come on, Ania. You need to sleep.'

He held out a big hand of his and I took it and allowed him to take me into the warmth of the house, closing the red door behind us.

To the right was a small kitchen with a wooden table and mismatched chairs of different sizes and styles. Gosia was already in the kitchen with a grey-haired woman, the pair of them talking loudly – Gosia the loudest.

As we entered the kitchen, the old woman sharply turned to look at us. 'Who are you?' she demanded, her lips pursed into a thin line.

'It's Ania and Benjamin,' Gosia said, taking potatoes from her pockets and placing them on the kitchen table.

'I don't know you! Why are you here, who are you?' the woman asked. She opened her mouth to say something else but then caught sight of Benj's face and her lips made a perfect O of surprise.

Benj held out his sizeable paw for her to take, but she stared at it then back at his face. He then dropped it to his side and tried to smile. Her reaction to the smile was one of disgust on seeing half the face raise, the other half sag.

'Aldona.' Gosia sighed. 'I just told you. That is Ania and that is Benjamin.' She pointed at us both. 'And she's not a boy although she looks a little like one. And she's not a girl either – would you credit it, she's a woman. Almost twenty, indeed. And he's nice, just don't worry about his face.'

Gosia's voice had broken Aldona from staring at Benj and she turned to her and shook her head, her eyes half closing with perhaps tiredness. 'You can't do this, Gosia, you can't bring more people here.'

'It's all right,' Gosia said. 'They'll sleep with me in the attic.'

'I'm sorry, Gosia, I can't do this any more!' Aldona cried. 'Every day you do something. Like you go out and come back with a chicken that you've stolen; or you find strangers on the road! And all the while you're meant to be hiding. If they see you, if they come here...' She trailed off and raised her arms as if in defeat. 'I'm sorry, Gosia. I can't have you here any more.'

'You say that every day,' Gosia cackled. She went to Aldona and patted her arm. 'It'll be fine.'

Gosia, seemingly not understanding what Aldona was saying, went to the stove and filled a pan with water.

'You,' Aldona whispered at me, 'come here.' She wiggled a finger and I followed her into a small sitting room, a fire ablaze in the hearth. Framed photographs of family members hung on the walls alongside watercolour paintings of fields, of the sea and one of an owl.

Aldona sank into one of the chairs with a sigh. 'How old are you, *really*?' she asked me.

I stood in the middle of the room, unsure of whether I should sit too. I eyed a tattered green armchair and waited for her to tell me to sit. She didn't.

'Almost twenty,' I said.

'You look like a child – how odd,' she said. 'And that man in there, with the face.' She reached up and touched her cheek. 'Who's he?'

'My friend,' I said.

'A Jew?'

I nodded.

'And you? Jewish?'

'No,' I answered. 'Catholic.'

She nodded. 'Not very chatty, are you?' she said, then sighed. 'And where are you going?'

'Away,' I said. I did not want to tell her about the forest, about Bartok. There was something about her that I just didn't trust.

'Where are you from?'

'A small village,' I answered, delighting that I saw her grasp the arm rests of the chair. I knew she was annoyed. That was something Isaac had done when I had annoyed him too.

'Fine,' she said. 'Don't tell me, I don't care. But I do care that you're going somewhere. It's time for Gosia to leave. You can take her with you.'

'I am not sure that she wants to leave.'

She placed her hands either side of the chair and raised herself up. 'I tried to help her, God knows I did. Turned up on my doorstep one morning, wearing that awful yellow dress, dirty and cold. I couldn't turn her away, could I? Others in town have helped, you know, hiding people, Jews and some others part of the resistance. Gosia told me how they took the other patients at the hospital – they want the mad ones too! And I thought, why not? I'm alone, in the middle of nowhere. But Gosia, Gosia.' She stopped. 'She's *different. Too different.*'

Different. Strange. *Szalony.* I knew all the words.

'I can't cope with her. She won't stay hidden. Wanders about and sometimes she is gone for days then she turns back up here and tells me she was talking with people. I ask her who these people are but she never says! I mean, doesn't she realise the danger she's putting me in, herself in?' Aldona wrung her hands and looked to the kitchen where we could hear Gosia telling Benj how to boil potatoes.

'You'll take her with you.' She stepped towards me and took my hands in hers. 'Please. She'll be better with her own kind – find others like her, find a doctor to help her. I can't help her. Please.'

I could see two things at once in this woman – the way she wanted to help and her own fear. I could almost feel the anxiety coming off her. 'We'll take her,' I said. 'But she's already with her own kind,' I added, watching as Aldona's eyes widened, her mouth opening and closing.

'I didn't mean—' she said.

'It's okay,' I told her. 'I *understand*.'

I felt her flinch as I told her I understood. The same flinch that Basia would give when my voice became cold, sharper than normal. It would stop her in her tracks, make her think again about what she was about to do. I liked it when Basia did that – it gave me a feeling of power over her. But it never lasted long; the next day she would find something to say, a hairbrush to throw at me, and I would wish for that cold, stony voice to come back once more. But it could not be trusted to appear at will; instead, it appeared without me even thinking of it.

'We should eat. You can stay tonight and then tomorrow you'll be gone?'

I didn't answer and watched her walk out of the room, noting that she looked over her shoulder at me and gave a weak grin.

As I followed her and sat on a chair with a high back, watching the three of them get plates, go into a larder and return with jars, I thought of Basia. All those times she had been mean to me, punched me, and yet knowing that she no longer existed in this world made me discombobulated. Whether I had enjoyed my life or not, whether I had been happy or not, Basia and Tata had been my world, my anchor. With them gone, I wasn't sure who I was, what I was supposed to say, what I was supposed to do even. They would tell me when I said something out of turn, when my ramblings went on for too long, when they felt I was being lazy and needed to help clean or dig for pota-toes. I'd relied on them for that guidance – even Isaac too – helping me not to get frustrated to see the other side of things. 'They are as frustrated as you, Ania,' he told me once. 'That frustration you feel at the lack of books, of stimulation, that then presents itself in tantrums and fits; imagine how they feel having to witness that all the time.'

'Well, they should get me more books. Basia shouldn't hit me,' I had told him.

'Your father has little money, no wife. Basia, she is looking to carry on with her life now she is almost a woman – she wants to get married, have children of her own and yet she is stuck helping your father, taking care of you too. Imagine how frustrating that must be? They love you, Ania, they do love you and want the best for you, it's simply that they are not sure what to do with you.'

As I sat in Aldona's kitchen, with Isaac's voice in my head, I came to realise that I had most likely been awful to live with. Selfish, absorbed in my own mind all the time. I suddenly had a new feeling, one I had never experienced before. It wriggled around in my stomach and made me feel nauseous. I wanted to tell Tata and Basia I was sorry. I wanted to go back in time and change my behaviour and make it easier for them.

'Guilt,' I suddenly said out loud, making the trio look at me.

'What?' Aldona asked.

'Nothing. Just thinking.'

She gave me that weak, almost scared, smile again and went back to shelling peas into a bowl.

Guilt. Shame, perhaps too? I didn't like either feeling and tried to push them back down and instead looked at Gosia's red coat, thought of the red apple and allowed the bigger feeling of rage to take front and centre instead. This was a feeling that, although it made me uncomfortable, was much better than anything else that was trying to break free.

* * *

Dinner was boiled potatoes, sauerkraut, pickled fish and peas. The potatoes I immediately pushed to the side of my plate. As we ate, a comforting quiet came over the room. The warmth from the fireplace, the food that was beginning to fill my stomach, made me come over all sleepy, so I found that I wasn't particularly aware when Gosia was talking, nor taking in much of what she was saying.

'The last supper,' she said. 'Ania. It was the last supper, wasn't it?'

'Hmmm?'

Gosia rolled her eyes at me. 'The last supper. They ate fish and potatoes. I know they did. It's in the Bible.' Then she looked at Benj. 'Not your book. The one you don't read. There was this man, Jesus, and they had this dinner one night before he died and there was fish and potatoes. I'm right, Ania, aren't I?'

'They ate bread and drank wine,' I said, then yawned. 'Matthew 26:17–29; Mark 14:12–25; Luke 22:7–38; and I Corinthians 11:23–25. Not sure about the fishes or potatoes.'

'You know your scripture,' Aldona said, seemingly impressed.

'I know a lot of things,' I said.

'Oh,' she replied, then stuck a forkful of sauerkraut in her mouth.

'We need to sleep before our adventure tomorrow.' Gosia leaned back in her chair and rubbed her stomach.

'It's not an adventure,' Benj said.

'Oh rubbish. It will be with old Gosia here, you'll see. Look at us: nice supper, full bellies – like the last supper. Then off we go on a new adventure.'

I didn't bother reminding Gosia that the following day Christ had died.

* * *

We climbed the narrow staircase to the attic, each holding a candle to light the way, mine worn almost to a nub. As soon as Aldona closed the door and wished us a restful sleep, I heard the click of a lock from the outside. She had locked us in.

Gosia seemed not to mind that she had been locked into an attic and made her way to a heap of blankets in a corner and sank down on top of them, sighing.

Benjamin, ever curious, and bent almost double, went from corner to corner, crevice to crevice, his candle in his hands, seeking out anything else that was in this space. There was nothing of interest and soon, he slumped down, his back against an eave, and stretched his legs out in front of him.

'I like it here,' Gosia said, her voice softer now. She yawned. 'It reminds me of my home once, before... before everything changed.'

Benjamin yawned loudly.

'Here.' She handed him one of her blankets. 'You get some sleep.'

He took the blanket from her and curled up into a tight ball, his eyes on the candle that sat on the dusty floorboards, his lids heavy and closing.

'He had a home too,' she whispered as Benj succumbed to sleep, his breathing ragged within seconds.

'So did I,' I said.

'Who with?' Gosia asked, shifting her weight a little.

I told her about the farm, about my father and sister. I told her about the men with their voices and what they did.

She never interrupted me as I spoke, nodding along as if she knew it was what I was going to say.

'I didn't have that; I almost did, but not quite. You know,

Ania, when I was young, like you, I was beautiful!' She grinned and the candlelight caught her gold tooth, which winked at me.

'Beautiful, I was. Married my husband – and he was handsome. All the girls in the village were jealous. They wanted him but I got him. And I had a plan too, to have children and live this happy life. But then things changed.'

'The war.' I nodded sagely.

'Oh, God no!' Gosia laughed and Benj stirred in his sleep. She lowered her voice. 'It happened a long, long time ago. He ran off, you see. He left poor Gosia all alone and ran away with another woman who he'd met in Warsaw. Said he'd made a mistake. A mistake, I ask you! He was my husband. *Mine.*' She stabbed at her chest. 'And he took off. She took him from me.'

'He never came back?' I asked.

'No,' she said. 'Never. And me, I was left alone. Parents were dead, one sister, and this feeling – this thing – in my brain telling me how I wanted him back, but at the same time how I wanted to kill him.'

'Kill him?'

'Of course!' She laughed again and Benj turned onto his side. 'Why not? He deserved it. Leaving me all alone. But then some people came' – she shook her head – 'said I needed to see a doctor – something about me shouting things in the street, but I'm sure I didn't do that – I'm sure Gosia would never shout things in the street and upset people. So they took me. Put me in hospitals. All my life, nearly. I thought my sister would save me from it but she put me in them too. But then those soldiers came and I hid!' She winked at me. 'Hid. Gosia hid and then she ran. So now I can do what I want.'

'What do you want?' I asked.

She shrugged. 'I still love him, you know. Maybe I will find him. Maybe make him love me. Maybe kill him though.' She shrugged again. 'And you. What do you want? What will you do? Me, I know what I would do if someone did that to my family.'

'Kill them?' I suggested.

'Of course!' She laughed then settled herself down on her heap of blankets, pulling and stretching at the red coat to cover her body as much as possible.

I managed to free a blanket and place it over her.

'Kill them,' I said to myself, but I must have said it aloud, as Gosia's eyes widened.

'*Exactly*, Ania.' She grabbed at my hand; her skin was cold and dry. 'You have to have a purpose, see. I had one but it was taken from me, and now I need a new one. And you need one too.'

'I never thought of having one,' I said. 'A purpose.'

'Now, see...' She let go of my hand and propped herself up on her elbow, her head resting in her hand. 'Some women's purpose is just to get married and have babies. I suppose that was my purpose to begin with, but it sent me all wrong. Now, even though all that nonsense is going on out there, you still have to find a purpose.'

'So I have to get married?' I asked, not quite grasping what she meant.

'No, no! None of that. Revenge, dear girl! Revenge! All those soldiers out there and some of them took your sister – even the police chief was in on it, you said. Traitors out there too. You find them and make them pay.'

'And what would I do after that?' I asked. 'My purpose would be over.'

'Oh, there's plenty of them, girl. Plenty of those men and their guns out there – you'll never be able to get them all!' She cackled again, rousing Benj, who rolled over, opened his eyes to look at us and then fitfully fell back to sleep.

I scuffled away from Gosia and lay down next to her, staring at her as she spoke. 'You stick with me, girl. Old Gosia here will teach you all sorts of things. Old Gosia will show you how to be a woman – a strong woman – no more of you talking like a little girl any more. No. None of that. You'll show them all, my dear. They'll see a child walking towards them and then you'll show them all.'

Her eyes began to close and I let her talk until there was nothing but her heavy breathing.

I closed my eyes and tried to sleep but Gosia's voice rang in my mind: *You're not a little girl*, the voice said. *You can show them. You can have a purpose.* I thought back over the years, how I had never grown up – not properly – how I had leaned into being taken care of, coddled, misunderstood and yelled at. How that wasn't my life any more and I could decide what I did now.

But could I kill someone?

Then a new thought, in my voice: *You already killed your mother.*

## 10

## A NEW ROAD AND A NEW ANIA

*5 December 1942*
*Lublin Voivodeship, Poland*
*Ania*

That night, I dreamt of Tata and Basia. They were in the farmhouse, at the kitchen table. I went to join them, dragging out my chair ready to sit down. But I never sat. I looked at them. My father's eyes were open, his mouth was slack and blood dripped from his head onto the table. Basia's face was covered in red. But she could still talk, still blink. She grinned at me.

'Sister,' she said. 'It's all your fault. Why did you do this to us?'

I think I screamed. I reached out to Tata and tried to wake him but all I did was make his head loll to one side.

'Why did you do it, Ania? Why?'

Behind me I could hear other voices speaking in German. I turned to try to see the faces but there was no one there but the voices – the voices were clear, loud, and it felt like they were getting closer.

'Why did you do it, Ania?' Basia asked me again. 'Why did you let it happen?'

I woke, started and sat bolt upright and looked about me. Both Gosia and Benj were still asleep, Benj whimpering in his dreams like a puppy, and I wondered whether he was having the same vision I had had.

I went to the small window that looked out onto the fields below. The morning mist was thick, the weak winter sun too slow to rise and burn it away. I watched the mist for some time, my warm breath steaming up the window now and then so that I had to wipe it away with my hand. Feeling the cold glass on my skin made me wake up a little. I stopped thinking so much of the dream and thought more to who I was today. I was new. A new Ania. I wasn't a child, like Gosia had said, but I wasn't completely sure how to be an adult either. I was somewhere in between, with an ache in my chest for my family, a burning deep down to find some way to make the ache go away, and the distant voice of Basia in my head: *Why did you do it Ania, why?*

What had I done? Had it been my fault? Had they sacrificed themselves for me, or if I hadn't come too early, arriving on that winter wind, would everything be different – would we all be different? As if I had summoned it, a wind whipped up the trees outside and whistled through the crack in the windowpane. I listened to it, trying to hear its secrets, or perhaps its warnings. Then as suddenly as it had arrived, it departed, making me wonder if it had ever been there at all.

'Ania.' Benj's voice was heavy with sleep. I turned to see him sitting, rubbing at his eyes. 'Ania, I don't want to leave here,' he said.

I went and sat next to him. 'We can't stay here,' I said. 'We have to keep going, find Bartok. Gosia, she talked to me last night and said that I had a purpose. I have to help, to fight these men that have come here and taken so much away, Benj. Tata, Basia, your parents. It's the right thing for me, isn't it, Benj?'

I felt his body stiffen next to me. 'I don't like it, Ania,' he said. 'It's dangerous and we should just hide and wait and one day it will be over.'

'But what if it never ends, Benj? Think about it. Think. They might not stop until we are all gone, and we can't just sit back and wait for it to happen. We have to do something.'

'I don't want to kill anyone, Ania.' Benj's voice had taken on that lament of a child – one I myself had cultivated over the years with Tata and Basia so they could be content with their vision of me as a small child instead of an adult. I didn't think that Benj was doing it on purpose though. It was like the more time we spent together, the more he was relying on me, making sure I knew that he needed me.

'You don't have to, Benj. I'll do it.'

'It's not right, Ania. It's not right to kill people.'

'I know, Benj.' I sighed and placed my hand on his. 'But it has to be done and it's something I think I will be good at.'

* * *

After a quick breakfast of boiled eggs, bread and water, we set out.

'I hope you find your way,' Aldona said as we left, then grabbed my hand as Gosia cackled at some joke she had just told Benj.

'I am sorry about this – I am,' she said, her eyes not on me, but on Gosia. 'I have to let her go. I just can't...' She trailed off.

I didn't allay her fears. I said nothing and turned away from her and the red door, my compass in my hand.

We three headed further east to the thicker forests still some ten miles away. I wanted to make it before dark – I wanted to do what Gosia had said I needed to do – avenge my father's and sister's deaths. As we walked, keeping to small roads, thickets of trees, I thought some more about what Gosia and I had discussed – how you had to have a purpose in life. I had to admit, as soon as I had decided what my purpose was, that niggly burning feeling I had had in my chest since finding Tata and Basia on the farmhouse floor had abated somewhat.

How I was going to kill Nazis I had no idea. There were guns, but I did not have one. A knife would work, but it would be messy, I was sure, and would require physical strength to plunge a blade deep through skin, tissue and muscle, a physicality I was not sure that I possessed. I had killed chickens before, but it was easy when you knew what you were doing, and they were much smaller than a grown man and did not have weapons. Either you twisted the neck until it snapped, or you used Tata's sharp knife, taking the head clear off, letting the rest of the body run around for a moment before it stopped.

This wouldn't be easy though. I knew that it would take much more force to take a man's head off, for example. The human head weighed eleven pounds or thereabouts; the neck contained twenty muscles. Perhaps taking off someone's head wasn't the way to go – it wasn't something I could do.

'Ania!' Benj drew me out of my thoughts.

I looked at him and saw he was pointing at the road that we were nearing, a hedgerow running the length of it, but there in the distance, a grey-green German truck barrelled towards us.

I grabbed Gosia and sat close to the hedgerow with Benj following suit.

'Stay still,' I commanded.

'They'll just drive past. You'll see. They drive past all day every day. Never once stopped for Gosia,' she said.

I held tightly onto her and could feel Benj's warm breath on the nape of my neck.

The truck did keep on going; whoever was driving it crunched their gears a few times, causing Benj to flinch.

But it did not go far.

I looked through a gap in the hawthorn and saw that the truck had stopped on the side of the road. Two German soldiers had got out and were looking underneath the chassis.

'You did that,' one of them said. 'Learn how to fucking drive, would you?'

'What are they saying?' Gosia asked.

'Hush!' I whispered to her.

'I know how to drive. It was like that when we picked it up from the camp this morning. Who was the mechanic?' the second voice said.

'How should I know? Some Jew, or Pole, or Russian.'

'Yeah, well. I say we crawl this thing back there and make sure they don't have a job any more. Don't know what they've done to it, but it isn't me. It isn't my driving.'

'Whatever you say,' the first voice said. 'But it is your driving.'

Slowly, ever so slowly, the truck turned in the road, wheezing and crunching with whatever ailed it. Then it travelled right past us once more, back to where it had come from.

I made sure that we waited a few minutes until it was definitely safe for us to stand up and continue on. As we walked, I told them both what the two soldiers had said.

'Camp?' Gosia asked.

'They're talking about Konzentrationslager Lublin,' I said. 'But Bartok said that the locals call it Majdanek – little Majdan,' I said. 'Bartok said in the spring that it was in Lublin, on the road to Zamość and Lwów. I remembered because my uncle lived in Czerniejów. Same road.'

'Majdanek,' Gosia repeated. 'It sounds nice. Like Majdan but smaller I expect. Like a little town.'

I looked at her, really looked at her. Was she really that *szalony*?

'A camp,' Benj said.

'For prisoners of war, that was what Bartok said. Some of his friends were there. He said that he threw food over the fence, letters even, and asked Tata if he had any spare potatoes he could take.'

'So we are near there?' Benj asked worriedly.

'No. We are—' Then I stopped and looked at the compass. 'We are heading northeast still. Majdanek is south of Lublin.'

'So why are they here?' Benj asked. 'Do you think it's for me, Ania? Do you think it's the same ones again?'

'No, Benj, not for you. I don't know why they're here. I have no idea.'

'Majdanek,' Gosia said again in a dreamy way. 'Are we there yet?'

I didn't bother explaining to Gosia that we were not going to Majdanek, and made her carry on alongside me, my eyes seeking out tips of pine firs, oaks, ashes, maples, anything clumped together to suggest that we were near where we needed to be.

'Are you sure they weren't coming for me?' Benj whispered, pressing his arm against mine as we walked.

'I'm sure, Benj.'

'But you'll tell me if they are here for me?'

'I won't need to, Benj. I'll keep you safe.'

He didn't respond but I knew he would have given one of his heavy nods. Then it hit me. I had promised now to keep him safe, taken Gosia on too. It made the burning feeling in my chest ease a little more. I felt different too – older, stronger. Is this what Basia had felt looking after me, perhaps? Had it made her walk a bit taller, feel superior in some way? I hoped it had. I hoped it always hadn't been a burden on her. But then, maybe, the burden only came later. Maybe it took time for this proud feeling to dissipate and in its place sit a feeling of resentment.

By noon, we had managed to avoid any towns and villages and twice more had to throw ourselves into ditches to avoid cars, trucks and people. Some were soldiers, others simply going about their day, but either way I did not want anyone to see us – not only did we not look German enough, but we also stood out as something unusual – Gosia in her summer dress, Benj with his face and me dressed in oversized men's clothes.

The snow, which Benj had predicted, began to fall, each flake dancing in the air before settling softly on the ground. It was quiet, the kind of quiet that only comes with winter, when the world seems to hold its breath. I pulled my coat tighter around me and glanced at Benjamin, who shivered despite his layers. Gosia too was cold and held the ratty red coat tight around her, her legs pink and white, her socks slipping down from their moorings on her calves.

Ahead, a small stone bridge led off our track and into a village that sat between us and the next patch of farmland that we sorely had to get to.

I veered off the road in the direction of an overgrowth of blackberry bushes and brambles next to the small stream that bubbled over small rocks and stones. I told Gosia and Benj to sit amongst the brush as much as possible, hopefully hiding ourselves from any eyes.

'It's cold, Ania,' Benj said, his bottom lip trembling.

'We'll wait here,' I said, my voice barely more than a whisper. 'We'll wait here until it gets dark then we have to move quickly through. Don't stop, just keep walking to the next fields.'

'But we have money,' Benj said. 'We could buy some food?' he asked hopefully.

He was right, but I could not walk into that village with Benj and Gosia in tow.

'I'll go,' I said and found the pouch with the few coins inside. 'Gosia and Benj, stay put,' I told them. 'I'll go and be back soon.'

But even as I spoke, I knew it was no use. Gosia was already moving, her breath visible in the cold air as she turned to the village.

'Gosia, no!' I hissed, but she didn't listen. I watched her back recede into the distance, feeling a knot of dread tighten in my stomach.

'Stay here,' I told Benjamin again, as if repeating the command would somehow make it easier. Then, with one last look at him, I followed Gosia, my feet crunching softly in the fresh snow.

I trailed her, keeping to the shadows, the falling snow muffling my steps. She moved quickly, too quickly, and disappeared down a tight alleyway next to a bakery. I could smell the aroma of freshly baked bread, and my stomach rumbled.

'Gosia!' I half shouted down the alleyway, then turned and found that I had a watcher. A small boy stood there, a patch sewn into the knee of his trousers, staring at me, looking me up and down. Then a woman appeared, took the boy's hand in hers and stared at me too. It was a peculiar moment. Each of us waited for someone to speak, to say something that would ease the tension, but none of us did. The woman raised her eyebrows at me and tugged on the boy's hand, then the pair disappeared onto the whitened street.

I couldn't stay here. I needed to find Gosia, but God only

knew where she had gone and what she would do, and I couldn't scour the streets for her, nor could I buy food now. This village was small, too small, and I knew that within minutes that woman would be telling people that she either saw a small girl dressed in men's clothing or a boy with a yellow hat on his head, and soon someone might come looking for me.

I retraced my steps back over the bridge and to Benj, who had backed so far into the overgrowth that it took me a minute to find him.

As soon as I reappeared, he looked up at me and I could see that he had been crying. He tried to give me a smile, but all it did was add to the fear that was so visible on his face.

I sat down next to him, both of us taking each other's warmth for ourselves. Soon the shadows started to lengthen, the sun dipped below the horizon and Benj and I were left sat in a cold, silent world, snow thickening on the ground second after second, the only noise to be heard the soft patter of each flake as it landed on the leaves behind us.

'We should leave,' I whispered. 'She's not coming back.'

'We have to wait, Ania,' Benj said, although his teeth chattered so much that it took him a while to say it. 'She needs us. She needs you. When she gets back, you just need to tell her that she can't do it again, that it's not safe. She'll listen if you explain it to her.'

I agreed to wait one hour, and I counted the seconds in my mind as we sat together, wriggling my toes in my boots every now and then to check that the blood was still flowing.

Gosia returned to us as I reached fifty-five minutes and ten seconds.

I was ready to do as Benj had said and tell her that she could not just wander off, that it wasn't safe, that it made us all unsafe. The words were there, sitting patiently on my tongue, but they could not, would not, come. Because before us, Gosia stood, wrapped in a light-brown fur coat, grinning madly and telling Benj to stroke it – to feel its softness.

'Come on! See what I got for Gosia? I wanted to get one for you too, Benjamin, and you, Ania, but I only found this. But I got us some food, see.' She drew out two bread rolls from her pocket.

'Gosia.' I stood and placed my hands on each of her arms to stop her, just like Tata did with me when he wanted me to listen to him.

'Gosia,' I said again. 'Where did you get this?'

'I found it,' she said, then grinned.

'Where did you find it?'

She shrugged my hands away. 'I was cold, Ania. Cold. So I went and got Gosia a coat. That's what you do when you're cold, don't you know that? You go and get more clothes.'

'But you stole it, didn't you?' I insisted.

'No, Gosia is no thief.'

'So how did you get it?' I stressed, exasperated with her reticence.

'I told you. I found it. There was a door and it was open and there it was on a hook, so I took it and put my coat there so they still have a coat, but I have a warmer one. And there was bread on the side, so I took that too.'

'Gosia! That is still stealing! And you can't just run off like that!' I yelled at her. 'Do you know what could have happened? My father and sister were shot, in their own home, for no reason. So you have to understand that they can kill us for no reason too.'

'Ania.' Gosia spoke but she wasn't looking at me; she looked at Benj instead. 'You worry too much. I have a coat now. A good coat, so we can leave.'

I grabbed Gosia's arm hard then felt Benj's hand on my shoulder. 'Leave it for now, Ania,' Benj said. 'She doesn't understand.'

Gosia was already striding ahead, following the bank of the stream – something we should have done earlier. I chastised myself for not thinking of it, for saying we needed to wait to sneak through the village.

Benj and I followed her, the coat making her look like a wild animal prowling in the night.

We walked for hours, and my legs ached with each step, my feet blistered still, in my too-large boots. Gosia wore her fur coat; Benj ambled along and kept asking when we were going to stop, where we were going to sleep. I couldn't answer him; my mind was buzzing with its wasp's nest again. Tata. Basia. Gosia's words of having a purpose, of killing people. Of Gosia in her coat and how she was going to be hard to manage and yet we couldn't not take care of her. How Benj needed me. How I was hungry too, and tired, and also wondered where we were going to sleep and when. Each thought hit like a punch into my forehead, and as soon as I grabbed hold of one thought and tried to bring about a solution, it zipped away, leaving a new problem that I had no answer to. It was the first time in my life that my brain had acted in this way. Thoughts reeling and bumping into each other, the red apple randomly appearing, then the red door too. Was this how other people thought?, I wondered. If so, I wanted my old mind back again.

'Ania, look.' Benj pointed off into the night where the silhouette of a stone shepherd's hut sat, half crumbling into the dirt.

Gosia had already spotted it, and on her bowed legs she made her way as quickly as she could towards it.

When we reached her, the stench of animals, of straw,

pricked at my nostrils, but it was not an unpleasant smell – it reminded me of the barn, of home.

'This will do.' Gosia's disembodied voice called to us. 'Come on inside, you two. You stick with old Gosia now, and she'll see you right.'

That night, we slept, Benj and I curled tight against Gosia and her coat. Benj snuffled in his sleep again. And I dreamt of Tata and Basia again. But this time, I found the voices of Krzysztof and Rolf. I found them and I killed them, and in my dream I felt at peace.

# 11

## THE PARTISANS

*6 December 1942*
*Parczew Forest, Lublin Voivodeship, Poland*
*Ania*

The midday sun afforded us some warmth the following day, melting some of the snow that had fallen overnight, making it wink and sparkle in the sunlight. The sun's rays also made Gosia shed her new coat, revealing all its ugliness as she carried it like a baby in her arms. The coat was mink, but had lost some of its elegance having been eaten by moths over the years, which had gnawed small holes and torn away clumps of fur. The former owner of the coat must have worn it often, as embedded within the pelts were clumps of dirt, even remnants of food. It smelled too. A smell I had not noticed the night before in the bothy. But now, it stank like a rotting animal and twice I told Gosia to throw it to the side of the road. Both times she ignored me.

The scenery had changed somewhat now. Small copses of trees became larger, firs mostly that held a density about them that made me uneasy. I could imagine eyes watching us as we passed, hidden in amongst all that green. Open fields became smaller and smaller, the pines, oaks and elms taking over the land instead, their trunks covered in moss and lichen, the ground becoming covered in ferns, dead leaves and yellow and white mushrooms that sprouted from damp logs.

The terrain took us through these smaller woods, and each time I hoped they would never end, signalling that we were in the forest. But three times we found ourselves emerging from the trees and onto either dusty tracks or, once, a main road whose traffic was sparse save for a family approaching us.

I could see in the distance that the trees became thicker once more, the landscape beyond showing the density that a forest would provide. We had to use the road.

The family got closer to us. The father, a suitcase in each hand, his brow sweating, a yellow star of David stitched into his coat. The mother carried a baby, and behind her a small boy straggled, who stopped every few minutes to pick at grass or break a twig free from a branch.

Upon them seeing us, I saw the man stop, raise his eyebrows and say something to the woman.

'What do we do?' Benj whispered.

Before I could answer him and tell him to keep going, to not say a word, Gosia had shot forward to talk to them.

'Jews, are you?' she asked the man, who seemed terrified of her, not least because she had decided to adorn herself with her fur coat once more.

He nodded.

'I heard about what they're doing to you,' she said. 'Me too. They came for me. Him over there, with the face, he's Jewish too, so you don't have to worry!' She patted his arm and I saw him flinch.

'We're just moving on,' he said. 'Just moving on.'

'Same, same. Say, do you know a man called Bartok?' she asked him, then turned to the wife and interrogated her too. 'Lives in a forest. A forest man. Lots of people go there. You heard of it?'

In the distance, there was a rumble of an engine. The man looked behind him then back at us, wide eyed.

'Gosia! Come!' I ran forward and grabbed her arm, climbing up a thick grassy verge that led us away from the road. Behind me, I could hear Benj breathing heavily, the child crying, the man's voice as he told his son to hurry.

As the engine got closer, we all lay flat, Gosia trying to say something to the boy next to her, who was stroking at her coat.

'Hush now!' I told her, and thankfully, for once, she listened.

I watched the road as the truck rumbled past followed by a jeep, then another jeep. Even when the engines had dulled, and then disappeared, none of us moved for some time.

Eventually, the man sat up and leaned backwards, dragging a hand over his tired face.

'They're everywhere,' he said almost to himself. 'Everywhere. We were hiding at a neighbour's, but then we heard they were coming so we left.'

'Where will you go?' I sat up too and saw that his wife was cradling the baby, who whimpered into her breast.

'I don't know – I don't know.'

'Gosia, you know, she was right about what she said, about the forests, about how there are people hiding there. You should come with us.'

The man looked to his wife and then at me. 'And you're really going there?'

I nodded.

'We have heard about it, but I didn't think with children in tow it would be a good thing – but now I don't know. I don't even know where we are going – just wandering the roads and trying to hide. Maybe it's a good thing that we met you?' he said.

'Ania,' I said, introducing myself to him. 'That's me. Gosia you met. That's Benjamin. You should come with us.'

The man looked at his wife again and then went to her, the pair of them talking in hushed voices.

'No,' the man said. 'No, she's right. The baby, you see, the baby is sick. We can't go to the forests. We have to find somewhere else. But you, you go. You're not far away now. Go up high – get off the road. Stay in the trees and keep in them. Before long, you'll find them or they'll find you. Just keep moving through the woods. They're there, they'll find you,' he repeated.

We said our goodbyes to the family and left them sat on the high verge, the three of us climbing higher until we reached the few trees that sat above the road.

'I was scared, Ania,' Benj said. 'Were you scared?'

'I was scared, Benj. Or I think I was. My heart was racing.'

'My heart was racing too,' Benj said.

'I know that we are in danger,' I told him, 'I know it, and yet at the same time, it feels like it will never happen – like maybe we are immune to it.' I looked at the ribbon on my wrist. 'I know what happened to Basia and Tata, and I know that it makes me angry, but I don't know whether I am more angry than scared, or just...'

'Numb,' Gosia chimed in. 'Numb. You're numb. I was numb too when my husband left. I was angry then sad then everything. But then I was numb. You'll find a feeling, a strong one, again soon. And when you do, you'd best hope it's a nice one.'

'What do you mean?' Benj asked.

'I mean' – she turned and looked at us – 'I mean that the first feeling that comes after being numb, that's the one that will consume you. Maybe you will feel at peace, maybe you will be terrified; maybe though, just maybe, Ania, the best feeling that can come for you is one of anger – then the world will see, won't they? What a woman like you can do?'

* * *

Benj and I played a game as we walked, the sunlight dipping away, the trees getting thicker. Benj asked me to name all the cities in Poland, never knowing whether the answers were correct. And I asked him about feelings – about how he knew which was which and what he did with them.

'You know what anger is?' he asked me.

Yes. I knew anger. The more I thought about it, the more I realised that I had been full to the brim of anger all my life. The tantrums, the hitting, the shouting. I had been angry and frustrated.

'And happiness?' he asked.

'No,' I said. 'Unless it feels like just not being angry.'

'It's more than that,' Benj said. 'It's like it makes you smile, makes you – I don't know – happy.'

'I was happy with my husband,' Gosia added. 'All day, every day. I smiled and danced and couldn't wait to wake up in the morning.'

I had never felt that. I am sure I had smiled – perhaps at the fair with Tata and at the red apple, but was that really happiness?

'And fear,' Gosia said, joining in with the game. 'You know fear.'

Did I? Was I scared when I had heard those voices in the barn? I thought for a moment – yes, I had been scared, but not for me, for Benj.

'I'm scared for other people, I think,' I admitted. 'Not for me.'

'Why not?' Gosia asked.

I shrugged but I couldn't help but finger the red ribbon on my wrist.

'What about guilt? Or pride? Or envy?' Gosia prodded still.

Guilt, yes. I knew that one now. Pride, yes, that too. Proud that I was taking care of Benj and Gosia, but envy?

'Not envy,' I said.

'Not even envious of my coat?' Gosia cackled and I saw Benj smile.

'Never,' I said, making them both laugh more.

Soon, we were in amongst the forest. There now seemed no way out of it, no road or dusty track suddenly appearing – it was like we had happened upon another world. Moonlight filtered through the branches of the pines to create a mosaic of silvery beams, illuminating our path as we threaded through the forest. Ghostly shadows of tree trunks, the discerning rustle of leaves, the hoot of an owl were all that we had. Benj moved closer to me, Gosia on my other side. They were scared; I could feel their fear. But I felt strangely at peace with the damp earth muffling my steps, and the chill of the night air biting at my cheeks.

Suddenly, there was a rustle to my left. It was too much of a noise to be a rabbit, too much of a noise for this quiet wood. I slowly turned my head, eyes scanning the shadows. Out of the darkness, a figure emerged, then another, and another – until half a dozen men and women stood before me, their faces gaunt but eyes sharp.

Someone shone a torch into my face. 'Who are you?' one of them demanded. I could see the shadowy figure of a woman with a rifle slung over her shoulder, but I could not make out the others. She stepped closer.

'Ania,' I replied. The torch moved off my face.

'And you?' She pointed to Benj and then Gosia.

It took Gosia less than a second to walk up to this woman, ignoring the men, and offer her outstretched hand. 'Gosia,' she said confidently. 'And you are?'

I noticed a flicker of a smile on the woman's lips, but she didn't give in to it. 'That's none of your business.'

One of the manly shadows moved closer to Benj, his gun in his hands, and poked at Benj's stomach as if testing to see if he was real.

'I'm a Jew!' Benj suddenly screamed. 'I know Bartok! Bartok said he was here and we're here because her father and sister are dead! All shot in the head. And we hid, we hid from them and then we found Gosia in a potato field and then some man on the road told us where we could find you!' His words came so quickly that most of them were slurred by the slack of the right side of his mouth.

The shadow man lowered his gun and looked to the woman who was staring not at Benj but at Gosia's fur coat.

'Well, I've seen some things,' she said. 'Seen a lot of people, but this' – she gave a sharp laugh – 'this is new.'

I felt the need to take charge of the situation, and I explained properly what Benj had tried to say. The woman listened patiently and then said to me, 'How old are you?'

'Almost twenty,' I said, getting a bit tired of saying it all the time.

'Is that so?'

'And she's a genius!' Benj barked. 'She knows maps and books and languages – ask her to name all the cities in Poland and she can tell you.'

'How interesting,' the woman said.

'She can fight. She's killed before,' Gosia added, her hand

reaching out to touch the gun on the woman's shoulder, which she quickly shrugged away. Not that it deterred Gosia, who tried again. 'I can fight too. I wanted to kill my husband but he'd gone away with the whore of his so I couldn't get at him.'

I didn't know what had happened; I hadn't heard or seen anything, but collectively all the shadows and their guns and the woman with the face like flint shifted left and trained their guns on the darkness.

'Go, now!' the flint-faced woman said. She turned to the shadows, pointed at something, whispered to them, and they followed her orders, disappearing into the nothingness.

'Come with me,' she hissed. 'And stay quiet.'

Gosia opened her mouth to say something, then thought better of it and smacked her lips together.

Benj was by my side as we followed the woman, Gosia behind us, she holding on to my coat so that it felt as though I were leading a small child. Twice I tripped on warped tree roots, sending both Gosia and me to the forest floor. A muscle pulled in my thigh, but I knew not to cry out in pain, to just keep moving.

It felt as though we had walked for hours, but I am sure it wasn't that long – if it had been, Gosia would not have been able to stay quiet. Perhaps it was the dark that became heavier and more impenetrable as we walked so that we had to concentrate on each step with such focus that time became something else altogether.

'Wait here.' The flint woman turned to us, her face half obscured by the dark.

'Ania,' Benj whispered to me. 'I don't like this. I don't think they like us.'

I didn't answer, but I knew what he meant. I saw the look in the flint woman's eyes; I understood that she probably saw the three of us as some sort of troupe of misfits. But I was used to those looks, and I expected that Benj and Gosia were used to them too. We had never fitted in and I was slowly coming to realise that even with the war, with people disappearing just because they were clever, mad, Jewish, Gypsy, or for no reason whatsoever, we would still not be able to find a place for ourselves.

'Just let's see,' I told him. 'Let's just see what they say.'

'I'll tell you what they'll say.' Gosia leaned into me, her warm breath tickling my skin. 'They'll say they want my coat. That's what they'll say. I saw them looking at it. You have to tell them though, Ania, that this is Gosia's coat and they can't have it.'

Flint Face came back and told us to follow her again. This time there was a flicker of orange and red through the trees, the scent of burning logs.

Sat around the fire were two or three others who stared at us as we approached: one, a boy, I thought, of perhaps no more than fifteen; a man with a bushy black moustache and stubbled cheeks; and the other, another man, slight and sickly looking.

The man with the moustache came to us.

'Wojtek,' he said. 'Who sent you?'

'No one did,' I said.

'So you found us by accident?'

'I'm looking for Bartok Nowak,' I told him.

'From where? I know a few by that name,' he said with a smile.

'Nałęczów. But he's not been there for a while. He came to the woods – brought Jews to our farm.'

'I know of him,' he said. 'But he's not here, not part of this group.'

'What group is he part of?' I asked.

Wojtek opened his mouth to speak but then his eyes caught

on Gosia, who was grabbing hold of the young boy's arm, telling him to sit with her so she could tell him about her husband and what he had done.

The boy, although holding on to a gun, looked frightened.

'Leave him be,' Wojtek told her, then looked to Benj, who had sat by the fire, cradling his head in his hands.

'Those two are a pair,' he said, looking at me once more.

'So where is he? Bartok?'

Wojtek shrugged. 'You have to understand, little girl, there are groups everywhere. Changing each day. Some Jewish, some AK, some mixed. Everyone is fighting for survival.'

'I know. Against the Germans.'

'Not just them,' he said. 'There's fighting amongst the groups too.' He shook his head. 'Everyone wants to survive. It's complicated.'

'If you don't know where Bartok is,' I said, 'then we will just stay here and join your group.'

My statement made him laugh. 'This is not the place for you.'

'I am not a child,' I started, then he held up his hand to cut me off.

'Doesn't matter if you are or not. I've got children here who are fighting, who are helping to get food, ammunition – all sorts of things. That's not why this is not the place for you.'

'Where is it then?'

'Look. I know a fighter when I see one. I was in the army. I know how hard it is to survive and do what is needed. You just don't have it. And certainly your friends do not.' He waved in the general direction of Benj and Gosia. 'But there's a family camp, not run by me, but not too far away. For the elderly and infirm. Young children too. You'd be better off there. I'm sure they'll take you.'

'We can fight,' I said. 'Gosia is very good at stealing things, and Benj...' Well, what could I say about Benj? 'He could help cook maybe. Forage for food. He's a good man.'

As soon as I had said those words, a wail came from Benj's direction and Gosia rushed to him, holding him to her. 'The guns,' he sobbed. 'I don't like them.'

I clenched my jaw. 'He'll get used to them,' I told Wojtek.

'Ania, was it? Yes. Well, Ania, this just isn't the place for you. You can stay tonight, and tomorrow we'll get someone to take you to the family camp. Trust me, you'll be safer there and those two friends of yours will be looked after.'

'I—' I started, ready to argue my point again. But Wojtek had already tired of me and walked away to where the flint woman stood, whispered something to her then pointed at me. Then, I heard it: *szalony*.

'All of them. *Szalony*,' he said to her, making her smile. She did not take her eyes off me. She knew I had heard him.

I had no trouble understanding why they thought we were mad – all of us – but what I could not understand was how, in this bunch of people, all of whom were supposedly banding together to fight for their very existence, they would turn their backs on me. I knew what their perception of me was. A girl, not a woman. A girl who had found two outcasts just like her. More trouble than they were worth. I had heard it all my life and I was tired of it.

'Come. Sit. Warm yourself.' Wojtek waved me over.

I went to sit next to Benj and the sickly man. Gosia sat the other side of Benj, Wojtek across from me with the boy. Flint Face and the other shadows seemed to have disappeared into the darkness.

'Hungry?' Wojtek asked.

I did not answer. I did not need to. Gosia was already speaking on our behalf, accepting bread, cheese even.

'Bartok Nowak, eh?' Wojtek said, then shook his head. 'Good man. Shame about his brothers.'

'His brothers?' I asked.

'Taken to a prisoner-of-war camp. Bartok, he wanted to get them out; that's what I heard, anyway. But by the time he went there, they were dead.' He shook his head again.

'My father and sister were killed,' I said. 'The Germans.'

'Mine too,' the sickly man next to me said. 'Wife as well.'

For a moment no one spoke, letting the crackle of the fire, the hoot of an owl, fill the silence.

'My father,' I said, 'he wanted to help. We hid Jews. I want to help too. To fight. We have nowhere else to go, me, Benj and Gosia. We thought we would be safe here with you.'

'We are a small group,' Wojtek said. 'To the east there are bigger groups, more men, more ammunition, more food to go around. Resistance in all forms – Russians, Jews, Poles, all sorts. But I don't know where you'd fit in best, if at all.'

Gosia handed me some of her bread. 'Eat,' she said.

I took it from her and chewed. My stomach rumbled with the promise of food, yet the anger, the burning sensation in my chest, was preventing me from swallowing. I spat out the clump of bread.

'Don't waste it,' Wojtek said. 'Are you sick, child?'

'No,' I said. 'Not sick. Not a child.' My voice had taken on the coldness that had made Aldona flinch.

Wojtek stroked his moustache, then sat back, found a cigarette in his jacket pocket, lit it and then handed it to the sickly man, who took one puff and began to hand it to the rest of us – none of us taking it so that it went straight back to Wojtek.

'Family camp,' he said, screwing up his eyes against the

cigarette smoke, then he spat on the ground. 'Family camp is the best place for you.'

He stood, passed the cigarette to the sickly man again and came towards me. He stood above me, then placed his hand on my head. 'You'll see. I'm looking out for you, and your friends. This is no place for you. I'm taking care of you by sending you to the family camp. You'll thank me one day.'

Wojtek then turned to the boy and told him to take us to his bunker. The boy did not speak, just nodded, his face a perfect picture of seriousness and devotion to Wojtek. I had seen that look before, many times, when Father had taken me to a priest, or a doctor. He had trusted them implicitly.

'Family camp,' Benj said as we followed the boy away from the fire. 'That will be good for us, won't it, Ania? I mean, no guns?'

'They'll all want my coat,' Gosia said.

*'No guns, Ania.'*

*'My coat, Ania.'*

*'I'm taking care of you, Ania.'*

*'You'll thank me one day, Ania.'*

*'Szalony, Ania.'*

*'A burden, Ania.'*

*'You make it hard to love you, Ania.'*

*'Take the red apple, Ania.'*

*'They're dead, Ania.'*

Voices, all the voices, swirled in my mind, one after the other. I kept walking. One step, two steps, Gosia and Benj still talking, Basia's voice talking too. Father's. Wojtek's.

The boy opened something in the ground. Gosia went first, then Benj. Then me, followed by the dumb boy.

Then, darkness. And one last harmonious voice of everyone I had ever heard it from, said with perfect pitch.

'*Szalony.*'

## 12

## SOCRATES AND THE HEMLOCK

*7 December 1942*
*Parczew Forest, Lublin Voivodeship, Poland*
*Ania*

It had started to snow again. I stood outside the shelter breathing in the crisp air. I couldn't bear the smell of Gosia's coat inside that bunker, Benj's snorting and whistling, the damp earth and wondering about the worms and other insects that were embedded within. The voices were too loud down there too. *Szalony, szalony*, they called to me in a sing-song way that made me want to scream.

The cold bit at my skin as I slipped out of our hidden refuge, pulling my father's coat tightly around me.

All was quiet. Moonlight lit tiny pools of light on the leaf-strewn ground, shadows danced and weaved in between the trunks, leaves whispered in the air, and whoomphs of snow could be heard as branches shed their loads.

I decided to walk. Not far. Just a little, to stretch my legs, clear my mind of the voices. As I walked, snowflakes spiralled down and I held out my palm for one to land on. I stared at it as it melted, recollecting a picture of a snowflake I had seen in a book once, how each one was unique, their tiny patterns unbelievably beautiful. It was annoying that one would need a microscope to see the beauty, that we had to make do with just a blob of white.

The forest was a maze of dark trunks and ghostly shapes. I knew that some of the shadowy people would be there too – somewhere in amongst all these ghosts. But I could not see them, could not hear them.

I paused for a moment, closing my eyes, letting the stillness wash over me. It was as if the forest was holding its breath, as if at any moment, this secretive place would be found.

I opened my eyes and trudged on, the cold seeping through my coat, my painful feet shunting against the toe caps of the boots.

I thought of what Gosia had said, how I was numb and that soon one feeling would overwhelm the others. I hadn't told Gosia or Benj that a feeling had been creeping up – not just the burning grief or anger which was physical – but a thought – perhaps a feeling – that had nestled itself in my mind. A thought brewing into a feeling that was slowly getting bigger, and from talking with Gosia about revenge, about killing others, and then seeing that flinty woman with her gun, I could now identify it was a feeling of pure rage. Not anger like Gosia had said – this was a rage that made my muscles tense under my skin, how when I had lain down earlier to sleep, it had made my legs twitch and dance. Wojtek telling me we had to go to the family camp, that once more I was a burden, useless, *szalony*, had added to this rage that was slowly but ever so surely beginning to consume me.

A bramble caught on my hand, tearing into the skin of my

palm. I stopped and looked at it. I could not see the blood, but I could feel its warmth. I made a closed fist then opened it again. The pain felt almost welcome, settling the frantic voices in my head. I did it again, tighter this time, concentrating on the pain, on the warmth of my own blood.

Soon, the cold became too much and I reluctantly retraced my steps to the bunker and found Benj sat up, holding a candle.

'Ania,' he said quietly. 'I don't want to be here, Ania. I want to go home. I don't even want to go to the family camp. I don't want this any more.'

I sat beside him and undid his hands, taking one of them in mine. 'I want to go home too, Benj. But we can't. There is no home any more.'

'I know,' he said, sobbing.

'Benj,' I said to him. 'Remember how brave you were and how you hid us both?'

He nodded.

'You're changing too quickly – you're not being the Benj I met. You're getting upset all the time. You need to be that brave Benj again now.'

'I was never brave, Ania, never. I just thought I was for a minute but then I saw... I saw—'

I knew what he was trying to say – my father and sister.

'I wasn't brave before that, either, Ania.' He took a hand away from me and wiped his nose with his sleeve. 'I just wanted you to be safe and I was scared. I had made a hole before in that straw because I could hide in there. I wanted you to think that I was a man – a proper man – not one that everyone used to say was simple, or stupid, or weak. I wanted to be normal for you.'

I could feel that rage bubbling again. Rage now for Benj and how he had been treated. How he was still being treated.

'You are normal,' I told him. 'You are just like me, like Gosia.'

'Gosia's mad.' He sniffed and nodded at the old woman, who looked like a sleeping bear under her coat.

'People say I'm mad too though, Benj.'

'Not like her, you're not.'

'Maybe not. But I'm the same, and so are you – we are different from other people and that makes them scared because they don't understand us.' I parroted Isaac's words from years ago. 'We will make our own home, all right?'

'We will?' he asked, raising his eyes and looking at me hopefully.

'We will,' I said.

'Your hand.' He looked down. 'Ania, you're hurt. You're bleeding.' His voice wobbled again and I could see that he was about to cry once more.

'It's nothing, Benj. Really, this is a good thing.'

He shook his head and wiped at my hand with the cuff of his coat. 'I'll clean it for you,' he said. 'I'll make it better.'

I let my friend wipe at the blood. I let him worry about it for a few minutes, as I rummaged around in my mind and found that I now felt some sort of peace about everything. I saw it all so clearly now – what Gosia had said about letting a feeling overtake you, how Isaac had told me about people not under-standing, and finally, how Wojtek had treated me, and the others, and how I wasn't going to let it happen any more. All of these things, happening randomly, had culminated into bringing about a change in me – setting me on a new path.

As I lay down next to Benj, I thought of religion, of fate, of rituals, and how perhaps me coming into the world too early had been my fate – it had all had to happen this way and I could no longer resist it.

* * *

I walked in the woods that morning, knowing that we would soon be leaving – I just wasn't sure when or how it was going to happen. And I had no idea where we would be going either. All I knew was that so far, life had found a way to piece things together for me, and I just had to be patient and it would all soon happen to me, or I would have an idea of how to make it happen.

The sun rose, the mist floated up from the damp leaves, and the naked trunks stood high and proud. A stream nearby bubbled, birds made weak calls to each other and now and then, like there was in the woods, a random snap of a twig or crumple of leaves could be heard. Otherwise, all was quiet.

I walked carefully to the stream, my eyes roving about to constantly check for anyone who shouldn't be there. I saw one man, a lookout, smoking a cigarette and leaning against a tree, enjoying the moment of silence as dawn broke.

He pretended not to see me, and I him. I was glad it wasn't Flint Face.

Overnight, frost had clung to branches, spiderwebs and the ground, creating ghostly patterns that winked at me in the morning light.

Over the stream, a branch hung low, icicles dripping from it into the water. I knelt down, placed my hands in the stream, feeling the freshness on my skin, washing away the remnants of blood, tinging the water pink.

Then at the side of the stream I saw *Cicuta virosa*, northern water hemlock. The book on fauna and flora Isaac had given to me had been read, of course it had, and had lodged itself into my brain. I knew too that Socrates had chosen it as his preferred method of execution and I had always wondered why, as it was not an easy death.

As a child, I had been warned when swimming in the river,

or playing in streams, to never, ever ingest it, and I knew not to if I didn't want to end up like Socrates.

'It sends you *szalony*,' Basia would say, then laugh. 'But then you already are, so it won't matter.'

*Szalej* was its name colloquially. A plant that once ingested would kill you, but not before making you look as if you had gone totally mad. Salivation, foaming at the mouth, convulsions, gasping for breath.

Then, suddenly I thought of my uncle, Jan, my mother's brother, who had had a small holding in Czerniejów. He had once told me the story of a boy he knew at school who had eaten some of the hemlock as a joke, thinking that a small amount would not kill him.

'Sent him mad, Ania,' my uncle had said. 'I saw it before my eyes. If that's madness for you, then you certainly are not mad. Don't let people call you that. *Szalony*,' he'd said then spat on the ground.

Yes! Czerniejów. Why hadn't it occurred to me before now?

My uncle, a bachelor, had died five years ago, leaving his property to my father. He had been a short but stocky man who continually smoked pipes, and would put us to work whenever we went to visit him. He had been the first to show me how to kill a chicken with my bare hands, delighting in how quick I was and how I didn't cry.

'She's like a son, Marek,' he would say to my father. 'You should be proud of her.'

But after he had died, Father had not gotten round to selling the land, nor the house, and wasn't sure he ever would be able to sell it, so dilapidated as it was. The last time we had visited, the roof had half of its tiles missing, and two windows had no glass in them.

'It's becoming a *dom cieni*,' my uncle would say. 'A house of shadows. Full of ghosts and whisperings.'

'You need to fix it,' my father had told him.

'I like that it's a *dom cieni,*' my uncle had puffed. 'It's my house. I can do what I like with it.'

Basia was scared of the house of shadows and had barely slept, crying that she wanted to go home. I'd liked it though, the way the cracks in the walls would almost whisper to you, how it creaked and sighed as if it were alive.

When the war came, the house of shadows drifted from Father's mind, just as it had mine. But now, sat by the stream, fate had brought together two things.

*Szalej* and a house of shadows.

I knew then where we would go and exactly what we would do. I broke off a piece of the hemlock and placed it in my pocket, patting it down.

There was no need for guns. For bloodshed.

It was simple.

I'd send them all mad.

# 13

## THE OUTCASTS

*7 December 1942*
*Parczew Forest, Lublin Voivodeship, Poland*
*Ania*

Wojtek was standing ready at the opening to the bunker when I returned. Benj stared at his shoes. Gosia for once was quiet, sullen even.

'You ready?' he asked as I approached.

'We're not going,' I said.

'You have to. I told you, you can't stay here. We can't have you here.'

'We're going to Czerniejów,' I said.

'What's in Czerniejów?'

'Can I have a gun?' I asked. 'Food perhaps too, for the journey?'

My questions took him by surprise and he looked to Gosia and Benj, then back at me.

'Do you know how to use a gun?' he asked, smiling.

'Can't be that hard. You learned how to.' I let the coldness creep into my voice.

I could see that Wojtek wasn't sure how to react to me now. The sickly man came to see what we were all talking about and stood by Wojtek's side.

'She wants a gun, she says,' he told him.

'She can have mine,' the sickly man said, and drew out a small revolver. 'Only has one bullet in it though.'

'Why are you doing that?' Wojtek went to snatch the gun from him, but the sickly man was quick and handed it to me.

'She'll need it if she's on her own. If she were my sister, I'd want her to have a gun. My sister didn't. She's dead.'

Before Wojtek could take it away from me, I placed it in my pocket next to the hemlock.

'Come, let's go,' I told Gosia and Benj, who began to follow me. 'Don't worry about the food,' I called back to Wojtek. 'We can take care of ourselves.'

Neither Benj nor Gosia spoke as I marched them through the trees, stopping every now and then to look at the compass. It would take us probably a day or more of continual walking until we would get to my uncle's house.

We trudged through the melting snow, away from the protection that the trees and undergrowth had offered us, sticking to rutted farm tracks away from the main road.

'Ania.' Finally, Benj spoke. 'Where are we going?'

'To my uncle's house. We'll be safe there.'

'So we won't need to fight?' He breathed a heavy sigh.

'We will. Just in a different way.'

Abruptly, Benj stopped and Gosia stopped too.

'I don't want to,' Benj said. 'I told you. I don't want to, Ania.'

'And me. And Gosia,' Gosia said. 'I don't know what's happening. One minute in the fields, the next the woods, and then they say we are going to see family, and now you say an uncle!' She raised her arms up. 'Gosia is tired and she is hungry.'

The burning in my chest suddenly exploded.

'Are you not sick of this?' I yelled at them, causing their eyes to widen, their mouths to slacken. 'Are you not tired, Gosia, of everyone calling you *szalony*? And you, Benj, staring at you, not wanting to be near you? Could you not see that they didn't want us, just like everyone else, and if we went to the family camp, do you really think it would have been any different? Are you not tired of it all?'

I waited for them to respond and when they didn't, I couldn't help but continue. 'You Gosia. You. You're not as mad as you make yourself out to be. How could you be when you told me about your husband, about the things that have happened to you, and how you willingly came with us? There's something in you that is still you, underneath everything that made you like this. You still have a mind, can steal things, know things that perhaps I do not. You still have a brain, Gosia, and you know how to use it.'

'I'm just tired,' she said again, quieter.

'But you weren't tired yesterday, nor the day before. Why now? What's changed? It was you that said we can fight the Germans – revenge, you said.'

She pulled the coat tightly around herself. 'That boy,' she said. 'The one who didn't talk, the one with the gun, with that man, Wojtek. I don't know. He reminded me of someone and now I don't feel well. I feel tired.'

'Who did he remind you of, Gosia?'

'I don't know,' she said and looked to Benj.

'Ania,' Benj said. 'Why are you so angry?'

I laughed then. I couldn't help it. All the years that people had asked me that. Why are you angry? Why are you, *you*? Why do you act that way?

The laughter died down. 'Let's go,' I said. 'We're all tired. Hungry. Let's get there and discuss all this later.'

I knew they would follow me so I did not wait for them. They had no other option and we all knew it, but I wanted them to want to come with me, or at least feel like they had a choice.

As we walked in silence, I remembered a time that Tata had taken Basia and me into a town to a market to sell our potatoes. I supposed it was a place that Tata had been before because everyone knew him and he them.

\* \* \*

'Marek, so good to see you.' A man in a dirty white shirt stopped as we piled potatoes into their wooden crates.

'And you.' My father wiped his hand on his trousers before taking the other man's hand.

'And you brought your daughters! A family affair, how lovely to see. My daughter wouldn't be seen close to a vegetable, let alone help me unpack and sell them.' He chuckled. 'All she wants to do is play with her dolls. Girls!' He grinned at Father and raised his eyebrows.

'Girls,' Tata agreed.

'It's hard right now, isn't it?' the man asked Father.

'It is,' my father agreed once more, and began moving potatoes from one crate to another even though there was no need to do it.

'Prices are going up, yet demand is not. You must find it hard,' he pushed.

'I do.'

'And with two daughters.'

'Indeed,' Tata said.

'Is she—' The man looked at me and cocked his head. 'You know?'

'No. She's much the same.'

'Ah. Must be hard,' the man said.

'It will be all right,' Tata said, but he barely moved his lips as he spoke.

'I tell you what, why don't you let me take Basia to my house for the day, eh? She can play with Marlena and I'll bring her back later?'

My father looked to Basia, who was grinning. He smiled at her. 'Yes, I think that will be fine,' he said. 'Thank you.'

'And me?' I asked, stepping forward. Basia grabbed my arm tightly and pulled me back.

'Ah. You'd be better staying here,' the man said. 'Stay with your father.'

'Why?' I asked. 'Why can't I come?'

The man ignored me, laughed, took Basia's hand and left.

'Why couldn't I go, Tata?' I asked him once they had gone.

'Because it's not right that you go. You'll upset people,' he said as he worked, hauling another full crate on top of another. Then he stopped, smashed the crate down so that a few potatoes rolled away and knelt down in front of me. 'Sorry, Ania,' he said, shaking his head. 'I shouldn't have said it like that. It's just you don't fit in with those people. Basia does. So you need to stay here with me.'

'How does one fit in?' I asked him. 'What would I have to do to not upset people?'

He shook his head again. 'Nothing. There's nothing you can do. It's just the way it is.'

'Like how they won't let me go to school?' I asked, remembering how I had gone there a few years ago for one day and been sent home and asked not to return.

'Yes. Like that.'

'And how Basia's friends won't let me play with them?'

'Like that too.'

'And how when we are in church, no one speaks to me but they all say how sorry they are to you?' I asked, knowing exactly what he would say.

'Like that.' He stood and got back to the business of selling potatoes and did not offer me any words of comfort, nor did he offer a place where I might fit in. I knew what he meant. I knew how people looked at me, how they would whisper '*Szalony*' to each other, how they would take a step away from me when I passed in case somehow my otherness rubbed off on them. I wasn't welcome. I knew that.

\* \* \*

Memories stacked themselves on top of each other, all reinforcing what I had come to realise – we could only be accepted, be safe, if we stuck together. No one else was going to invite us in, no one else was going to understand us. We had to show them – just like Gosia had said – what a woman like me could do.

We walked on for hours, each of us locked into our own thoughts. As the day wore on, the snow became thicker, the air freezing, meaning that we had no option but to keep walking. We could not sleep outdoors; we would not survive. It was only when we stopped briefly, each of us picking up snow and placing it into our mouths to quench our thirsts, that we talked to each other again.

'Ania.' Gosia was by my side, then I felt Benj on the other. 'We're sorry,' she said.

'You don't have to apologise, Gosia, you did nothing wrong.'

'But we made you angry.'

'It wasn't you. It was other things.'

'You're right about me, you know that, Ania? I mean, I am mad, don't get me wrong. But then when I saw that boy it was like I was the old me, not the mad me.'

'Who did he remind you of, Gosia?' I asked gently.

'My son,' she said, her voice breaking ever so slightly. 'My sister took him when everything went wrong. I tried not to think about him. To forget that he had ever existed. I knew he did, of course I did. But it was only when I saw that boy, I really remembered.'

'You haven't seen him since when?' Benj asked.

'Since he was five years old. That boy in the forest and in the bunker with us last night. He was older of course. But he had a way about him, quiet, thinking, and his eyes. At first, I thought maybe it was him, my baby boy, but then it couldn't be because he would be a man now – what, thirty or forty years old. It wasn't him, but it made everything go a bit strange in my head, Ania.'

'I know how that feels,' I said.

'But we'll be fine now. We'll get to your uncle's house and make it all nice and just live there,' she said.

I didn't bother to argue with her, or correct her. That wasn't what we were going to do, but I let Benj and her daydream about it, talk about it even, how we would have meals together, sleep in warm beds. It comforted them and they needed it. There was no point telling them that we were nearing the house of shadows, and what we were about to do.

I patted the hemlock in my pocket again and smiled.

**14**

THE HOUSE OF SHADOWS

*8 December 1942*
*Czerniejów, Lublin Voivodeship, Poland*
*Ania*

The moon hung high above us, casting a silvery glow over our path. The night was quiet except for the occasional rustle of leaves and the soft whisper of the wind. Our small group moved slowly, all of us worn out from trudging through snow that was now shin deep. As the sky became prickled with stars, we reached my uncle's house at the bottom of a two-mile farm track.

'I don't like it here,' Benj whispered. 'Too much dark – too many shadows.'

The past five years had not been kind to the main house, and even in the dark I could see that nature was taking over. Ivy clothed half of the house, and the right side of the roof was worse than just a few tiles missing; now it sagged into the top floor. In the daytime, it would look much worse, and yet, it was perfect. If anyone were to come down the long track and find it, they would immediately think that no one lived there, and that's exactly what we needed.

'I like it!' Gosia became excited, pushing open the front door that hung half off its hinges. 'Full of ghosts, I think.' Her voice echoed off bare brick walls as we followed her inside.

The darkness was complete. We needed matches, a lamp. I placed my right hand on the damp wall, following it with my fingertips until it stopped. The doorway led into the kitchen, I knew. I turned into it and smelled something that should not be there.

'Smoke,' I said, but no-one answered.

'Benj, Gosia?' I called out, hearing my own voice in an echoey response.

'Benj,' I tried again.

'Ania,' he called back. His voice was near, but there was something wrong with it – it was higher than usual.

I turned and looked into the black and saw a dark lump a few feet away. 'Oh Benj,' I said, placing my hand on his back. 'There's no need to be scared.'

'Ania,' he said again.

'What is it, Benj?'

'Look what I found!' Suddenly Gosia was there, a gas lamp in her hands, a weak flicker coming from the wick showing the lamp to be dirty and covered with cobwebs.

'Under the stairs,' she said as she reached us. 'I had matches. Took them from that woman in the woods – she didn't see me do it, Ania, so don't get all angry. I knew we'd need them...'

Then she trailed off, held the lamp higher to illuminate the living room, showing two figures that were not us.

'Ania,' Benj said. 'Do you see them too or are they ghosts?'

I took a step nearer to the figures then heard a click.

'Don't come any much closer,' a male voice said in broken Polish. 'You come to be much closer then I shooting the gun.'

I felt around in my pocket for my own gun, but as I drew it out it slipped from my hand and clattered to the floor.

One figure stepped forward, quickly bent down and picked it up then stepped back into the shadows.

'You must leave now,' another voice, a woman, said. Perfect Polish but a hint of something else lay in the accent.

Gosia stepped forward and held the lamp high. 'Who are you?' she said to them. It was then that we could see the faces of the pair in front of us – one a man, his face angular, his eyes a little too close together, then the woman. Her hair was black – blacker than my own, or any hair I had ever seen. It was like it almost shone blue. Her eyes were large, almond shaped, with thick lashes, her lips plumped into a cupid's bow. I licked my own thin lips then pursed them a little.

'You have to leave,' the woman said again.

'This is my uncle's home,' I said.

'Yes – *you* need to leave!' Gosia barked at them.

The woman smiled without a hint of fear. I liked her. I liked that she was not scared.

'You're young,' she said to me. 'Your uncle's house, you said?' She stepped closer to me. Her eyes looked me up and down, then she raised her hand and took Basia's yellow hat from my head. 'A girl,' she said. 'I thought so.'

She smiled again at me and stroked my hair. 'You cut it yourself?'

It was as though I had suddenly turned to stone. I could not speak, could not move. But it was not unpleasant having this woman so close to me, unafraid, stroking my hair.

'You don't have to be afraid,' she said, then turned to the man. 'Aleksi, take this.' She handed him my gun that she had picked up from the floor. 'Drop your own. They won't harm us and we won't harm them.'

'I'm not afraid.' I managed to find my voice.

'I know you are not, but the other two. You two. You don't need to be afraid,' she told Gosia and Benj.

She moved away from me, went to Benj and stroked the scar on his face. Then to Gosia, touched the coat as if it were some sort of ritual.

Finally, she went back to the man she called Aleksi. 'I'm Wanda,' she said. 'This is Aleksi, he's Russian – you can tell, no? Hear it in his voice when he speaks Polish. Not quite there yet, are you, Aleksi?'

Aleksi grunted and I noticed he had lowered his gun but still held it.

'Don't worry too much about him.' She sighed. 'He doesn't talk much anyway. Can be a bit grumpy. Don't mind him at all.'

'Where did you come from?' Benj asked wistfully as if she were not real.

'What are your names?' she asked, looking at me.

'Ania,' I said.

Benjamin and Gosia answered for themselves.

'I am so sorry, Ania, that we are in your uncle's house. We have been here for a while now. Months, in fact. Hiding away as they hunt us out there. And I can see that you haven't come here for a holiday.' She let out a tinkling laugh. 'You're like us,' she said. 'Ania, can I ask, can I ask if we can stay here with you tonight? Tomorrow we can talk, and perhaps you will let us stay a little longer. Outside it's snowing, there is nowhere for us to go, so is it all right if we stay?'

'Of course it is!' Gosia cried out and went to Wanda. This time it was her turn to touch Wanda – stroking her hair, marvelling at how long it was, how shiny. 'How do you keep it so clean?' Gosia asked.

It did not seem to bother Wanda one bit, who smiled and indulged Gosia's touch and questions.

'Aleksi,' Wanda said as Gosia stood on tiptoes so she could look straight into Wanda's eyes, wanting to see those almond shapes up close. 'Go light the fire again, light the candles for Ania. It is her house.'

Aleksi nodded, grunted again then as he walked past me, handed me my gun back.

'Good boy,' Wanda called after him. 'He is gruff but I knew he would give it you back. Just a bit wary, sometimes too much so.'

'Ania.' Benj stood by me and whispered in my ear, 'I need the toilet.'

'Go outside,' I said. 'To the outhouse.'

'Can you come?' he asked.

I looked to Wanda, who was indulging Gosia still, who now was opening and closing her fur coat, showing Wanda how big it was, telling her how warm it was, and if Wanda ever needed anything like it herself, she would get one for her.

I went outside with Benj, allowing him to walk a few feet away to the barn that stood a dark lump in the night. 'I can't find the outhouse, Ania,' he said.

'Just go wherever,' I told him and blew warm air into my cupped hands.

'You think we can trust them?' His voice sang to me from the darkness.

'I do,' I said, my breath curling up and away from me. 'They are like us. I saw it in her.'

'But the other one – Aleksi?' Benj said.

'I don't know about him,' I said.

'Russian—'

'Russian,' I agreed. 'Benj, can you hurry up?'

'It's cold,' he replied. 'And when it's cold it takes time.'

'Want me to whistle?' I asked. I used to do this for Basia when she found it hard to go in the outhouse at home. Scared of the wind, the rain, the cold, the dark. She'd make me stand outside and whistle a tune.

'Can you?'

I began to whistle a folk tune that Isaac played on his violin, a song about home and country, a song that didn't mean much any more.

I heard the stream of piss hit the ground and stopped. 'You good?' I called to Benj.

'All done.' He came up to me and grinned.

Inside, they had the fire roaring in the kitchen, candles lit on the table where pools of hardened wax showed how much time the pair had spent here.

On the floor were a mattress and blankets taken from upstairs. I recognised the purple blanket that would have been on the guest bed.

'We're sorry.' Wanda saw me looking at the mattress then at the stairs. 'We helped ourselves. Couldn't get to part of the house. The roof. But the other part is fine, but cold. No fire so we thought to camp down here.'

'That's fine,' I said, sitting down on a small milking stool that was still in its rightful place next to the fire. It had once been used for purpose, but when Uncle got a cat, a cat he named Kita, he brought the stool inside, placed it next to the fire for her to sleep on.

Kita was long gone.

Wanda sat, legs crossed on the mattress. I could see she was wearing men's trousers but they looked much better on her than me, and a thick grey jumper which I was sure used to be Uncle's. Yes! There, on the elbow, a hole. It was his. But despite what she wore, she was still beautiful. Her legs long, her hands slim. I was sure I had never seen anyone who looked like her before.

Gosia sat next to her and tried to mimic her slick action but couldn't quite manage to get her legs to bend the right way. Benj sat at the kitchen table, Aleksi on a chair next to the stove, long legs stretched out in front of him, his arms folded.

It all felt oddly comfortable. It shouldn't have, meeting two strangers in this house. I should have asked more questions, demanded to know who they were. I yawned. Maybe tomorrow.

Gosia began to talk about her husband, delighting in having a new audience. Benj, I noticed, would look at Wanda, begin to smile, then look to Aleksi, who seemed to be looking directly at us all at once. How was he doing that, I wondered. And how dare he sit there, arms folded, looking at us as if we were encroaching on his home? He was the guest.

'My uncle died five years ago,' I suddenly said, staring at Aleksi, challenging him to look away first. 'I would come here to visit. I can tell you that the woodshed is out back, to the right of the house. The barn is twenty steps south-south-east. Inside the barn you will find rusting tools and junk that my uncle saved over the years. He never threw anything away. You'll also find an old chicken coop to the left of the barn, and if you walk ten yards down behind the barn, you'll find a small pond that he once kept geese and ducks in. The perimeter of the rear and sides of the property are flanked with oaks, elms and firs. Just in case you were wondering if I was lying,' I added, still staring at Aleksi.

'I never said you were,' he said, then grinned. 'Is your house. I agree. I never say no it was not.'

It was then that I saw his hand – his left. Only his thumb and pinkie finger remained. Where the rest of his fingers should be were red nubs. He saw me look at them, frowned, then reset his arms so that his other hand was the one visible with all five of its digits.

'Ania,' Wanda said, making me look away from Aleksi. 'Why are you here though? Where is your family – your father, mother?'

'Dead,' I told her.

She nodded.

'And you?' I asked.

'I lost all my friends,' she said. 'My family, some of them might be alive but most are gone.'

'Where are you from?' I asked, keen to hear if she were from somewhere exotic that I had read about.

'I was born here, in Poland. My mother was from Hungary, my father said he was Polish but he also said, sometimes, that he came from Romania. Each time he told us his stories, things changed, families changed, sometimes even names.'

'So when did you lose people?' Gosia asked impatiently.

Wanda smiled then took Gosia's hand in hers. 'Sometimes you need to hear where people started from to understand how they ended up where they did. Just like you and your husband – you had to tell me about him first, so I could understand why you had to stay in hospitals.'

The simple explanation seemed to make sense to Gosia, who stayed quiet and let Wanda continue.

'Anyway. We travelled, me, my father and mother. I had no siblings – a cousin, I had one of those, though. His name was Kapaldi and we were close when we were young, but then he left with a woman he had met and I never saw him again. So he was the first one to leave – to disappear.

'Then my father died and it was just my mother and me, and

then she died and so I had to find a new family. And I did. Over the years, we had travelled with so many others – meeting them time and time again, so it did not take long for me to come across some more of my own.

'We did what we always had done: go from place to place, never staying too long, never really belonging anywhere. But then, when the war started, some of them wanted to come back here, to Poland, to find their families – to try to keep them safe.'

'But they died,' Gosia said sadly.

'I don't know if they did,' Wanda said. 'I expect so. About four months ago, what was left of the family I had created were stopped as we tried to begin a journey south, hoping to get out of the country. There were soldiers. There were guns. Dogs that strained on their chains and barked at us. They made us leave our wagons, our horses, and made us sit on the ground, our hands on our heads. Then a truck came and one by one we were told to get in.'

'But you didn't?' I asked.

'I didn't,' Wanda said. 'One soldier, he liked the look of me, he said. He wanted me to stay behind with him. Just him in amongst the trees. He told the others he would escort me himself.'

'And he brought you there?' Benj asked hopefully.

Wanda shook her head. 'I escaped,' was all she said.

'And the soldier, where did he go?' Benj asked.

'Into the ground.' She sighed as if she were sad about it. 'Afterwards, he went into the ground.'

'Dead,' Gosia said and nodded.

'Dead,' Wanda agreed.

'And you?' Gosia barked at Aleksi, making him jump ever so slightly in his chair.

'Majdanek,' he answered, offering no more.

'But you're *Ruski*!' Gosia said.

'Escaped,' he said.

'From Russia?' Gosia asked, confused.

He sighed. 'From camp. In July. Me and some others. We make to run away.'

'The camp, Ania, the one you said about—' Gosia was abruptly cut off by Wanda.

'Aleksi, go back upstairs, see if you can get the other mattress from the other bit of the house for everyone. We'll light a fire in the living room, give everyone somewhere to sleep.'

Aleksi nodded and went to the rickety staircase.

'Benjamin,' Wanda said. 'Perhaps you can help?'

Benj smiled at her in his lopsided way, but it was a smile I had not seen on him before – bigger, brighter somehow. He stood and followed Aleksi.

'Sorry about that,' Wanda said. 'Sorry for interrupting you, Gosia,' she added. 'Aleksi does not like to talk about it. And it is late and with everything that has happened, perhaps we should sleep.'

'I'm hungry,' Gosia said.

'Of course!' Wanda jumped up, went to the stove top and brought a cast-iron pan and set it over the flames. 'It won't get too warm – hard to light that stove as it is. I made a broth. It's not great but it will do. Carrots, potatoes, onions and some herbs. I wanted to get a chicken but Aleksi said we had taken enough.'

'Taken it from where?' I asked.

Wanda shrugged. 'A farm. They had plenty.'

As the broth warmed a little, I asked her how she had met Aleksi. 'Found him in here,' she said. 'At first, well, you saw, he held a gun to me and then soon dropped it. Realised I was like him. Just trying to survive. And we've done all right so far. Get a bit of food here and there from other farmhouses – never the same one, mind you, and always at night. It's funny how many things you can get for free when you really need them.'

'I understand that,' Gosia said, her eyes fixed on the pot. 'I can get anything. Everyone is so busy looking at me, wondering who this mad woman is, that they don't notice when I slip my hand into their pockets. I'm old but I'm quick,' she said.

Soon Aleksi and Benj returned, heaving my uncle's mattress down the stairs and placing it in the dark sitting room.

Wanda made Benj sit at the table and placed the pot in the middle, got us bowls and spoons and told us to eat as she and Aleksi made the other room comfortable.

'You're quiet, Ania,' Benj said as he slurped at his soup.

'Tired,' I told him. And I was. My mind felt stuffed. Thoughts were hard to come by. I just wanted to sleep.

'Is it not strange,' Gosia said, 'how this is your house but we are the guests?'

'If I wasn't so tired I might care,' I said. 'I might find it strange.'

'I like them,' Gosia said, then yawned. 'They're just right for us. Just the right fit.'

'Right fit?' Benj asked.

'Like a glove. They fit. All five of us now. Like a hand,' Gosia blathered.

Benj nodded, slurped again at his soup. Me, I felt a hand on my arm. My eyes were closing.

'Come, Ania.' Wanda's voice was like sugar syrup.

I yawned.

'Come, Ania.'

Then I was lying down. A blanket, a crackle of a log on the fire. Heat seeping through every part of my body.

'Sleep, Ania,' she whispered, sending me away into blackness.

## 15

### WANDA AND ALEKSI

*9 December 1942*
*Czerniejów, Lublin Voivodeship, Poland*
*Ania*

The wind woke me. It had blown down the chimney, causing the fire to smoke. I sat up, rubbed at my eyes and saw that the fire was almost out. There was no need to douse it; the smoke would soon dissipate through the draughty house. Benj's feet were near my head, and so were Gosia's. The pair of them had fallen asleep tightly next to each other, the ratty purple blanket I had seen on Wanda's mattress tucked firmly around them.

For a moment, I listened to the wind as it whistled its way through gaps in the mortar, as it rustled leaves outside. Then I rolled off the mattress and stood, noticing that my feet were bare. Someone had removed Tata's boots.

The room was beginning to lighten as the night was taken away by the day. I saw my boots placed neatly next to the wall. The sofa that had once been there was gone; so was the side table and the painting of a black horse that had adorned the wall. Who had taken them?

As I picked up my boots, I looked across the hall into the kitchen and saw that it was empty. There was no Aleksi, no Wanda on the mattress. Had they left? Were they upstairs? I had no time to dwell on the thought too much, nor look for them. The call of nature was upon me, and my stomach was cramping.

I shoved my feet into the boots and clomped outside to the outhouse that I hoped was still standing. It had been oddly built out of the front door instead of the rear, over the small grassy garden, around the side of the house to the left. Most were in the back, but my uncle, with the ways that he had had, said he wanted to be able to sit on the toilet and look at his barn, the meadow beyond it, down to the pond. 'It is a nice thing to look at when you are doing your business,' he would say. 'I look at my barn, built with my own hands, and think of the things inside that I have kept over the years and wonder to myself what I could make with those odds and ends of metal and wood. Then I look to the pond, and if the sun is rising I see my ducks swimming about, the geese honking, and I think to myself, what more could a man want in this life!'

My father said my uncle had a problem. Not as big as mine, but a problem nonetheless. He once said he wondered whether it all stemmed from my mother's side of the family. 'Her father, your grandfather, wasn't right either.'

The air outside was crisp, a biting cold that I quite liked. I breathed it in, let it sting at my throat and lungs for a moment, then headed to the left of the house.

There, the outhouse still stood, but with no door. It mattered little – who would see me anyway?

I sat on the rim of the toilet, the cold nibbling at my skin, and saw that Aleksi or Wanda had found newspapers and ripped them up and placed them to the side. It was all well and good that they had, as Wanda's broth did not agree with my stomach.

I noticed as I sat there that the wind had dropped. A wind that had woken me, that had smoked the room, had disappeared. I looked to the ribbon on my wrist and fingered it. Then hurried myself along as the cold began to seep under my skin.

As I finished and tidied myself, I saw a glimpse of orange, red, down near the pond.

I stepped out, made my way nearer to it. The light stayed, then it flickered – a fire. As I crunched my way over the frozen snow, I saw two figures, huddled close next to the flames. A branch cracked underfoot, a noise so loud in that silent forest that it made the two look at me – Wanda and Aleksi.

She waved me over.

'Ania,' she said, then patted the ground next to her. 'Up early.'

'I wondered where you had gone,' I said.

Aleksi shuffled over, letting me sit in the gap between them.

'I like to come outside and have a fire sometimes. Especially to watch the sun rise. It's important to see the new day come – especially now, when you are not so sure if there will be another sunrise for you.'

'Too cold and too early,' Aleksi grumbled. 'You Poles all with your strange thinking,' he said, then looked at me.

'No one made you come with me.' Wanda half laughed.

Aleksi shrugged. 'I am to keep you safe.'

'Aleksi here was in the army.' Wanda took my hand in hers. 'Weren't you, Aleksi? A proper soldier. Saw battle, all brave and things. He still thinks he is in the army, I think.'

Aleksi shook his head as if he had heard it all before.

I could smell her – Wanda as she sat next to me and gently

stroked my palm, then the back of my hand. She smelled of the earth on a summer's day, and of something sweeter that I could not place. I wanted to place my nose against her skin and inhale her.

'You're not as young as you look, are you?' she said. She stared at my palm and traced lines and creases.

'Nineteen,' I said. 'Twenty soon – March.'

'But it has been hard for you, hasn't it? Everyone thinking you are younger. They underestimate you, don't they, Ania?'

Wanda had this strange effect on me, I was coming to realise. Not just like the night before when I was tired and found that I did not speak much, or let her take charge, or even think properly. It was the same now as she held my hand in hers. My thoughts drifted away, the chatter, the noise, the voices that were always there but at different volumes, telling me I was *szalony* – they all disappeared.

'But you have made a decision, haven't you?' she asked. 'You're not going to be the same Ania as before.'

'Yes,' I managed to say.

'You know why I really come out here, Ania? Why I like the fire outside so much? I need it. I *need* the flames.' She let go of my hand and beat at her chest. 'I need them, Ania. Without them, there's a part of me missing.'

As soon as she said those words, I felt something shift inside me.

'I'm missing parts too,' I said.

'I know,' she said. 'I saw it earlier with the others. I saw you have something missing; so does Benjamin and so does Gosia. Aleksi too.'

'I am fine,' Aleksi said. 'She is thinking she can see things in the flames. Magic woman!' He laughed.

'Go inside if you don't want to hear it,' she told him, her voice a little edgier.

It did something to him. I felt him tense. 'I will stay,' he said. 'Keep talking, Ania. Tell me about the missing part of you.'

I felt comfortable and uncomfortable all at once. I wanted to speak to Wanda, I wanted her to hold my hand in hers again. But on the other hand, it all felt a bit much – a bit like I was in a foreign country, and as much as it was beautiful, I didn't really understand anything.

'Go on,' Wanda urged. 'You can say it. You'll feel better when it is out of you. Don't keep it all locked away.'

I swallowed. May as well give it a go, I thought. No one had ever wanted to listen to me before, save for Isaac.

'My father tried to find it,' I told her. 'My missing thing. But we never found it and now he's gone, so I will have to find it myself.'

'And have you?'

I shook my head. 'I don't think so. But there's something – a part of me that is starting to feel something – and I think it's been there this whole time. But I'm a little afraid of it. Like, if I let it out, I won't be able to stop it. It will just keep taking me.' I shook my head again and laughed. 'I'm sorry. My thoughts must sound insane to you.'

'They sound normal to me,' she said, then threw something onto the flames so that the logs crackled and hissed, sending sparks into the cold, crisp early morning air. The flames danced, casting flickering shadows on the pond's iced surface and illuminating her face. She took my hand back in hers and placed it on her chest. Her heart started to beat faster and faster and I could feel my own following suit. Her breathing became quicker; so did mine. Then all of a sudden, as if she willed it so, her heart seemed to stop. Her breathing became quiet. She stared at the flames as they danced.

'I can see it,' she whispered. 'The missing part of you. You shouldn't be afraid of it, Ania. It is your purpose. It is your fate. You cannot ignore it any longer. You cannot let others direct you any more. You are now the leader. I can see you, wandering down a road. It is dark, dangerous, but you keep walking. You feel no fear. No sadness. Begging you, people follow. They are attached to you – they need you. Without you their own fates are sealed. You must keep going, Ania, down that road, into the dark...' She stopped for a moment and her eyes narrowed. 'A woman waits for you. She has a red ribbon. She said it is yours. Behind you, a man holds one too. You have to decide to go with her or stay.'

'What do I decide?' I whispered, staring too at the fire, wanting to see what she saw.

'You decide to do the right thing,' she said, but her voice had changed. It was no longer whispering, no longer magically lyrical. Now it was flat, and she did not look into the fire any more; she looked at me. 'You decide to do the right thing,' she repeated. Then she let go of my hand, placing it on my knee, and patted it.

'See?' Aleksi broke the stillness. 'She is thinking she is magical. She say she see me too. She see me with wife and children,' he guffawed. 'In this time. With war. With Germans! Wife and children,' he said again.

'I said in the future,' Wanda stubbornly said. 'I never said now.'

'Future?' Aleksi stood and wiped his hands on his trousers. 'Is no future, Wanda. Is not for us.'

I watched him walk back to the house, but Wanda had turned her head back to the flames. Her softness had gone.

'Are you all right?' I asked.

'I need to be alone for a moment. Sorry, Ania. He just makes me so...' She balled up her fists like I had done so many times in my life.

I nodded, stood and patted her shoulder and went back inside, finding Aleksi lying on the mattress, curled tightly into a ball.

I removed my boots and got back into my own bed, fighting a bit of the blankets away from Benj and Gosia to cover myself.

My nose was cold and I dipped my head into my chest, pulling the blanket over my head as much as I could to feel the warmth of my breath on my skin.

Sleep was not going to come back now, I knew. It was too cold with the fire out. Then my thoughts that had been quietened with Wanda came back. This time it was about what she had said. I wasn't sure whether I believed her or not – whether she had really seen something or whether she just needed this to feel as though she was whole. I recalled when once Isaac had told me about his beliefs – about why he felt it important to be Jewish, to have a ritual each Friday, to pray and to sing to God.

'It makes you feel whole,' he had said. 'As if you are not alone.'

'Maybe I should be Jewish,' I had childishly told him. 'Maybe that is the missing part of me.'

He had smiled indulgently at me. 'Maybe God will fill a part of you, Ania, but I can promise you that what your father said is not true – you are not missing something. If anything, you have more than most people. Your intelligence worries him because he does not understand it. Fear is born from ignorance, or sometimes simply feeling inferior to someone else. For example, an unhappy man can see a happy man and wonder what makes him happy—'

'So he is jealous,' I had said, cutting him off.

'No, not jealous. He is curious. He wants to know what makes this man so happy. So he asks him and the man explains. He says that it is his religion, or maybe it is his family, or maybe it is a way he lives his life that differs from the unhappy man. The unhappy man does not understand this – he thinks it is strange and unusual and he does not think that it will make him happy. This unhappy man sees the happy man each day, and resentment starts to build. Perhaps now he becomes jealous, but really, his anger is fuelled by his ignorance.

'One day, the unhappy man sees that the happy man has fallen down. He is injured and in pain. The unhappy man feels something in his breast – a lightness. This man's misfortune has brought about a sense of joy – he is glad that finally the happy man is now as unhappy as him. So he seeks out to make sure that the happy man is brought down to his level.'

'So it makes him happy – this unhappy man is happy because the other man is now sad?' I had asked.

'No. The unhappy man is still unhappy.'

'So why does he wish the happy man ill? Why does he want him to become like him?'

'Because, Ania, it's the only thing that makes sense to him. It is logical for the unhappy man that everyone be as unhappy as he.'

Isaac's explaining to me, when I was a child, what ignorance was, what feelings did to people, made me glad that I was less emotional. It was better to not feel but to have rational thought, I decided. But now, with Wanda and her ritual that gave her comfort, and Isaac's religion that made him whole, I wondered whether I had missed out on something that could have helped me.

It was then I thought of something – the ribbons – how had she known? I placed my hand on my wrist and could not feel the material, then I ruffled up my sleeve and found it on my forearm. She hadn't seen it. Wanda hadn't seen the ribbon. So how had she known, and who, in this vision of hers, had the woman been? My mother? Basia?

I heard footsteps. Wanda was returning. Then I felt her above me, then her hand on my head.

'Sleep, Ania.'

Before I could say anything, do anything, I felt myself fall away into a dream that did not make sense, into a dream where I ran after my mother, Benj following me, a red ribbon drifting off into the sky.

## 16

### ANIA THE LEADER

*9 December 1942*
*Czerniejów, Lublin Voivodeship, Poland*
*Ania*

My dreams continued into the morning. Merging from one to another, so quickly that I tried to grasp at them, tried to make sense of them even in my sleep, but they slipped through my fingers like water.

When I woke I did not feel rested, and all I could recall from the dreams was red – the colour red – everywhere – people's faces, the sky – everything was scarlet.

I looked about me, wanting to tell Wanda about this dream, about all the red, and to see if she thought it held any meaning, but the room was empty, the fireplace cold and vacant. For a second I almost thought I must have imagined Wanda and the others – perhaps they had never been with me at all.

Then, I heard heavy footsteps and knew that Benj was close by.

'Ania,' he said. I looked up to see him standing in the doorway, his face bright red – just like in my dream. 'Wanda is making me chop wood – we found an axe outside and I'm chopping it.' Then he grinned. A wide grin that I had never seen on him before. 'Wanda says that I am really strong – stronger even than Aleksi.'

'That's good, Benj. That's good that you can chop the wood.'

I eased myself up off the mattress, stood for a moment and stretched my arms above my head.

'Where's Gosia?' I asked.

'In the kitchen, with Wanda. It's gone eleven, you know. You slept and slept and Wanda said to leave you. I chopped wood. Aleksi, he went somewhere and came back with a chicken! A chicken, Ania! Wanda and Gosia are cooking it now. They say we will eat a feast tonight. But there is bread and cheese and milk! Aleksi finds it all, that's what Wanda says, but she told me not to ask how he does it.'

I had never seen Benj so energised, so happy before, that it took me a moment to take it all in.

I went to the kitchen and found Gosia and Wanda talking as they chopped vegetables. The mattress had been propped against the wall. Aleksi sat by the fire in what was once an old rocking chair with a rocker broken, which had been banished into the ever fuller barn. Now though, it was fixed.

Aleksi looked up at me briefly as I entered the room, nodded, then placed a sliver of wood in his mouth and chewed at it.

'Sit, sit.' Gosia came to me, fussed at me. Made me sit at the table and placed a hunk of fresh bread in front of me, cheese, a mug of milk.

I ate, marvelling at the scene in front of me. It was as though I were still dreaming.

'Quiet today,' Aleksi said. 'No words from you?'

I wasn't sure whether he was joking with me, so I just nodded at him.

'You have to tell her,' Wanda said, tuning to look at me, smile. Then she went back to chopping whatever vegetable was in front of her.

'I will,' Aleksi said.

'We've all been talking this morning,' Gosia said. 'When you were sleeping.'

Benj sat down next to me and eyed the cheese. I pushed it towards him.

'Is that so,' I said, my mouth half full of bread.

'I told them all about your father and sister and then we spoke about Benjamin, and then we spoke about the men in the forests and how you said that you were going to take revenge.'

'I never said that, you did,' I told Gosia. 'It was your idea.'

'My idea, your idea, who cares? Anyway, Wanda, she likes it. Even Aleksi too.'

I looked at him, but he was staring at Wanda.

'Not me.' Benj sat, a crumb of cheese falling out of his mouth. 'But Wanda said I didn't have to fight if I didn't want to. My job is to chop wood. Stay here. Keep it warm and safe.'

*Wanda said, did she?*

'But Wanda says that Aleksi has to tell you about the camp. She says it is a good place to start.'

'I think Ania might have her own ideas,' Wanda said. 'But I thought it couldn't hurt to hear what Aleksi thinks. He was there, knows the layout, was in the army. He knows what is needed.'

All of a sudden it was as though I were no longer needed. Wanda had taken Benj and Gosia, made them happy, made them feel safe. Wasn't that supposed to be my job?

'I—' I started.

But Aleksi was speaking too. His voice carried better, made everyone stop what they were doing and look at him.

'The camp, Majdanek, not too far from here. Maybe half a day walk. Hour in a car. Me and my soldiers, we built it – made to built it,' he said. 'They take us, the Germans, and take us here, and say, "Build your own housing." So we build and build and fences come, wire on the top, all of us prisoners of war. No food, so many die from no food or illness. Every day, death. Wake up, death. Go to bed, more death.' He stopped and shook his head. 'I not say more on that. I not say more. Doesn't matter for what you need to know.

'They say many more coming here so we build more and more. Poles, they come. Jews. So many beaten every day for no reason. Just the Germans like it, you know, to hit and to hit, and they see the blood and they laugh. Anyway.' He shook his head again. 'Me and some others, not many of us left then, we say no more. We must to leave. To escape. And if they shoot at us, and we die, at least we die like men. We die because we are trying. So is July, yes, this July. We at night go to the south of the field and we all throw anything we can at the fence, you know, to climb over, to knock it down, to make the wire covered so it did not hurt us. Eighty-six of us. Eighty-six. All of us quickly, quickly, throwing things, and then we realise it is working, and we run. My God, we run. Only two guards that night, thinking we are too weak so not many guards needed, so they did not know what to do. They shoot, try to shoot, and some yes get hit, but most, we get away. Some men, they go to the forest. I go too. I meet with resistance – Russian resistance, but—' Then he stopped again and looked at Wanda.

'It wasn't for him,' she finished for him. 'He didn't want to stay with them.'

He nodded his thanks at her.

'So you came here?' I asked.

'I find.' He shrugged. 'The men in forest give me gun, clothes, wish me well. I find this place here and I think maybe I stay. Be quiet for a time. And then Wanda, she comes and we stay together all quiet. But then you come.' He sighed. 'Now no more time to be quiet.'

'The partisans were helping the inmates at the camp, weren't they, Aleksi?' Wanda prompted him.

'Yes. Food, you know. Thrown over fences. Sometimes we can write letter and they take for us. But they never attack guards, you know. Help inmates, yes, is good. But the guards...'

'Gosia said you wanted to fight back?' Wanda said, looking at me, her eyes bright, wide. 'Me too. Aleksi too. We can do it, I think, us five.'

'I get more guns,' Aleksi offered. 'Very good at getting things – food, clothes. Not so hard, you know. You not go to same town or village twice. You take from richer people. You never take from very poor. I can get guns from partisans if we need them. I think we need them.'

'And do what?' Gosia asked. 'You need to tell me specifically. Who are we going to kill?'

'Not kill. For defence,' Aleksi said. 'We can help inmates too. We need gun to stop trucks, maybe save people in them from going to camp. Maybe kill,' he suggested, and shrugged. 'Guards, yes, kill them if we can, but not at camp – they leave camp, go to Lublin, to villages, to their houses. They go restaurants, bars. We find them there. Never at camp. Too many guards now. Too many guns.'

It was all spiralling quickly. Yes, I wanted to fight. I wanted to prove to everyone that I was not a child, I would not sit back and do nothing any more. But I had not yet formed a plan, and planning, thinking, were everything to me, and it all felt a bit rushed.

'Ania.' Wanda placed her hand on my shoulder.

'I need air,' I said. I scraped back my chair and went outside.

I walked to the barn and looked inside at all the things my uncle had saved over the years. A broken windowpane, sheet metal, a mouldy bale of straw. To calm the thoughts in my mind, or to at least give myself a chance to understand what was happening and the feelings that went along with them, I picked my way through the detritus.

A picket fence rested against a wall, a fence that had once surrounded the front garden of the house that was blown down in the wind and never fixed. Slabs of wood, nails, screws scattered about the floor, so I had to manoeuvre carefully. On the far-right wall was something I knew, something that had once been in our home and had been spirited away. An old grandfather clock. It had been my mother's, that I knew, and had never worked. I remembered it had lived with us until I was perhaps seven or eight, then my uncle came on his horse and cart and told my father he would fix it and return it to us. Of course, he never had. I went to the clock and smeared the grime from its face. The time read 11.05. I wondered what had happened in that moment of the clock stopping. Had it been 11.05 in the morning, at night? Had it been the exact time of my mother's death perhaps? Had the clock somehow known...

'Ania,' Wanda called to me. 'Are you all right?'

She carefully squeezed her way through all the junk and reached my side. 'I didn't mean to upset you. It was just that Gosia was talking all morning, saying that you were going to do something, that you were clever, she said, and that you were angry. As soon as she said it, I knew. I knew you had been brought here for a reason. Me and Aleksi, we feel the same way. Aleksi, well, it took him time to feel that way again – but that's not my story to tell.' She reached up and tucked her hair behind her ears. 'I just thought if you heard about the camp, about how Aleksi knows how to get things, how he can teach us how to use the guns, then we could piece it all together. *Together*,' she added.

'This was my mother's,' I said, gesturing at the clock. 'It stopped. It died.'

Wanda nodded.

'I am angry,' I said. 'Not at you. I don't think so. It takes me time, sometimes, to know what I am feeling and why. The anger that is in me, I mean, the apple, the red, all of that, it all comes together and I feel rage. Like a rage where I could do something but I am not sure what it is. And then I had a thought, in the forest. I was tired of it all, you see, of being called a child, of being called *szalony*, and I saw this.' I felt around in my pocket and drew out the hemlock.

'*Szalej*,' Wanda said.

'I had this thought. This thought that I could do something with it. I'm rambling, I know. You have to stop me when you don't understand.' I waved the hemlock about. 'It was this thought, born from the rage, this thought that wouldn't it be perfect to send them mad, to kill them with madness?' Then I laughed. 'I'm sorry,' I said again. 'My thoughts. I told you they sound insane. They dance about, all jostling and pushing each other, and then recently, well, since Tata and Basia, there are these feelings too that I am trying to understand, control, and they affect the thoughts. Normally, I can think, you know, logically. I can make sense of everything. If it is in a book, I understand it. I can understand these strange, big, wonderful things that people write about. But then, like I said, you know. The apple and all that. And Tata and Basia. It's like I'm actually losing my mind. I'm actually *szalony* now. Isn't that ironic?'

It was the longest I had ever spoken to anyone about what

went on in my head. Especially since Tata's and Basia's deaths. But as I had spoken, as nonsensical as the sentences sounded, it all started to fit together in my brain – like I was finally understanding what had happened.

'Shock,' Wanda said and placed her hand on my cheek. 'I know the feeling. It's shock. That's what word you need to describe all that's going on in your head. After the soldier – well – I won't say, but you know, after that, I mean, I wasn't myself. I couldn't understand things either. Aleksi too – but like I said, that's his story to tell, not mine. It's normal to feel this way, Ania. You're not losing your mind.'

'Really?' I asked.

'Not at all. Your mind is just dealing with what happened to you. And Gosia was right about you being clever.' She grinned and touched the hemlock. 'I don't think I've ever heard of a more perfect idea!'

\* \* \*

For the next two hours we all sat at the kitchen table and spoke about what we could do. What *we* could do that perhaps the partisans could not. How we could make our feelings, our thoughts, either go away or at least dull them by knowing that we were finally fighting back, doing something.

In the centre of the table sat the hemlock. They all liked my idea, bar Benj, who stood up and busied himself chopping more wood when talk went to revenge, to killing guards.

'Can you imagine?' Aleksi said. 'They sit there and turn mad, die; we know they are to die, and they know we know but they do nothing. Is better than guns, than shooting, Ania. Very much better.'

For the first time, Aleksi smiled, lighting up his face,

changing it from that sullen, grumpy man, to perhaps one that was younger, perhaps full of hope.

'But how do we get them to drink it?' Gosia asked. 'You can't just walk up to them and say, here, take this, and they take it and that's that.'

'I've been thinking about that,' I said. 'I think there are a few ways. Aleksi, you said that the guards from the camp are billeted either in Lublin or in villages, yes?'

'Yes. They everywhere. Like rats. You not go far to find one.'

'We need to get into those bars, get close to them.' I looked to Wanda. I could see the effect she had on Aleksi, on Benj. Even on me.

'Me?' she asked, then grinned. 'Oh, I suppose I could chat with them a little, pour something into their drinks? But I can't go like this!' She looked down at the jumper.

I thought that perhaps she could. I was sure men would still look at her regardless of what she wore.

'You need nice clothes,' Gosia mused. 'Nice, like the German ladies wear. All nice and clean. I'll get them for you.'

'And how will you do that?' I asked Gosia.

'Never you mind. You saw the coat I got?'

I had. And if that was Gosia's interpretation of nice and clean, it was a bad idea.

'The coat is old, Ania,' Gosia said and patted my hand. 'I know it is. You think I am mad or something?' She cackled, showing us her gold tooth. 'Can't go into the big towns to shops so have to go into homes. Say, you *Ruski*.' She looked at Aleksi.

'Aleksi,' he reminded her.

'Sure. Sure. Any big houses you have seen? Any nice rich people about? Must be a couple. We only need one, maybe two at most.'

'Maybe,' he said. 'There was this one house. Not so far from here. Maybe five, six miles. Big. All trees and gardens. I don't know who is living there. Maybe a woman? Maybe. Then one more house, maybe ten miles. But smaller homes good too. In the town. Not in the country like here. No good for those homes. No one will be having the nice clothes there. But maybe not in Lublin city we go, just before city. Just on edge. Some big places there. Not farmers. Not poor. Big, you know. But is risk because closer you are getting to the city, more Germans you see.'

'Do you think you could do it though?' I asked.

'I think, yes, I can. I still go tomorrow, yes, to see partisans in forest. Take me two, maybe three days. I go and come back. I see old commander. He was sorry I leave. But he understand why. I ask him for favour. He will do for me, because I help him get free from camp. He owe me something.'

'What was the other idea you had?' Wanda fingered the hemlock then drew her hand back as if it bit her.

'The nails, the wood in the barn. You said, Aleksi, about stopping trucks from taking people to the camp. When I saw the nails, the wood, I thought that if they were on the road, and the tyres blew, they would be forced to stop. We don't try to blow all the tyres. Just one. Make it look like an accident. When they get out to look at it, we have Wanda, come down the road, soup in hand. Says she saw them and worried for them in the cold. She gives them the soup. They'll take it. They wouldn't not take it from her. And then, give it ten minutes or so to start getting into their bloodstream, we release people, if that's what they have in the truck, or if it's food, weapons, whatever it is, we take it. Give it to the inmates.'

No one spoke for a moment and I wondered whether it all sounded too far-fetched. In my mind it was clear. I could see it happening. I could plan it out so that it worked. I knew I could.

'Binoculars,' Aleksi said, leaning back in the chair and

looking at the ceiling. 'Need them. We must to watch the roads of the camp. Learn routines. See what is happening and when. We don't do anything until we know as much as we can know. Yes?'

'Agreed,' I said. 'I'll plan it. I'll watch the roads. I know the way.'

'You have map?' he asked.

I pointed at my head. 'In here. I can find my way. Trust me.'

'And what is my job?' Gosia asked. '*Ruski* is going to the partisans, and to Lublin for the clothes, even though he is not a woman,' she spat. 'Then Wanda, you are going to go to bars. Ania, you are going to watch roads and cars and other things and plan it all. What will Gosia do?'

I looked at her and smiled, then inched the hemlock closer to her with my index finger. 'You have the job of finding more of this, down near the river, not far from here, and then making it into something that we can feed to the Germans.'

Gosia regarded the hemlock, then grinned. 'Gosia always was a good cook,' she said. 'Right up until her husband left her. But she remembers.' Then she corrected herself and stared at me. 'I remember. I remember how to do it. And I remember who the old Gosia used to be.'

## 17

## THE BLUE POLICE

*11 December 1942*
*Czerniejów, Lublin Voivodeship, Poland*
*Ania*

Two days later my plan was coming together. Aleksi had gone to see his old commander, assuring us that he would be able to find him quickly, and that he would do his best to find suitable clothing for Wanda.

Before he left, I watched as he kissed her forehead, then laid a kiss on each cheek. She blushed and stroked his face, then told him that she would miss him.

The second evening that he was gone, after going to the outhouse, I found Wanda sat in front of the fire, a cream blanket wrapped around her shoulders.

'You can't sleep?' I whispered to her.

She turned and I saw that her eyes were red, watery. 'Come sit with me. Sleep with me tonight. I find I cannot sleep alone.'

I sat next to her and she placed some of the blanket around my shoulders.

'You and he?' I asked.

She nodded. Then, 'I don't know.'

'Why don't you know?' I asked, genuinely intrigued. I had never seen Basia with a boy, although I knew of the ones she had had her eye on. I really wanted to know what it was like to be with someone, how people found each other, got married, had children. I had never seen it, so how could I know?

'It is complicated. He is complicated. His hand, you know.' She raised her own hand and bent three fingers away. 'Things happened to him when he was fighting, and then at the camp. He is better than he was but sometimes he slips away again.' She shook her head and laughed. 'I fall in love with the wrong men all the time; why should this time be any different?'

'What does it feel like?' I asked.

'What? Falling in love?'

I nodded.

'Like... I don't know. Like you sort of go a bit mad. Like you said before, when you were trying to explain your thoughts to me, it's sort of like that, but it makes your chest ache too, and makes you nervous and happy all at the same time. You've never been in love, Ania?'

'No,' I said. I then told her about my life. About how I had been isolated in the farm, how I was treated like a child, and had perhaps acted like one too. 'I had no one to look at – to see what I was meant to be.'

'Your sister though? She did not tell you about things, about being a woman?'

I thought of Basia. She had explained sex to me. She had explained why each month my stomach cramped, how to pad my underwear with old cloths that I then had to boil wash. She had talked of boys, of one day being a mother, but not often enough that it had ever really meant anything to me.

'She told me how babies were made,' I said.

'What did you think to that when she told you?'

'Not much. It sounded, really to me, the same as what the pigs did, or the cows. I knew about all that for years so it didn't come as much of a shock when she said that people did the same as animals. It's just necessary, isn't it, to be able to have children.'

'It is,' Wanda said. 'But it can be much, much more than that. It's an expression of love, when you are that close to someone that you let them know you. Let them know every part of you.' She sighed sadly. 'But then it can make things worse too. Make it all the more confusing.'

I did not respond. I wasn't sure what to say. I really did not understand what she was talking about, and I knew I would either have to ask a very direct question to get the straight answer I needed or leave well alone. I decided on the latter, mainly because she started to cry.

She rested her head on my shoulder and cried for a few minutes, then wiped at her face with the back of her hand.

'You see those flames, Ania,' she said. 'How beautiful they are. How they flicker and change. Whenever I need to think, whenever I get upset, or even angry, I find that just by looking into the flames it calms my mind. What calms yours?'

*You*, I wanted to tell her. But I said, 'Sleep.'

She laughed and raised her head. 'Then we must go to sleep. There is much to do. Much to plan. Although you seem to have a hold on it all.'

'I like planning. It calms me too, I suppose.'

'I hate it. Planning. Knowing what will happen. Sometimes it takes the joy out of life. But then again, there is no real joy now, is there? Come, Ania, lie next to me.'

I did as she told me. She wrapped her arms around me, and her fingers found the ribbon on my wrist.

'Did you really see those things in the fire the other day – about me and the woman and the ribbons?' I whispered as she stroked at the material.

'I did,' she whispered back, her voice becoming heavier with the promise of sleep. 'This is your mother's,' she said, tapping the ribbon. 'It was meant to be for her.'

I opened my mouth to say something, but nothing came out. How did she know?

'It's all right. It's strange, isn't it, when someone can see things about you. That's my gift – my burden. All these years I have tried to help people, to show them things, warn them about things – some listen, others don't believe.'

'Did you see anything else?' I asked, finding my voice at last.

'No,' she said.

'Not the purpose you spoke of?' I pushed her.

'Only you can know your own purpose. But I told you about leading people, and that's what you are doing. With us. With all these plans.'

'I worry though,' I said. 'That the rage I feel, the anger that drives it all will get too much, too big. I learned before to control my temper. But this isn't temper. This burns my chest. And I haven't let it go yet. And I'm afraid and excited to at the same time.'

She nodded. 'Rage is powerful. But it's dangerous too. It changes you. Once you give in, it's hard to not let it consume you.'

'Did you feel rage, that time in the woods with the soldier?'

'I did.' She sighed.

'But now you don't feel it?'

'I do. All the time.'

'But you don't act on it?'

'I will again. I know I will. But not yet.'

Neither of us spoke for a while, letting the crackle of the wood in the fireplace fill the silent room.

'Tell me about your mother, Ania,' Wanda suddenly said. 'Tell me why you think that ribbon belongs to her.'

'Because I killed her,' I said.

'You didn't. She knows you didn't. She knows that that ribbon is for you. She thinks it was not meant for her at all.'

'How do you know that? You saw her?'

'I told you – I hear, see things. I don't know. All I can say is that the ribbon is yours, not hers. She already has one, she says.'

I shook my head. 'No. I owe a life. I took hers and now I owe one.'

Wanda let out a slight laugh. 'Says who?'

'A woman. She was like you. My father took me to see her once to find the piece of me that was missing. He thought she would be able to explain me to him, I think. She read cards and she told me that I owe a life for the one I took. Tata got mad. He took me home and he never took me back to the woman again.'

'I don't think that's right,' Wanda said. 'It doesn't sound right.'

'It is,' I insisted. 'My father was scared to go. Maybe I was twelve or younger, I don't know. But we went on the cart and I remember that the horse did not want to go into the village. He snorted and bucked, and it made my father suck hard on his cigarette so that it burned quickly, and suddenly he yelled from the pain as it touched his lip with its ash. We stopped outside this house. A small house, so small I wasn't sure it was even a house. Inside, the rooms were covered with all sorts of strange carvings – wooden heads, stone sculptures of people dancing, but their faces had been carved in such a way that they were grimacing in pain.

'There was a strong smell of lavender and something else – something burning that she kept in a small dish on a table covered with a red and purple cloth. She made us both sit, took out her cards and asked me to cut the pack in half. I did and that's when she said it. She said that I would never be whole because I had taken a life, and that one day, I would have to owe mine – give it to someone else so that I could go to heaven and be with Mother.'

Wanda sat up and took my hand in hers and turned it over to trace the lines and creases in my palm like she had done before. 'She was wrong, Ania, to say that to you in that way. You're not missing a part because your mother died.'

'I know. I know it wasn't true. It didn't make sense. I told Tata that too – he was so frightened afterwards that I had to keep telling him over and over that it wasn't true. But now, I don't know. Now I think she might have been right – maybe I do owe a life. Not to get me to heaven, not to make me whole – but maybe it's part of this purpose of mine, part of this rage that is growing. I'm sorry.' I shook my head. 'I can't explain – my mind, you see – there are so many things, thoughts in there, that I can't make sense of things at the moment.'

I could feel the weight of tiredness on my shoulders and head.

'Sleep, Ania.' Wanda lay down next to me. 'Sleep now. Things will become clearer soon.'

As I drifted away, I felt her fingers stroking my hair, I could hear her humming something wild and mystical, I could smell the burning logs, and suddenly I drifted into a dreamless sleep.

\* \* \*

The following morning, I woke to find Benj sat at the kitchen table watching me.

'You slept here,' he said.

I yawned, sat up. 'Where's Wanda? Gosia?'

'They found pheasants – saw one and they both took after it.'

Pheasant for dinner. Sounded good. I stretched, feeling somewhat different. Stronger, quieter mind?

'Ania,' Benj said. 'This house. This house of shadows that you called it. Last night there were noises and Gosia said that there were ghosts here. Is that true? Do you believe in ghosts?'

'I don't, Benj.' I stood.

He chewed at his thumbnail. 'I think maybe there are. When will Aleksi be back? Will you still be going to the camp? Will I be here alone?'

I could see that even though Benj enjoyed being around Wanda, having a job to do, whether chopping wood, making fires, trying to fix the front door, or shoving bits of wood, leaves, anything he could find into the gaps in the walls, he was still Benj. Still Benj who was afraid. Still Benj who needed me.

I mimicked Wanda, placed my hand on his head and stroked his hair. 'I promise you will never be left alone, Benj. I promise.'

'At night too. You must promise that. I don't like the dark, Ania. And here, there are shadows everywhere.'

'I promise,' I said again.

'Good. That's good.'

'How about, Benj, you go into the barn, see what's in there. Maybe there are things we could use in the house? It would be helpful to Wanda, I know.'

Benj nodded and made his way outside, seeming happier now he had something to do – some way in which to be useful.

I followed Benj outside and saw Wanda and Gosia

approaching me, feathered bundles in their arms. As they neared, I saw the necks of the pheasants lolling.

'She's old but she's quick,' Wanda said, her face red and sweating despite the cold. 'She got them both.' They placed the pheasants down and rubbed at the dirt on their palms.

'The trick is to let them think you're their friend – you mean them no harm – and then!' Gosia mimed snapping a neck. 'We need some other things.'

I looked at the two dead birds, there in the grey sludge of snow, their eyes open, looking at me.

'Ania, are you listening?' Gosia asked. 'We need other things, I said. Ask Wanda what we need and she'll send you on your way.' She bustled past me, a few feathers drifting behind her, caught in the air.

'Can you go into the village?' Wanda asked. 'You must know it well enough from being here before. We need you to go to find flour, if you can, vegetables, anything really if there is anything. We have no ration cards so you'll have to use whatever money you have – Benjamin said you had some. It might raise some eyebrows so be careful how you go about it.'

I hadn't been into the village for what, perhaps ten years, and when we had visited Uncle before, we had rarely gone in anyway. However, it was not lost on me that someone could recognise me, wonder what I was doing here, then tongues would be sent wagging and the whole village would soon know that Ania, the mad niece, was back.

'It might be better for you to go.' I explained it all to Wanda.

'Trust me, I would stand out too much,' she said without a hint of narcissism. It was simply a fact – Wanda was beautiful and she was well aware of the effect she had on people. 'We can't send Benjamin or Gosia. Aleksi will be back soon and then we won't need to go into the village again. It's just this once.'

I wasn't sure about it, but I agreed that I would go. It hadn't been planned, thought through, making my palms itch.

'Take this.' She handed me Tata's knife that I had taken and placed in our sack. 'Benjamin got it out when he was showing me this bear of his.'

'I have a gun,' I said and patted my pocket, but it was empty.

'It's in the house,' she said. 'Aleksi said he would fix it – something wrong with the coil or something.' She looked to Benj, who was heaving things out of the barn, seemingly bored now of our discussion.

'You'll be fine, Ania.' She then looked at me and gave me one of her smiles that made me feel strange. 'You'll be fine,' she said again.

I took the knife from her, went inside, found the money that we had taken when we left the farm, and set off into the village.

\* \* \*

Czerniejów was a small village of perhaps only 400 inhabitants, mostly farmers, so that the village itself sprawled over fertile fields, edging towards the Wieprz River, a tributary of the Vistula. Some summers when we visited, we would sit on the riverbank watching for otters, swimming in the lazy currents and picking at daisies in the grass. There had been a farm on the other side of the bank, Old Man Kaminski's farm, where we sometimes got eggs and milk, which was probably gone by now – Kaminski had been almost bent double with age when I was a child; I doubted he was still around.

As I walked, fields on either side, I could smell the freshness of water and knew if I turned left I would soon be stood on the riverbank again. Although the pull to see the water was strong, that memory of those lazy days with Basia, Tata and Uncle needed to be preserved. I didn't want to see the river without them. Without Tata and Uncle, sitting with their fishing rods, grumbling to each other about the weather, the farm, the soil. Without Basia, who was nice to me on those days and would make me jump off the bank into the water where she stood, waiting for me, then would splash me with cool drops and laugh. That memory, that one memory of perhaps happiness, needed to stay perfect for me because there were so few of them; so few that I could recall anyway.

Perhaps there had been more days like this. I wracked my brain thinking of nicer things that Basia had said or done, Tata even. It was then, as I scanned through memories, I saw that they had not been as mean to me as I had always assumed they were. It was me in those memories that was difficult, yelling at Basia for nothing in particular, moaning to Tata as he whistled as he worked, telling him that the noise was annoying me, the day was too hot, and how much I hated his beloved potatoes.

Even our meals that started pleasantly enough, sitting around the table, Tata talking about the farm, Basia listening and occasionally suggesting that we perhaps get some more help, or maybe get the pigs back that we once had had – it was all normal, serene even. Then, it would be me who had not eaten her dinner, who would leave the table, dinner untouched, roam about the house, find a book I had read then throw it to the floor in frustration.

The more the memories came to me, the more that Isaac's advice resonated – he had asked me to look at things from their points of view and I very rarely had. It had been all about me, my anger, my frustration, and I had blamed them when they had got irritated with me.

That walk, past the fields, the farmhouses, slowly reaching the denser village itself that was peppered with a few houses, a bakery, butcher and grocer; my history, my memories, began to rewrite themselves. I had not been unloved. Treated badly. There were good days with my family, perhaps happy ones. It hadn't all been what I thought it had.

I passed the cemetery and thought to stop, to find my uncle's grave that was within the tooth-like tombstones that jutted above the snow-laden ground. As I turned to the railings, a woman, old, a red headscarf tied tightly under her chin, carrying not flowers but a small fir branch that was tied with yellow ribbons, stepped in front of me.

'Please,' I said, gesturing that she should go in front of me.

'Who are you?' Her eyes scrunched up, causing her face to break into a million creases.

'Please,' I said again, then turned away towards the bakery that was crammed between two small houses.

I looked over my shoulder and saw she was still standing at the entrance to the graveyard, watching me walk away.

I knew it! This village was too small. Gossip would fly from lip to lip within the hour, I was sure of it.

I needed to be quick. No more dwelling on the past, no more dawdling. *Quick, Ania.*

The bakery was open but looked closed from the street. The window dark, no bread display, no welcoming light coming from inside. The aroma still held though. As soon as I walked in, the smell of baking bread, yeast, rushed at me, making my stomach growl.

Behind the counter was a woman I had never seen before, or perhaps I had and had forgotten her. I was sure that the bakery had once been run by a man – Piotr?

'Not much left,' the woman said, scanning the empty shelves, her black hair streaked with white pulled sharply at the nape of her neck. 'Should have come early.' She held out her hand to me. When I didn't move, she said, 'Ration coupon!'

I felt about in my pocket for the few notes I had. I had no idea how much bread would cost or even if she would want the money. We had had ration coupons at the farm, but we had rarely used them. Father had bartered for food, said the rations that were allotted us wouldn't feed one person let alone three. Sometimes he even bartered the ration coupons themselves, and any money he did receive he hid in tins about the house and under his mattress.

'I need whatever you have,' I said and handed her one note. She looked at it, at me, at my hand that was grimy, thick black dirt underneath the fingernails.

'Jew?' she asked, not taking the money.

I shook my head.

She grabbed the money and handed me a large round loaf. 'Don't come back,' she said. 'I don't want you here. I don't want to know.'

She came out from behind the counter and followed me out of the shop.

Outside, I breathed a sigh of relief. I had managed to do it, given her twelve zlotys, which I knew was too much but I had no way to argue with her.

The grocer, a man who resembled a carrot, tall, thin, with a crop of orange hair, treated me a bit better.

'Jew?' he asked, just like the baker.

'No,' I said.

'You can tell me,' he said. 'They come here, sometimes. I help. Not many others do, you know. But I help.'

I did not engage him with a conversation that he was dearly yearning for; instead, I handed him a note and took a brown paper bag filled with vegetables, some of which I could see were already turning to rot.

'Here.' He handed me the money back. 'Keep it. Come back if you need anything more.'

I decided to stop whilst I was ahead. I had bread, vegetables; that would have to be enough.

I looked left, then right, and saw that the street was empty. Too empty. Not a horse and cart, no one going to work, going to church.

I turned back the way I had come, walked past the graveyard and did not see the woman in her red headscarf, of which I was glad.

The scent of the bread was too much, and as I continued on, I tore a piece away for myself, delighting that it was fresh and still a little warm.

There was a hum behind me, a hum that got louder and louder. A motorcycle. I did not look behind me; I carried on the road, then saw a few yards ahead an opening into a field. I would go in there, wait for it to pass.

I crossed the road and the hum had stopped. Only when I reached the field did I look back to the village, and there stood a police officer, dressed in his navy-blue long coat, pointing at me in the distance, the woman with the bun from the bakery standing next to him.

I knew that uniform. The *Granatowa policja* – Blue Police. Krzysztof had worn that same uniform. A uniform that marked him out as a traitor to his own people – a man who welcomed the German control, understood what they wanted from him, and was happy to do as they asked.

The bread was still in my mouth, tucked against my cheek turning into mush. The police officer began to near me. Four yards away. Three. I did not move. It was one thing that I knew not to do – Tata had told me that. 'If anyone, a soldier, a police officer, *anyone*, comes up to you, do not run. Running makes it look like you have something to hide. Promise me, Ania, if I am in the fields, if Basia is in the house and someone turns up – DO NOT RUN. Stand there. Answer questions and direct them to wherever I am.'

The problem I had now was that I did not have Tata to direct this officer to. I would have to stand my ground.

Two yards.

One.

'*Dzień dobry*. You new here?' he asked.

'Just passing through,' I said.

'Is that so.' Then he looked me up and down. I could see that he was trying to decide who I was. Girl? Boy? Jew? He stepped closer and I could smell something familiar – pig fat. I looked at the little hair that peeked out from under his cap. He gelled it just like Krzysztof had.

'I'm visiting my grandmother in Żabia Wola,' I said and took a step back.

'Quite a walk to come to this bakery.' He stepped forward again.

'We ran out of coupons and the village bakery would not take money. My grandmother is old. Blind. I said I would find somewhere to get some food.'

'*Kennkarten*,' he said and waited.

I held the bag in my left hand, placed my right into my pocket and felt around for the two notes I had left.

'I'm afraid I don't have my identification,' I said. 'It's at my grandmother's.'

'That's a shame,' he said and smiled. 'You know that's against the law?'

'Please,' I said, and scrunched my eyes up like I was crying. 'I'm just twelve years old. Please!' I started to sob.

'Twelve? I would have thought fourteen.' He stepped too close. Placed his hand on my shoulder. 'A shame. Twelve, are you sure? Not fourteen?'

'I'm twelve.' I tried to sound innocent, wheedling like I did when I had wanted something from Tata. 'It's just me and my grandmother. She'll be getting worried.'

He did not move his hand away. His breathing was warm, heavy on the top of my head. I did not want to look up at his face.

'So small, so slight,' he whispered, then he took his hand from my shoulder and touched the front of my coat, unbuttoning the top button. 'You are sure you are twelve?'

I swallowed. Hard. I knew what he wanted. But this wasn't what Wanda had said it was like with Aleksi – showing love. This was the same as what had happened to Wanda in the woods.

'Please.' I made my voice as childlike as I could. 'I want to go home. I want my grandmother.'

Whether it was the childish pleading that did it, I do not know. But he stepped back. 'Twelve. Shame,' he said. 'So what are we going to do with you?' He tilted his head to the side then whistled. 'You see, the thing is, what should be done is that I come with you to your grandmother's and take a look at your *Kennkarten* and that would be that. But I have to get back to headquarters in Dziesiąta. I only stopped because that woman waved me down. So lucky and unlucky all at the same time, eh?'

'Can I go home? I can go home and I will give you her address and you can come and see her?'

'Tell you what.' He looked in the bag, then pulled a face.

'What money have you got left? I'd take the food but it looks rotten to me.'

I pulled out one note and handed it to him.

'That all?' he asked.

I nodded.

'Fine.' He sighed. 'It will do. But I'll tell you something now.' He prodded a finger into my chest. 'I see you again, I hear about you again, then I won't be as friendly, all right?'

I nodded again.

He turned to leave, then suddenly whipped back, grabbed the bag out of my hands then walked away throwing the food into the bushes as he continued, looking back over his shoulder to make sure that I was watching him.

I watched him.

*Red apple.*

*Red door.*

*Red headscarf.*

*Tata. Basia and all the red.*

*Pig fat. Krzysztof.*

I let the rage build as I thought of each one. It started in my chest as usual, but this time I did not try to control it. Bit by bit it rose. Soon it was in my throat, then my mouth. I did not let it out. I let it continue upwards into my mind until it hummed like the electric light Isaac had had at his home.

As soon as the officer was back talking to the bun woman, I ran. I ran across the field, then turned left, down a track. I stopped only once to check my compass. I knew where he was going; I knew the roads and tracks he would take to get there.

I was only perhaps half a mile in front of him when I stopped where the main road jutted right down a narrower, bumpier road that would soon lead him onto the bigger roads that led to Lublin and Dziesiąta.

I found a fallen branch, sturdy, thick. It might work, it might not, but I had little choice. The humming in my head was too much. I had to do this.

I crouched low in a drainage ditch and waited.

Counting to 100, then 300, then 500. Perhaps I had been wrong; perhaps he would not come this way. Then, the thrum of a motorcycle. I looked over the ditch, seeing him in his blue uniform approaching me. Ten yards, nine, eight, seven, six, five, four, three – then I threw the heavy branch out into the middle of the road and watched as he tried to swerve to avoid it, but it was too late. The front wheel caught on the branch and would have normally only maybe made him wobble slightly, but he had pulled the handlebars too sharply as he saw the branch thrown onto the road, surprised at where it had come from.

The motorcycle skidded to the right, then ejected its rider and fell onto its side, his engine still ticking over.

'What the fuck?' He pushed himself up to stand and I knew I did not have much time.

I stood up. He looked at me, completely dumbfounded. 'What?' he asked.

I walked slowly towards him.

One step, *red apple*.

Next step, *red door*.

Next, *pig fat*.

Next, *Krzysztof. Basia. Tata*.

He did not move as I got closer; he seemed confused, or even perhaps intrigued by what was happening.

Then, the knife in my hand, a final thought: *szalony*. I plunged the knife upwards under his chin, through the muscles, the tendons.

The look of shock on his face was slightly amusing. He looked at my hand, at my face, and I could imagine what he was thinking: *How has this happened? How has this girl – this child done this?*

He dropped to his knees, his hands flailing about above him, trying to grab on to my clothes. He could not talk. Blood dripped from his mouth. But he would not die either.

I licked my lips, could feel sweat dripping down my back despite the cold.

Why was he not dead yet? There was blood, so much blood. Surely he should be dead by now?

He fell backwards. His hands had found the knife that stuck out from under his chin and I could see that he was trying to pull it free.

That's when I sat on top of him. I sat there and pushed the knife harder upwards. He let out a gurgled groan like an animal, but I did not stop. I kept pushing and pushing at that knife, imagining Tata's body on the floor, imagining that neat bullet hole in Basia's head.

But he would not die. The blood still came. His eyes were wide, but he kept right on breathing – granted shallower, almost gravelly, but he was still breathing.

I remembered Basia and the way she had taken too long killing the chickens – how Tata had said that it was cruel.

I withdrew the knife, watching it for a second as blood gushed out of the hole, into the grey slushed snow, splattering my coat, my face, my arms. The warmth of it made me feel oddly calm. Then, before he could move, before I could think too much, I plunged the knife deep into the side of his neck and dragged it across his throat as much as I could. Finally, he stopped moving. The gasping, gurgling, ended.

I waited a few minutes, sat there on top of him, listening to the sound of my own breathing that was coming fast through my open mouth.

I wiped my brow with the back of my hand, then stood, wiped the blade on my trousers and placed it into my pocket. I pulled at his arm but he was too heavy to move. I stepped back and looked at him. Then I sat on the ground and placed my feet against his body and began to push him nearer to the ditch. It took three or four efforts until he rolled away into the bracken.

Then, I looked at the motorcycle. This could prove useful.

I managed to turn off the engine, and with the last of my strength, I yanked it up from the ground, pushing it home. Not once did I look back. Not once did I think of what I had just done.

MEMORANDUM
Date: 13 December 1942

For the attention of Granatowa policja, Lublin,

Policing surrounding countryside areas of the General Gouvernement, Lublin district, must increase after the murder of a Polnische Polizei in the General Gouvernement last week.

Partisans are suspected of carrying out this attack utilising a child, who was seen in the vicinity prior to the murder.

The child is described as 14 to 15 years old, short black hair, wearing a yellow hat. It is not known whether the child is male or female.

Officers are advised to remain vigilant at all times and report any incidents of partisan activity in their districts.

## 18

*Autumn, 1969*
*Parczew Forest, Lublin Voivodeship, Poland*
*Benjamin*

'I can't remember,' Benjamin said. 'The blood that was on you that day. You killed someone, I think.'

'Did I?' Her voice was singsong, innocent.

'I think so.'

'I didn't tell you, did I, and you never asked. You said you couldn't bear knowing. Was it better that way, Benjamin, you not knowing?'

'I think so,' he said, but suddenly he wasn't so sure. 'Maybe. You must have told me something. How else would I have known how you did it – with that knife?'

'Perhaps Wanda told you. Or Gosia?' she suggested.

Benjamin didn't answer her straight away. He thought back over the years. Combing through each memory, trying to picture it, feel it.

She had come back, he remembered that. Blood on her arms. She had smiled; she was happy.

'Do you regret it?' he asked the grave.

'Not really. It had to happen, Benj, there was no other option. It had to happen. He could have found us. Could have come back. But even if he wasn't going to, even if I would never see him again, it just had to happen, Benj.'

'I wish things had been different for us, Ania. Sometimes I pretend that the war never happened and I imagine what my life would have been like. In this imagined past, I don't have a face like this and I am smart and people want to listen to me when I talk. I don't cry so much; I don't get scared of anything.'

'But, if this had happened, we would never have met, would we, Benj?' she said.

'I dream that we still did meet, but in a different way. That we met one day, just walking down the road. It is summer and it's warm and the birds are singing and on either side of us, the fields are full of corn and it's all golden and it whispers in the breeze – you know, each of the stalks talking to each other. And you stop and you ask me my name and I tell you it's Benjamin, and you say, "I'll call you Benj." And we become friends and because I am smart, I read a lot like you. And people come and listen to us and ask us advice because we are both so clever. And they invite us to these banquets, you know. All this food, and we dress up in nice clothes and no one cares that I'm a Jew and everyone thinks you're beautiful and smart and it's all perfect. And then one day, you marry Aleksi, and maybe I marry Wanda, and Gosia – she's there too, but she's not so mad any more and she doesn't want to kill her husband any more. In fact, she finds a new husband and she's very happy.'

'I like that, Benj,' she said. 'I like that. I had a vision for myself too. Do you remember how I told you about it – how I imagined what our future would be like one day? How we couldn't change the past but maybe we could have a different future – write it for ourselves?'

He nodded and closed his eyes and her voice, strong, almost joyous, took him back into the past where they were sat side by side, outside in the spring. He didn't know when exactly this conversation had happened or why it had, but he could hear it again – hear it as if he were there.

'I have a vision of myself. I can see it clearly – I sit on the steps of the farmhouse. It is a summer's dawn. The sun rises and begins to burn away the mist that is hanging above the fields beyond. I know, even though I cannot see them, who is there – out there, in the fields.

'I imagine them from my place on the steps. Aleksi talks to you, Benj. You pick potatoes, each of you happy with your work, your crop. Gosia helps, or at least tries to. She is not so quick any more, but she wants to help. Gone is that yellow stained dress of hers. Now she wears trousers and an old blue shirt that is tucked in. She has gotten fake teeth and she likes these teeth that can tear into meat, into anything, and she can smile and be happy about it.

'Inside the house, Wanda cooks. She is a good cook. She likes to sing as she chops onions, carrots and wild garlic, adding them to the pan, delighting when they hiss and sizzle in front of her.

'I sit and watch because I can. Because this is mine – you are all mine. Soon, though, I will have to work too. I will have to add some value to this life that we have all created together. Soon, I will retreat indoors and there I will sit at a desk, like Isaac's desk, and I will write, I will read. The letters and sentences I make on the page will be full of wonder and beauty. They will help others, of that I am sure.

'But for now, in this vision, I sit and watch the sun burn at the ground, at the mist, and imagine those that I cannot see but I know you are all there, somewhere in that mist of a summer dawn, just waiting – waiting for me.'

Benjamin must have told himself that story many times over the years. He had imagined it too, standing in the field, knowing that Ania sat on the steps, waiting for him.

'I like your story better,' he told the cold earth. 'I wish it had happened that way.'

'So do I, Benj. So do I.'

He wiped a tear from his eye. He hadn't even realised that he had started to cry.

'Ania,' he said, 'we have to keep going though. We have to finish like we always do. What do you think happened next?'

'What do you remember, Benj?' she asked.

He thought for a moment and a memory resurfaced. A memory that he really did not want to recollect.

'The bar,' he said. 'When you went to the bar. You came back, and your dress was torn.'

'It was, Benj. But I was all right.'

'You weren't, Ania. You weren't all right. And then you went to the camp, after the bar, and then things changed – it all got bad, Ania.'

'I know, Benj. We made some mistakes.'

'I don't like this part,' Benj said. 'I don't want to remember it.'

'We have to, Benj.' She sighed. 'We have to remember. That's all we have left.'

## 19

### MAJDANEK AND DANIIL

*23 December 1943*
*Czerniejów, Lublin Voivodeship, Poland*
*Ania*

Aleksi returned just before Christmas with two guns that were too large, too big, a bag full of clothes – women's, men's, children's too. He said he would be gone a few days, but had taken around two weeks.

'Is long way to walk in snow,' he said, letting Wanda rub at his feet. 'Is long way – fifty miles to forest, maybe more, then to Lublin, then back to them again and then here. Takes time.'

'This won't fit Wanda.' Gosia pulled a small coat from the bag, blue with brown buttons, then held it in front of me. 'Might fit her though. You should have taken the motorcycle, Aleksi. Much quicker than walking. This might fit me though.' Gosia held a light blue jumper in her hands that was far too small. 'I can fit myself into it, I'm sure.'

'A motorcycle?' Aleksi asked.

'This won't fit either.' Wanda was rummaging around the

clothes, picking things out she thought might fit her. Even Benj was animated having been quiet, withdrawn, since seeing me covered in blood a few days before, pushing the motorcycle up to the house. He delved into the bag and found a knitted black jumper and held it against his torso.

'A motorcycle?' Aleksi repeated.

'Don't look at me,' Wanda said. She kissed him on his cheek then went back to looking in the bag too.

'You?'

I nodded.

He shrugged. 'Good job.'

'Ask her how she did it,' Wanda said.

He waved his hand in dismissal. 'Be easier to get to the camp,' he said. 'We should go tomorrow, start watching. Take only maybe less an hour to get there. We go see.'

'It's Christmas Eve tomorrow,' Wanda said.

'So? We go. I have binoculars too. We go, two of us we go, me and Ania. Go, see, come back. We go early, Ania. Very early. Maybe leave two in morning. We must to go to East side. Commander says East side, 4 a.m., change guards at four and taking time. Gives inmates time to come to fence. One inmate, Russian, like me, very clever, very wise. He will come, take food, gun, anything we can give.'

'We have some vegetables,' Wanda said. 'Quite a lot, and some bread. We got flour.'

After I had come home with only a motorcycle, and after explaining myself to a wide-eyed Wanda and Gosia, who chuckled throughout as if I were telling her a joke, Gosia disappeared for a whole day and came back with supplies. We did not ask her how she had done it. All she said was that a nice man who was taking milk in a cart took her some-where, to a village, and then she decided to look about. 'I am good at looking, and found some things. It's easy,' she finished.

'Sounds good,' I agreed and placed my feet on a chair, crossing my legs.

Aleksi gave me a strange look, then drew out from his pocket three cigarettes. He raised his eyebrows in question at me. I took one.

I had never smoked before, not even when Basia had stolen one of Tata's and handed it to me. But since the policeman incident, I felt calmer, older. I would smoke, I decided. This new Ania would smoke.

I got questioning looks from the other three as Aleksi lit it for me and I dragged on it. Immediately, I coughed.

'You don't smoke, Ania,' Benj said.

'Leave her be. She's been a busy girl.' Gosia placed her hands on the floor and pushed herself up to stand. She came to me and kissed the top of my head. 'A busy girl. So proud. I'll get supper for us all.'

Benj shook his head. Wanda had gone back to looking at the clothes, drawing out a blue dress with a white belt.

'That would look lovely on you,' I told her.

'And this for you?' She drew out a red dress with tiny black buttons from the collar to the waist.

Red again.

'I don't think so,' I said, then looked at Tata's jumper that Gosia had scrubbed for me, getting rid of all the blood. But there was still a curious odour about it.

'Come on.' Wanda came to me. 'I was going to go to some bars soon, once Gosia and I have finished with the hemlock.'

'I need more!' Gosia called from where she stirred what was most likely a soup on the stove.

'I'm not going,' I said.

'Why not? We'll sort your hair, get some make-up – Gosia?' Wanda said.

'I'll get you some make-up,' Gosia said, as if it were as simple as walking down to the shop.

'Then you'll look the way you feel. You don't feel like a child any more, right? You feel different. It changed you, didn't it?' Wanda said.

I tried to take a smaller drag on the cigarette and did not cough as much this time. 'Maybe,' I said. 'Maybe I'll try it on.'

We ate early and retired by eight. I needed to sleep if I were going to be awake at two in the morning, but Benj would not stop fidgeting.

'Benj,' I whispered. 'You just kicked me again.'

'Sorry,' he mumbled.

I turned over and tried to get comfortable again.

'Ania?'

'Yes, Benj.' I sighed.

'You're different.'

'How am I different, Benj?' I could feel sleep starting to tug at my brain.

'I don't know. But I think to when we met and how you talked and how you were. And then Gosia said all those things to you about revenge and hurting people. And now, you did it, I think you did. All that blood on your clothes. But when you came back here, Ania, you were smiling, did you know that? You were smiling and happy. I had never seen you happy like that, but it made me nervous, because I don't think it was a good kind of happy. And now you talk differently. You talk less but when you talk it feels different. I don't know, Ania.'

'Everyone changes, Benj,' I mumbled. 'Gosia, she's like a mother now – at least I think so. Kissing the tops of our heads, cooking. She said she was proud of me tonight. You heard that,

Benj?' I yawned. 'It's nice, isn't it? Gosia a mother, me a daughter.' My voice was beginning to fade away. 'You my brother, Aleksi and Wanda...'

I could not finish the sentence. I was falling hard into that abyss of nothingness. But I thought I heard Benj again, but I could have imagined it. 'You scare me now, Ania. I'm scared.'

\* \* \*

Aleksi drove like a mad man. I sat behind him on the motorcycle, the freezing night air stinging my cheeks, my hands gripping his chest. I wanted to tell him to slow down, but my words became lost on the wind.

He kept to dirt tracks, skirting around villages, towns, anywhere he thought that we would be spotted. It took more than an hour to reach Majdanek with all this zigzagging about and by the time we stopped, my legs and arms were stiff with the cold.

'You could have killed us,' I said as soon as I managed to dismount.

'Hush!' He placed his finger on his lips then wheeled the motorcycle between the trees, standing it against a trunk.

'Come,' he said.

I followed him through the trees, keeping as close to him as possible. Then the trees stopped and beyond us was a field, then beyond that, razor-tipped wire that glinted as search lights passed over them, left to right.

'We come here to East because before' – he pointed to another part of the camp – 'that is where we escape and they watch more there now. This part, this part you see that building?' He handed me a pair of binoculars. 'You see?' he asked.

Through the lenses I could see the darkness of a building, a chimney jutting up to the sky.

'I build this. Me. Just before we decide to escape.'

'What is it?' I asked.

Aleksi looked at his watch. 'We still wait a little more,' he said, then sat down, resting his back against a trunk. 'Sit, sit,' he commanded.

'Is for the burning of bodies,' he said. 'You know, prisoners dead. Poison.'

'Poison?'

'Gas. They take them into a room, make the gas, then all dead. Before the chimney, we take to a pit and bury and then they make us build this thing and take bodies there instead.'

I knew about camps – who couldn't know? I had heard how people were forced to work, were starved and beaten. But I hadn't heard of what Aleksi was talking about.

'That's why I like your idea. You know, the the...' He thought for a moment for the right word.

'The hemlock,' I said for him.

'Yes. Good idea, I think. Very good. Make them poison instead and make them *szalony* like you say. I like this idea. Very good.'

'How long were you here?'

'Not long, you know. Before me, so many prisoners from army, but I come maybe March this year, and most of others already gone. First they build it, you know. No food, sleep outside then die. So we come, me and maybe a hundred more, and then we say on day one, Ania, day one, when we see all bodies and they talk of gas and burning, we say, we must to leave. So we do. We wait, we build and then July – yes, July, we leave.'

I wanted to ask Aleksi more. I wanted to know more, but he grabbed my arm. 'See. Look.'

The search light was no longer scanning the ground. 'The man we come to see, he come to the crematorium. His job to get fires ready. My commander, he says he is good man. Russian man. Name is Daniil. Good man. Come, we go now. Be quick. He say when light stop, guard comes to the ground, leaves. Daniil to start work. Maybe ten minutes, maybe less. Come, be quick.'

Aleksi was quick. Half bent, he raced across the field, holding the sack with bread, potatoes and a knife inside. I followed him as quickly as I could, the slushed snow from the recent rain splashing up onto my trousers.

We reached the fence and were completely out in the open.

'He here,' Aleksi said.

A lumpy figure was coming closer to us. It ran through the pool of light, showing a man in blue and white striped jacket and trousers. When he reached the fence, he placed his fingers in the holes.

'Friend?' Daniil asked.

'Friend,' Aleksi replied in Russian. He then spoke quickly, so quickly that I could not follow in its entirety.

'You've brought something?' Daniil asked after Aleksi had finished saying something about a commander, partisans and forests.

Aleksi emptied the sack and began to throw the food and knife over the fence, sending Daniil scuttling off in the darkness to find them. When Daniil returned, his jacket was bulging from where he had stashed everything.

'Thank you, my friend,' Daniil said, then, not being able to help himself, he placed his hand under his jacket and brought out a hunk of bread and gnawed at it.

'We need your help too,' Aleksi said.

Daniil nodded, his mouth full, and crouched down.

'How often are the deliveries? Still every morning?'

Another nod from Daniil. Then he swallowed. 'Morning for delivery of food, things, you know. All sorts. Afternoons and evenings at the moment for people. Trucks mostly. Some are marched in from a train.'

'Times?' Aleksi asked, then scanned left, right, behind us.

'Varies. But they say they are coming from the ghettos. So coming from the city.'

Daniil shoved more bread into his mouth then looked at me. 'And this?'

'Ania,' I answered him. 'A friend too.'

Aleksi opened his mouth then closed it.

'Polish?' Daniil asked.

'Yes. I speak enough Russian though.'

'You do?' Aleksi asked.

'I do,' I said.

'But why...' Then he shook his head and turned back to Daniil. 'They're coming from Lublin?' Aleksi asked.

'Yes. At least for now. Why? You going to stop them coming here?'

'Maybe,' Aleksi said.

'Watch the roads from Lublin. One came the other day, around six. It was dark. Means they left the city maybe twenty or thirty minutes before. It's not far.'

Suddenly, Daniil stood. 'Go. Now!'

He disappeared into the camp, leaving us just a fleeting glimpse of his back as he ran back through the pool of light.

'Ania, come!' Aleksi ran and I followed.

When we reached the safety of the trees, we stopped for a

moment to catch our breaths then saw the searchlight begin its sweep once more.

Aleksi laughed. 'We did it,' he said, still speaking in Russian to me.

'We did!'

'You feel it? That feeling? Exhilaration?' he asked.

'I feel it,' I said and turned to him. His eyes, which I had once thought too close together, were perfectly spaced now. They were bright even in the dark. 'I feel it,' I said again.

His smile wavered, then dropped. 'Come. We need to get back.'

He walked back through the trees, not waiting for me, so I had to half run to keep up with him. When we reached the motorcycle I began to tell him about the languages I knew, and how we could speak in Russian from now on if he preferred it.

He did not answer; he started up the motorcycle and I climbed on. 'Aleksi,' I said, before he sped off again. 'I enjoyed that.'

'That's good,' he said, in Polish now.

'You can speak Russian to me. It can be something between us,' I suggested. 'It's good for me to practise and must be nicer for you?'

'Polish is fine,' Aleksi said. He revved the engine, driving so fast once more that I could not talk to him in any language.

MEMORANDUM
Date: 26 December 1942

Urgent notice
Partisan movements

Attention all guards,

After the escape of Russian prisoners, security has been tightened. However, partisan operations in the Lublin, Majdan ghetto continue, and throughout Lublin itself.

Severe punishment must be served to any inmate who has any contraband on his person. Names of partisans who are still infiltrating the camp must be elicited from prisoners.

One child was seen wearing a yellow hat running from the camp's fences near to the chimneys at Konzentrationslager Lublin. Guards must remain vigilant at all times – the partisans will utilise children for their war against us and we must not hesitate in our reaction to this.

By order of the Commandant,
SS-Sturmbannführer Florstedt

Konzentrationslager Lublin

# 20

## WHAT IS LOVE?

*1 January 1943*
*Czerniejów, Lublin Voivodeship, Poland*
*Ania*

The first day of the new year brought a change in the weather.
The snow had finally stopped, letting a snippet of clean blue
streak across the sky. Benj stuck fast to Wanda as she tried to
explain to him how to make soup out of the meagre vegetables
and rabbit that we had. Gosia sat close by, telling Wanda that
soup should have chicken and not rabbit, and once, she made
rabbit soup for her husband and she was sure that was the
moment he had decided to leave her.

I stood in the doorway for a few minutes, not wanting to
interrupt the scene in front of me. Despite the cold, the
ramshackle house, the fire that barely burned in the grate,
these three, all huddled round, talking over each other, smiling
at each other, made me realise how much I not only missed
Tata and Basia, but I missed what we could have been. Why
hadn't Basia and I talked more? Why had I annoyed her so

much? I didn't seem to bother Wanda, Gosia or Benj. Aleksi had dropped his gruffness at first, but then after our first look at the camp, and me speaking Russian to him, he had resorted back to his sternness. I had no idea why. It had been a success – we had met Daniil, and his information had proved right, allowing us to go back four more times to watch the trucks arrive from a distance. In all those times we had been alone together, he had barely spoken to me, so soon I had given up trying.

Suddenly a memory assaulted me and I had to turn away from looking at the others and look outside instead, not wanting the image in my mind to ruin the serene scene of this strange family I had created.

I shook my head, hoping to shake the memory loose, make it fall to the ground and scuttle away into the undergrowth. But it would not and I could clearly see one of the evenings that Aleksi and I had shared at one of our visits to the camp.

The sky that night had been a purple bruise, as if the heavens themselves were in pain. I knew the clouds were full of snow and that a new flurry would soon be upon us. In the distance, the chimney from the camp spewed out grey smoke, as if someone were inside simply warming themselves against the cold. Most chimneys would evoke that in an onlooker, make them desperate to get inside and sit by the fire too. But this chimney was wrong here. What was burning inside was not wood, and it sent an acrid smell out into the cold air where it hung for too long.

Dogs barked now and then; lights too bright filled the grounds as if it were daylight and picked out the razor-topped fences.

Daniil we had not seen again, yet we still went back, or at least tried to, to see if he would come.

'Something is wrong,' Aleksi said. 'Something has gone wrong.'

We did not stay in the same lookout spot for too long – always moving, always.

As we sat there on that purple-skied evening, Aleksi pointed in the direction of the city. 'That's the ghetto,' he said. 'Lublin ghetto.'

'You've been there?' I asked.

'I've seen it. All people crammed in. Guards, noise.'

As I looked in the direction of the ghetto, in the corner of my eye I saw that there was movement inside the camp. Slowly, ever so slowly, hunched figures emerged from the shadows into a perfect circle of light created by one of the spotlights that now sat still. I looked through the binoculars, seeing a face I thought I knew – Daniil? No. Not Daniil, but a man with the same hanged look. The same dark eyes. Next to him, a young man stood, perhaps no more than my age. His head was bowed, then suddenly he looked up – looked straight at me; or at least that's what it felt like. I could see that his eyes were moist, his face. His bottom lip trembled.

More men lined up to result in ten altogether. All next to each other, waiting and blinking in that white light.

A guard, a gun in one hand, a dog straining at a leash in the other, stood in the centre of the light circle. Then two more guards appeared.

'Don't look.' Aleksi tried to grab the binoculars away from me, but I would not let him have them.

I kept watching the boy's face. He was crying now, mouth open, eyes scrunched.

Then, a pop, pop of gunfire rang out.

'Ania!' Aleksi tried again.

Bodies fell left and right to the side of the boy. He stood, crying. Then his eyes seemed to find mine again and in that moment, his mouth opened widely in surprise, then he fell to the ground.

'Ania.' Aleksi managed to relieve me of the binoculars.

We sat and waited and watched again. All the bodies slumped on the ground were left for an hour, then more prisoners came and hauled them into a cart. Throwing them in like Tata had done with the sacks of potatoes.

'Ovens,' Aleksi said. 'They're going to the ovens now.'

\* \* \*

Singing interrupted the memory, drawing me back to the house of shadows. That boy's face I knew I would never forget – that open mouth – the look of shock. I could not help but try to imagine how he would have felt standing there in the cold, knowing what was about to happen. Would I have been scared? Would I have cried?

'Ania.'

Aleksi called to me but I could not see him.

'Ania,' he said again.

It came from the direction of the wood pile where I soon found him sat, his back against the logs.

'Why you standing in the cold?' he said in his broken Polish.

I spoke back to him in his mother tongue. 'Why are *you* out here? Was that you singing?'

He shrugged. 'Where else should I be?' Finally, his voice, no longer broken, but in his own language.

'May I?' I asked, indicating the ground.

'Free country.' Then he laughed. 'Stupid joke,' he added.

I sat by his side and saw that he had been whittling a piece of wood, shavings scattered in the snow, a wonky piece of wood in one hand, a knife in the other.

'What is it?' I asked.

'Supposed to be a whistle.' He sighed. 'I used to be good at making things, but then...' He wiggled the red stumps at me.

'What happened?' I asked. 'Was it in the camp?'

'No. Just the war,' he said. 'Normal stuff. Fighting, guns. I was lucky.'

'I don't think I would feel lucky,' I said.

'I didn't at first,' he admitted, then looked at me and held my gaze a bit too long, then sighed. 'I should apologise to you, I think.'

'For ignoring me,' I suggested.

'Yes. That.'

'Why did you?'

He shrugged again. 'I just get grumpy sometimes. Wanda knows.'

'Is it because of the camp – what happened there – what you saw?'

'That and other things.'

I was beginning to get frustrated with his reticence. Why couldn't he just speak like anyone else? Then suddenly I saw the irony in it – that's what Basia had sometimes said to me.

'I'll leave you then.' I made to push myself up from the ground. I wasn't going to sit in the cold, on the snow, whilst he sat there in silence.

'Ania,' he said, his blue eyes locked onto mine. He smiled, a small smile, like a child did when they first met you – wanting to please you, yet scared of you being a stranger.

'Yes?'

'Sit. I'll tell you about my hand if you want. You keep asking

– I know you've asked Wanda before – better it all comes from me.'

I sat once more and drew my legs up to my chest and hugged them to me.

'The thing is,' he began, 'I never wanted to fight again, not after everything, but then you came along, with Benjamin and Gosia, and things changed. I think I've been a bit angry about it, but at the same time excited too. That first night at the camp, it all came back – the risk taking, the rush – but then I realised what I was getting myself into again. I think I blamed you and that wasn't right and I am sorry.' He looked at me, waited. 'And then that other night.' He shook his head as I had done, not wanting to remember.

'Forgiven,' I said.

'Good. Thank you. But you see, I get like this. I don't mean to. Wanda, she told me, or she tried to tell me, about how you described to her what was going on in your mind, how you deal with things, and you know, we are not that different, I think. I went to war, not because I wanted to, but because I had no choice – like so many others. I left home, left my mother and my younger brother, and came here and lost friends, my fingers.' He wiggled the stubs again. 'I saw so much death and it became almost normal. You go numb from it, numb so that you can get through the next day and then the next. But then I was captured and brought to the camp and saw a different kind of death.' He exhaled heavily. 'It's a kind of death that is inhumane. Not death on the battlefield where each person has a weapon and a fighting chance. This was different – extermination by working you hard, starving you, beating you, and then the gassing...'

He looked off into the bushes and I let the silence sit for a minute.

'The bodies were in pits. We had to build the ovens, get them ready to be burned,' he whispered, still looking far away into the bracken as if he were looking straight through it and all the way to Majdanek. 'I knew it was going to happen to me – to us – there were fewer than a hundred of us. They'd gotten rid of us, thousands of us, and they were soon bringing Jews, Romanians, Poles – anyone, for any reason. I saw them coming through those gates, I saw the fear in their eyes, but none of us told them what to expect – I don't think we could even put it into words ourselves.'

'But you got free. You're free now.' I placed my hand on his arm.

'Free. Ha,' he said. 'Not really. I am as free as a rat is when he gets out of the trap. He's not really free, is he, because now his whole life is hiding from that trap. He knows it is there, he knows that it could get him again.'

'But we're safe here,' I told him. I hadn't moved my hand from his arm.

'Are we?' Again, that long look, followed by a shake of the head, and back staring off into the distance.

'I thought I was going to be safe with the partisans. I found them, we all did. All ready to fight again. Then the next morning, they handed me a gun, and I just...'

'Just what?'

'I just couldn't do it. It was like all those months fighting, then the camp – I don't know. I just couldn't. I couldn't talk, couldn't sleep. It was like I was a ghost; no, like a shadow of myself, like a part of me was still there, in those cold, muddy fields, bullets constantly firing, plane engines whirring, constantly whirring above me. Then a part of me in the camp, in that crematorium.'

He hung his head and mumbled into his chest, 'I had to

leave. Get out. Be on my own. This house, when I found it I thought it was perfect, all cloaked in shadows.'

'That's what my uncle called it,' I said. '*Dom cieni*, a house of shadows.'

'Wise man,' he said.

'So what changed? What made you want to help – to fight again?'

He lifted his head. 'I don't know. No, I do know. You, I think.' He glanced at me, smiled then turned away again. 'You – this small little thing – so bold, not scared of anything. Then when the others spoke about you, that morning when you were still asleep, and Wanda asked me if she thought we should do something too, I don't know, I just thought maybe yes. And then you brought out that hemlock, and it was so strange, so brilliant in its way, that I felt something shift – or at least felt like myself again.'

'Ania!' Wanda shouted for me. 'Aleksi, you out here too? Food is ready.'

'Well,' he said, standing and offering me a hand to take. 'Best get inside?'

There was a moment, perhaps two seconds, nothing more than that, but it felt much longer, where he had my hand in his, his eyes on my face, and suddenly I felt something shift in me too. A warmth, then a sickness in my stomach that was not altogether unpleasant.

'Inside,' I said.

He gave a strange laugh and let go of my hand. I followed him inside, wondering what that was all about.

That night, I thought of Aleksi, which infuriated me as I had other things, more important things, to think about – like how between Gosia and Wanda they had managed to find enough hemlock, boil it down and stew it. They added more, just in case, they said, the poison was not strong enough. Then carefully they had poured it into two metal flasks – one that had belonged to Aleksi, the other found in my uncle's bedside table.

Wanda and I were to go to a bar on the outskirts of Lublin in a few evenings' time. She did not want to go alone, she had said, and had reasoned with me that this was all my plan and I should want to see it through. I did, but I was still aware of how I looked and was not sure that a change of clothes and some make-up would make that much of a difference.

So. There was that to think about and how to get the poison into a drink. Who to choose. How long to stay. So much to think about and yet that moment, those two seconds with Aleksi, continued to plague me.

It was irritating. Making my legs kick under the blankets, more than once disturbing Benj and Gosia. I flipped on one side, then the other, then lay flat on my back. Nothing worked.

I wanted to scream with this frustration. Why was I thinking about him? Why?

Then, it was as if I could hear Basia's voice – distant, whispering. 'Love.'

I turned on my side, trying to ignore it, but the word repeated again and again in my mind. *Love.*

This word dragged me back into a memory of when I was twelve years old, of when Basia, for once, had confided in me. One day, after church, Basia told me that you could not control who you fell in love with.

During the service, a boy called Piotr, a boy who was really a man at nineteen years old, had sat in the pew in front of my fourteen-year-old sister. He stood over six feet tall, his arms like knotted wood from days working in the fields, his blond hair almost white when the sun had bleached it in the summer months.

He had gone to our church for some time, and Basia had never said a thing about him. But this day, something about him had caught her eye and as we left church, her face was flushed and she could not stop smiling. On our walk home, she stopped twice to pick at the spring wildflowers, humming a tune under her breath, and gave me one of her posies.

I did not know at the time that it was Piotr who had made her happy – I just took the flowers and placed them in a vase in my bedroom when we returned home. The following Sunday, Basia was the first ready for church – scrubbed and dressed in one of Mother's old cornflower blue dresses, her hair brushed so that it shone – and she stood at the front door chivvying father to put on his boots quickly. He grunted his response, unsure of this change in Basia, and kept a close eye on her as we sat in the uncomfortable wooden pews and listened to the priest talk of hell and heaven, of sin and of good.

It was after this sermon that she stopped in the graveyard and made a beeline for Piotr. I don't know what she said to him, nor what he to her, but when she returned to Tata and me, her face had fallen and her eyes were full of tears that were ready to fall.

When we returned home, this time she ran to her bedroom, slammed the door and wept loudly.

'Go see what it's all about,' Tata told me.

'She won't want me to. You go,' I said.

Tata screwed up his face. 'It's not for me to go.' He stood behind me and gave me a little push towards her bedroom. 'You go, Ania. It's better that you go.'

I didn't think that it was better for me to go, but I shrugged at my father, who shifted awkwardly from foot to foot. 'Go on,' he chivvied. 'You go. Go on!'

I opened the door to find her face down on her bed. She

twisted her head to the side to look at me, displaying a red, mottled face. She sniffed loudly. 'What do you want?' she asked in a muffled voice.

'Tata told me to come,' I said. I closed the door and sat gently on her bed. 'Are you sick? Shall I get Tata to fetch a doctor?'

'I am sick but a doctor cannot help me!' she wailed dramatically, then stuffed her face back into her pillow and resumed her crying.

I reached out and patted her back – a gesture she gave to me when I was sick – and waited for her to stop.

'He's – he's courting that pig girl!' she finally yelled into her pillow. Her speech was muffled so I was sure that I had heard incorrectly.

'Pig girl?'

She flipped over and stared at the ceiling, now and then sniffling, but the crying at least had stopped for now. 'You know. Iza? The girl at the pig farm. She looks like a pig too. Why doesn't he want to see me? I'm much prettier than her, aren't I, Ania?'

'Yes, yes, you are,' I said, because I knew I should.

'So why doesn't he want me?' She raised her arms up as if imploring God to give her the answer from above.

'Why do you want *him*?' I asked.

'Oh, Ania, you can't help who you love! You just love them. And I love him. I do. I love him and I can't go on without him!'

The crying started again after this revelation. This time, she curled up into a ball and rocked and wailed and told me of her love for this Piotr, who she had only just noticed.

I couldn't understand Basia's feelings. I couldn't understand how love could make you so crazy and nor could I comprehend her statement that you could not choose who you loved; surely she was mistaken?

I thought about it a while and decided that Basia was wrong. You could choose anything – the clothes you wore each day, the food you ate; sometimes you could even choose your thoughts or at least calm them, control them in some way. There was nothing that you could not choose.

But something *was* happening to me. Aleksi made my stomach sick, my face warmer. I realised how over the weeks I had watched his every movement, how he would squint his eyes when he thought, how he would chew on his fingernails, how when he was tired, he would rub at his eyes with a balled-up fist like a small child.

Each and every movement had been interesting to me – why else had I kept looking at him, waiting for him to move? I didn't feel that way about anyone else. So, I had to ask myself – was this love and was Basia right? I hadn't chosen to love him; I hadn't even seen it coming. It was just here, this thing, this overwhelming feeling that made my already scrambled mind completely unfocused.

Was this love?

# 21

## THE BAR

4 January 1943
*Lublin, Poland*
*Ania*

The bar was packed. Aleksi had found it, scouted it and said that
many a guard from Majdanek drank there.

'How do you know?' I had asked.

'Trust me. There are many faces I will never forget.'

'Which one shall we choose?'

'Any. All,' he'd said.

Wanda had driven us on the motorcycle, a journey that was
more frightening than driving with Aleksi. She constantly
turned too quickly, wobbled the bike, then would laugh as we
nearly tumbled off it.

We left it three streets away from the tavern and walked our
way there in the outfits that Wanda had worked on with Gosia –
her in blue, me in red, my hair now cut neatly into a bob,
washed with freezing water and soap, make-up that Gosia had
stolen on my face, stockings too and shoes with a small heel.

Before we had left, Aleksi had looked at us both, declared that we looked beautiful, kissed Wanda on the cheek, then patted my shoulder a little too hard.

I had looked at my reflection in the grimy window at home before leaving, seeing someone I did not recognise, but quite liked. The face, although blurry, that looked back at me was not one of a child, but of a woman who was pretty, almost beautiful. Her body fit into the dress perfectly, skimming her calves, the heels making her that little bit taller. Even her breasts looked bigger. I had always thought mine small in comparison to Basia's, which had strained at shirts and dresses, almost begging to be set free. But this dress did something to them, made them look rounder, almost ripe somehow.

I had lost a bit of my swagger, however, as soon as we reached a piano bar on the outskirts of Lublin. It was busy – too busy. As soon as we walked in, the air was cloying – cigarette smoke hung in grey swirls from the ceiling, glasses clinked, people laughed. A man at the piano in the corner, a small man wearing glasses, battered away at the keys, sweat on his forehead and his top lip.

Chairs scraped back; voices talked over each other. It suddenly reminded me of the time that Tata had taken me to the fair in the city; how it was all overwhelming – the smells, the sounds.

'Come, Ania.' Wanda tugged at my arm, threading me through the tables until she found two seats at the bar and placed our handbags (once more stolen by Gosia off some unsuspecting woman who had left her front door unlocked) on the bar then hopped up onto the green cushioned seat with ease.

I was not so elegant at getting onto the stool and was sure

that people were looking at me, wondering who had brought a child into a place like this.

'You're doing fine,' Wanda whispered, leaning close to my ear. 'Just smile. Look like this is something you do all the time.'

Before the barman could come and take our drink order, a German in a field grey uniform, black lapels with two oak leaves on each of the collars sat next to us.

'Bogdan!' the man said in German, waving down the barman but at the same time did not take his eyes off us. 'These ladies are waiting.'

Bogdan rushed forward, all big smiles, showing nicotine-stained teeth, a white cloth in his hands.

'Yes, ladies?' he enquired.

'Don't ask them, Bogdan. Ask me. It's me that wants to get them a drink!' The German laughed, then said to us, 'Vodka? Polish, yes? Do you understand me?'

I felt Wanda elbow me. 'I do,' I said. 'I speak German, but my friend here only speaks a little.'

He eyed us both and for a moment I thought I had made some mistake and he would draw out his gun. As he looked at us, I could see that his features were not that interesting. Brown hair, dull brown eyes, thin lips – nothing remarkable. Nothing even what you would call handsome.

'I like that you can speak German.' He then grinned at me. His teeth were too big, too square for his mouth. 'Bogdan. Vodka it is!'

Within seconds, the glasses were on the bar, the clear alcohol poured into each glass. 'And one for me, of course,' the German told him.

Another glass appeared, this one filled to the brim.

'I'm Karl,' he said and offered me his hand. 'And you two beauties are?'

'Ania,' I said, immediately wanting to rip out my own tongue. Wanda and I had agreed to give fake names. Too late now. 'This is Celina.'

It was as though Karl had not really taken a proper look at Wanda when her face was in profile. But now, she turned to face him and all he could say was, '*Außergewöhnlich!*' Extraordinary.

I told Wanda in Polish what he had said. She smiled at him, tilted her head to the side and demurely offered him her hand to take.

He took her fingertips in hers, kissed them and held her hand for too long, making him laugh and apologise at the same time.

'Over there, I have a table. A table with my friend Christoph. Won't you join us?'

'Of course,' I said. He did not help me from my stool, but went straight to Wanda, guiding her through the throng as if she were a precious vase.

'Christoph. I have found us some friends. That is Ania, this, *this* is Celina.' Karl introduced us to his friend, who sat smoking, staring into an ashtray that overflowed with butts. He looked up, his eyes glassy, red spidery veins. His face had them too – these broken veins patterning his cheeks, his bulbous nose. He was older than Karl, who I'd thought was perhaps thirty or so. This man had greying hair, a thickened waist where his belt strained to keep it all in. His hair was slick too, just like Polish Krzysztof's, but I bet that he did not style it with pig fat.

I held out my hand for him to take. He grinned at it hungrily, then kissed it. Looked to Wanda, who was being carefully seated by Karl, who then said he would be back in one moment with the best vodka he could find, and scurried away, looking back over his shoulder every few seconds in case Wanda had disappeared.

'Christoph.' He introduced himself to Wanda.

'Celina,' she said.

'She does not speak much German,' I told him.

'Ah ha! Well, she won't understand when I say that I think my friend Karl has taken a liking to her!' He laughed, patted his belly then stubbed out one cigarette, brought out a packet and offered each of us one. Wanda declined. I took one, not because I particularly liked it, but because I felt more adult, and it gave me something to do with my hands.

'What's this?' Christoph saw the red ribbon on my wrist and immediately began to paw at it.

'It was a gift,' I said.

'Strange gift. You know, my last girlfriend, I bought her a pearl bracelet. Pearls.' He winked at me. 'Do you like pearls, Ania?'

'I don't think I have ever seen any before,' I said, trying to sound normal, trying not to think of the burning in my chest, how he still stroked my arm, how his name was Christoph. The noise, the music, everyone laughing. I could feel myself spiralling.

'Are you all right?' he asked. 'You look a little pale.'

'It's just a bit warm in here,' I said.

'Everything all right?' Karl was back, a bottle of vodka in his hands, his eyes darting from me to Wanda to his friend. 'Everything all right?'

'This little one is overcome by the heat,' Christoph said, then stroked my cheek.

'You'll be fine,' Karl told me.

I looked to Wanda. I could feel sweat dripping down my back, and my brain was beginning to fog over. The noise – the damned noise. The voices all talking at once!

'Forgive me, but my friend is unwell,' Wanda said, then stood.

'No! No.' Karl wasn't about to give in.

'I'll tell you what. You come back to Christoph's apartment. He has a nice one, just two streets away. I'd take you to mine, but I share with so many others,' he jabbered. 'Christoph has a nice place. His wife and children are away too. It's cooler in there, quieter.'

Wanda looked at me. I regained some form of composure. We could still do what we had come here to do, and this sounded better than what we had originally planned.

'That would be very kind, thank you,' I said and allowed a grinning Christoph to help me stand, then laced my arm through his.

As soon as the cold air hit me, it was as if I were back in my own body again. It was just too much in that bar. I could not cope and knew that if we were to do this again, we would have to find a quieter spot.

'Feeling better?' Christoph asked me as Karl blathered on more to Wanda, seemingly not caring that she might not under-stand. Wanda indulgently smiled sweetly and nodded at every-thing he said.

'Much better,' I said. 'Thank you.'

'You know,' he said, 'I have had many girlfriends before. I have a wife, of course, and children, because that's what you must do – what a man should do. But he still needs his girl-friends. I think you're adorable. So small, and me so round!' He laughed. 'So small. You could sit on my knee, couldn't you, when we get to my apartment. You could sit on it and let me tell you about all the types of jewellery I could buy you and where you'll wear them.' His other hand came out of nowhere and tickled at my neck. 'A diamond necklace,' he breathed heavily in my ear. His breath was sour.

I swallowed. Thought of the flask in my bag. Thought of the red apple, red door. Basia, Tata, *szalony*, letting the rage build and build.

* * *

His apartment was on the third floor. A doorman stood in the marbled foyer. 'Used to be a hotel,' Christoph said. 'Requisitioned for senior SS like me.' He then burped as we got into the lift.

I did not marvel at the lift – even though it was the first time that I had been in one. I did not notice the interior of his home, what the furnishings were like; I just repeated red apple, red door, Basia, Krzysztof, Tata, pig's fat, in my head over and over, letting the anger wash over me, making me oddly calm.

The memories of that night became like taking photographs one after the other.

*I'm sat on his lap. He smells of dried sweat. I let him place his hand on my knee, let him whisper something foul in my ear.*

*Click.*

*Wanda pours drinks for everyone. I do not drink; neither does Wanda, but we play with our glasses.*

*Click.*

*Wanda and I go to the bathroom together. She tells me we must get them more inebriated.*

*Click.*

*I'm sat on his knee again. I keep pouring him drinks, he knocks them back, I smile for the camera.*

*Click.*

'Let's go to the bedroom,' Christoph said. 'Leave these two out here.'

I looked to Wanda; she shook her head.

'One more drink,' I said, 'then I will sit on your lap in the bedroom.'

Now the camera stopped taking pictures. Now it was all in slow motion and I was aware of everything I was doing.

I went to the drinks trolley that he had positioned up against the wall in between two large bay windows. My bag I had already placed on the chair near it when we arrived. I looked behind me and nodded at Wanda. Suddenly, she started laughing and then fell off Karl's lap onto the floor. The two men scrambled around trying to help her up, both of them very unsteady on their feet. Quickly, I undid the cap and poured the contents of the flask into two tall glasses, half filling each. I hoped it would be enough. Then I topped each one off with vodka, placed the flask back in my bag and returned to them, the two men back on the sofa eyeing the tall glasses.

'Bit much, my dear,' Christoph said. 'I'll teach you how to pour shots of vodka. This is too much.'

'This is the Polish way,' I said. 'Polish men drink it like this – all of it in one go – and I thought to myself as I was pouring it, why, it actually might not be large enough, because you, being a big strong German man, would find this a child's drink!'

'Of course!' Christoph smacked his knee. 'Pass it to me. I'll show you how a German drinks.'

Both he and Karl took the glasses and knocked the drinks back in one go, and handed me the empty vessels. Each smacked their lips a little, ran their tongues over the roofs of their mouths.

'Bitter,' Christoph said, then belched. 'Excuse me, my dear!'

'Must have been a dirty glass?' I suggested.

'Quite, quite. I'll be telling the maid tomorrow to make sure she rinses them properly in future. Now. To bed?'

He did not wait for my answer, just held out his fat hand for me to drag him to his feet. Then he slung an arm over my shoulder and walked me to two double doors, opened them and pushed me gently inside.

Wanda and I had never discussed this happening. Our entire plan had been to poison drinks then get out of there. And although I did not like it when I had not planned something – this was working out much better – now we would actually get to see what it looked like when you were *szalony*.

He sat on the bed then patted the quilt. Red. Good.

I sat and he placed his hand on my knee and whispered that he liked that I was small, like a doll, like a child. He moved his hand further up my leg. I knew that the poison would take about twenty minutes to get into his system – to at least show some initial signs of discomfort. I did not want his hand on my leg, or have it moving upwards, for that amount of time.

I jumped up; his hand caught on the skirt and tore it slightly. 'What's the matter?' he slurred, blinking heavily.

'Nothing,' I said. 'I just wondered whether we could lie next to each other for a while. Hold me. Like a child,' I added. 'Then you can touch me like that again.'

He grinned. Licked his lips and shuffled his weight backwards until his head was on the plump white pillow and patted the bed again.

I lay down next to him and let him roll onto his side, placing a hefty weight of his arm across me.

'Do you like that?' he murmured. 'All safe. Like a little girl.'

*Red apple.*

*Red door.*

*Red dress.*

*Basia. Tata. Krzysztof.*

'Yes,' I said. Then, 'Tell me about your job. Tell me why you get such a lovely apartment and poor Karl must live with others.'

'Because I'm senior,' he said. 'One of the best. Karl is new, but he'll learn, though I doubt he will ever be as good as me.' He then belched again.

'What do you do?' I prodded.

'Work at the camp. I was in the ghettos with them all, but I got promoted. Now it's an easy job. I get to take them from the ghetto to the camp, do some paperwork, watch as they work. Sometimes' – he yawned – 'sometimes I oversee the other things – the things that no woman should want to hear about.'

'I want to know,' I said.

'They'll give you nightmares. Not good to know too much.' Another yawn. 'I mean, it's all necessary – all of it. Have to get rid of them somehow. So far it's just been the men and I'm fine with that, but they're moving women in now too. I'm not sure how I feel about that. But I'm sure I'll get used to it. Have we cuddled enough?'

Suddenly, he was on top of me, his weight pinning me down. His face lowered onto mine and I turned my head away.

'Now, now, don't be a tease.'

'A little more cuddling,' I said. 'Please. Just a little more, then you can do what you like.'

'Anything I like?' he asked, surprised.

'Anything,' I agreed.

'As you wish, my little one.' He rolled off me, his arm thrown over me again.

'Tell me about Germany.' I tried to find something, anything, to make the time pass. 'Tell me about what it is like to live there. I am sure it is better than here!'

'Of course it is!' he said. 'It's the only country worth living in.' He then told me about his life in Germany, of what the world would one day look like, how we would all be German, one nation, perfect. He loved to talk of it; would not stop until –

'My stomach,' he said and turned away from me onto his back. 'I think I need the bathroom. Excuse me.'

He tried to sit on the edge of the bed, but a cramp overcame him. He moaned, holding on to his stomach. Then, vomit spouted from his mouth, onto the hardwood floor, splattering itself everywhere.

I got off the bed and stood near the door and watched.

He wildly looked about as more vomit came, then more; saw me standing there and gurgled that I should get Karl. I didn't move.

More groaning, this time from the other side of the door, then it opened and Wanda stood there.

'We can go now,' she said, looking at Christoph, then back at Karl.

'No. I want to see it. I want to see it happen,' I told her.

'Ania.' She grabbed my arm, but I shook her away.

'We're waiting,' I commanded.

She nodded at me, wrapped her arms around herself and let her eyes flick from one man to the other. I had my eyes on Christoph.

A few minutes later, the vomiting stopped and foam began to sprout from the corners of his mouth. 'Get a doctor,' he groaned, then fell off the bed into his own vomit. There, he writhed about, his limbs stiffening then relaxing, stiffening then relaxing.

I walked up to him and stood over him.

'Ania,' Wanda pleaded. 'I don't want to see this.'

'Then don't look,' I said.

The vein in his neck was bulging blue against his skin. His breathing was ragged, the spittle at his mouth now and again replaced with vomit that exited him without him even trying.

'Please,' he said.

'I had a father,' I told him. 'And a sister.'

'Please,' he said again.

'A man called Krzysztof, he came and he shot them. Isn't that perfect that you're called Christoph?' I smiled at him. 'I mean, I like to plan things, but this, this was a gift – fate, even. Don't you think?'

His body convulsed more, his teeth chattered against each other, his breath came faster and faster.

'You're *verrückt*! What have you done?'

'It's *szalony* in Polish,' I said. 'Mad is what you just called me, yes? You want to know what I have done? Right now, in your bloodstream is *szalej*, a northern water hemlock. Do you know what hemlock is? You should. It killed Socrates. Poisons you. But you know why it's called *szalej*? No? Can't speak? Well, it's called that because when you take it, when it's killing you, it looks like you have gone mad! Isn't that perfect? Here's you, calling me mad, and yet it's you that is frothing at the mouth, shitting himself.'

His breathing was very laboured now and he could not talk. I looked to Wanda and saw that she had gone to stand near the front door, her back to Karl, who was going through the same slow death as Christoph.

I wasn't going to leave yet. I needed to see him dead.

It took time. Maybe another forty minutes of gasping and wheezing. I had to admit to myself that I was in fact getting a bit bored waiting, and I went through his drawers, finding his wife's jewellery, his wallet. I took a few things and went to the sitting room, where I placed them in my bag.

'You should take some things,' I told Wanda. 'Maybe some food? Anything.'

She turned to look at me and wiped her face.

'You're crying,' I said.

'And you're not,' she replied. 'Does this not upset you?'

I shrugged. 'I thought this is what we wanted – what you wanted too?'

'I did. I do,' she said. 'It's just a lot to see.'

'Don't look at it,' I told her. 'It doesn't bother me at all. Let me watch them. You go and see if there's anything we can take – there is a kitchen there. Look through that door. Get something we can take with us. We can wrap it in our coats so that the doorman downstairs doesn't see.'

She wiped her face again and went to the kitchen. I went back to look at Christoph, who was still but breathing shallowly, then to Karl; ah, young Karl, with so much promise to kill people in a camp.

'Shame you won't be able to see it through,' I told him and saw that his chest was no longer rising.

Back to Christoph. Finally! His large stomach raised heavenwards, his face slack, his eyes open.

'*Szalony*,' I whispered to him, then closed the bedroom door, found Wanda, and we two, slipped out into the night.

*Red apple.*

*Red door.*

*Red dress.*

*Basia. Tata.*

I sighed. A happy sigh. Wait – happy? Yes. I was.

MEMORANDUM
Date: 6 January 1943

Urgent notice
Internal communication
Confidential: Investigation into the deaths of Lagerführer
Christoph Schneider and Verwaltungsführer Karl Meyer

The investigation into the deaths of Lagerführer Christoph
Schneider and Verwaltungsführer Karl Meyer is ongoing.
Both men were last seen at a bar on Słoneczna with two
women – one described as tall with long dark hair, the other
short, wearing a red dress.

After leaving the bar, the men did not report to duty the
following day, and upon investigation were found in number
6 Ogrodowa apartments, both poisoned. It is thought not to
be a suicide.

An alert has been given out to all officers with the
descriptions of the two women, who remain at large.

## 22

### GOSIA'S MISTAKE

*2 February 1943*
*Majdanek Concentration Camp, Lublin, Poland*
*Ania*

Weeks went by before we did anything else. Our next plan – a big one – was to liberate prisoners being taken to Majdanek. Aleksi wanted as much information as he could get before we set out – and it would need four of us to take it on, Benj exempt from it. Aleksi went almost every day to the camp, watching it, noting down the who, the when. He went back to the partisans a few times too and tried to find out anything else that might be useful, and a week before the beginning of February, he found out that one of the ghettos was being liquidated on 2 February – most, including the elderly and children, would be taken by train across the country, and most of the men and some women would be brought by truck to Majdanek.

Convoys of them would begin to arrive around midday, and Aleksi's source explained that they would probably continue into the night.

'We need to get the last truck,' Aleksi said as we stood outside, shooting at a target he had made. 'The very last. Slow it down in some way so that the others are too far ahead.'

I shot the gun I had been given by the sickly man in the forest. Aleksi had fixed it, he said, got bullets from his commander.

'Good shot,' Aleksi said. 'Right in the head.'

'I won't be using it though,' I told him. 'I'll get the driver out of the truck with it, but I don't want to shoot him. Gosia has made a new batch – stronger, and she says it will work faster this time.'

'I know, but it might have to be done quickly, Ania.'

'And I know that if we shoot them, it makes them look for us. If they find them, sat in their truck keeled over, then they'll assume they both got sick and died.'

'Both, though? Bit convenient?'

'Maybe.' I shrugged. 'But it will keep them guessing for a while. Keep us safer.' I turned from him and shot the target again, this time in the heart.

Both Gosia and Wanda had been practising too, and since the night at the bar, Wanda had been a little different, quieter. I sometimes caught her looking at me as we ate supper, her face aglow under the candlelight, her eyes narrowed as if she were either trying to see something in the flame or in me.

She still talked to me, still kissed the top of my head, stroked my cheek, but there was just something missing that I could not quite understand. I thought of how Isaac had told me to watch people's movements to see what they were trying to say without actually saying it. I had thought I was getting much better at it, much quicker in being able to tell what someone's emotions were, but Wanda was hard to read.

As Aleksi was rarely home with us as he watched the camp, I

found that the feeling – that odd giddiness – had abated somewhat, and thoughts of him had been replaced with my snapshot
memories of the night at Christoph's house. I did not think of
each image, each scene, and revel in it. Rather, I looked to see
what I had done, and what could have been done better. I
looked at it from every angle, and then thought of Basia and
Tata and the bullet holes in their heads, then back to the lifeless
body of Christoph, and I felt calm and, yes, somewhat happy.

We woke early, 2 a.m. Aleksi bundled Wanda onto the back
of the motorcycle, took off and said he would be back soon for
Gosia, then another trip for me. I asked him where he was
getting all this fuel from. 'Stealing it from their cars,' he said
with a smile.

It was better that Wanda went first, ready to take care of
Gosia and keep her in line until Aleksi and I returned, then we
would all wait, watch from a hiding spot that Aleksi had scouted
in a drainage ditch that ran alongside a field, a hedgerow in
front of us. But over the weeks Gosia had been less *szalony* than
usual. She rarely talked about herself in the third person any
more, rarely mentioned the husband either. Instead, she seemed
to find some peace in cooking, getting the hemlock, stealing
things when needed, and generally clucking about us as if we
were all her children. Each day, she would tell me she was
proud of me, ask me to tell her about the policeman on the
motorcycle, or Christoph and Karl. She would sit, eyes closed as
if she were there herself, and then say, 'Well, they never saw you
coming, did they?'

So it was just us three, me, Gosia and Benj, sitting in the
house that morning, a wind whipping up the trees outside, a
freezing rain falling, as we waited for Aleksi to return.

Benj sat close to the fire, pulling at the edge of his jumper until he found a loose thread and then would wrap it around his finger.

'I'm not taking the coat, you'll be pleased to hear,' Gosia said. She had new clothes. The yellow sundress burned on one of Wanda's outdoor fires. Now she wore trousers, a shirt and a thick jumper, like the rest of us. Sometimes, it looked almost like we had inadvertently decided upon uniforms for ourselves, but these were just the clothes that Aleksi could get his hands on that both fitted us, and were suitable for the weather.

'Fur won't match what you've got on,' I told her. She laughed in reply.

'Benj,' I said, but he would not look at me. He had been sullen since Wanda and I had returned, and he'd started to say that the house was haunted and he could hear ghosts at night. He became needy, constantly following one of us around at all times, and had made Aleksi wake in the night to take him to the outhouse. It was as though whilst I had found my way into being an adult, he had regressed further, becoming a small boy again.

'Benj,' I tried again.

This time, he looked at me and gave me a lopsided smile.

'I'll come back, Benj, I promise I will if that's what you are worried about.'

The wind rattled at the window, begging to be let in. He looked to it and then to me, then to Gosia.

'How long will you be again?'

'This time tomorrow we will be back. Just one day, Benj. That's all. When we leave, go to sleep. Time will pass quickly. Then when you wake, light the fire, make some food. Just stay here and wait.'

'And if someone comes?'

I had decided not to give him Father's advice of staying put and not running. Benj needed to run.

'You hide, Benj if you can't run. You're good at it. But no one will come. No one knows we are here. We are too far from the road. There's no reason why anyone would come down here.'

I think I had repeated the same things to him now at least ten times, but he needed me to say it again and again to provide him with some form of comfort.

'You think it will all work?' Gosia asked, picking at something in her teeth. 'I mean, we place the nails down for the last truck – and boom – the tyre goes. But what if it doesn't go?' she asked.

'If it doesn't go, then we do what Aleksi said – we'll have to shoot at the tyres. But I'm sure it won't come to that.'

Gosia nodded. 'And then the truck stops and the guards – the soldiers – they get out. The back of the truck is where the people are and Aleksi says that there will be a driver, and another soldier, and maybe one in the back with the people, but he said he doesn't think so because he's watched the others, the ones that are all open at the back, and it's just people standing there. Like cattle being taken to market, he said. So we just have two of them to deal with.'

'Yes,' I said. I reached into my pocket and found a cigarette. It was starting to become a habit now.

'Then, we go to them with guns. Wait to surprise them. Then Aleksi and you, you will give them this' – she waved the silver flask at me – 'and me and Wanda, we open up the back and we give them the drawing of the map that Aleksi did of where to find the forests and we tell them to run, and keep running.'

'Yes.' I blew out a puff of smoke.

'And then when the men are dead, we put them inside the

cab again, leave them there. And Aleksi takes me home first and you and Wanda are going to go and hide.'

'Yes. That's everything.'

'But what if Aleksi can't find you?' Benj asked.

'I've told him that Wanda and I will find our way back. Don't worry, Benj. I can always find my way.' I took out the compass and showed him the engraving on the back. He stroked the inscription – *So you never lose your way in this life* – then went back to pulling at loose stiches of his jumper.

\* \* \*

Aleksi came back by three thirty and took off again with Gosia, leaving me to go over once more with Benj what he should do if anyone came, promising I would be home as soon as I could. And I told him to sleep to make the time pass.

By the time I was on the back of the motorcycle, the sky was beginning to lighten, but the rain still fell in sheets; the wind still knocked the bike to and fro.

As Aleksi drove, I began my ritual.

*Red apple.*

*Red door.*

*Red dress.*

*Basia. Tata.*

*Szalony.*

*Krzysztof.*

*Pig fat.*

*Rolf.*

I would add in extra too – things that Christoph had said about extermination, things that Aleksi had said about gassing and burning. I would sometimes picture Daniil's face, drawn and pale in those striped trousers and jacket, chewing on the bread as if he were eating the finest-tasting meal on this earth. And of that boy's face when he was shot. All of this helped the burning rage to wake up properly. It never slept – not properly – rather it eased a little and then could come back on its own, or sometimes needed a little prodding. In my mind I had decided that it was a creature. Not a cat, a dog, not even a snake. It didn't really have a form that I could describe, but in my head, it was red, it had talons, it breathed and grew and I nurtured it with my words, my thoughts. And I needed it to wake up today. Today was a big risk, I knew. So many things could go wrong but I needed it to be there, ready for anything. We had to – simply had to – help the people that were being sent to Majdanek. We could not save them all, but we could save some, and if all went well, we could do it again.

My creature was thumping at my chest, ready to be let out. Today we would find our way to not only satisfy my rage, but also save people and disrupt their killing machine. I liked that thought, of them all running around afterwards, in their shiny black boots, scratching at their heads, wondering what the hell had happened. It made it all the more enjoyable.

What wasn't enjoyable was the wait. From midday trucks began to rumble down the road. All of them like Aleksi had described, open at the back, just wooden slats holding these people in, who stood, crammed together like livestock. As they rushed past us, I could see the pale, drawn faces. Then another truck would come, more of the same.

'Why don't they just jump out?' Gosia had asked.

'Because they are tired. Starving. They do not know where they are going. They are too tired to do the fighting,' Aleksi explained to her in Polish. 'We must to do for them.'

Aleksi soon left the ditch and went to higher ground so that he could see the convoy coming closer to us – so that he could see the one in the rear that we were to stop.

I felt nauseous as perhaps ten or so trucks passed us that day. The rain drenching us, filling the drainage ditch up to our shins, soaking those people who stood in the back, taken to a place that they may never be able to get out of. The creature was burning hot today. Those trucks made it angry, made it wish it could stop them all, help them all, kill all the guards, but I had to be patient. We could only do so much.

Suddenly, Aleksi was back.

'Last truck, three miles away,' he said breathlessly. 'Ready?'

We nodded and Aleksi climbed back out of the ditch to the other side of the road. In the ditch with me was a plank of wood, nails sticking out of it. I picked it up, climbed out and placed it in the road, Aleksi doing the same on the other side.

I could hear the rumble of the engine. It was time.

I nodded at Wanda, who held her gun – a rifle – ready. Gosia had a small pistol. It was Aleksi who had a machine gun. When he showed me a demonstration, I had agreed that it should not be in our hands – it was far too powerful.

Despite his hand, Aleksi was adept with the gun. He found a way to hold it, to pull the trigger, that meant you would not even notice that he had three fingers missing. I doubted that if it were me, I would be so coordinated.

The engine was getting closer. I climbed up the ditch a little, just so that I could see over the top, my feet wedged into the mud of the bank, slipping every now and then.

I could see it. Ten yards. Now six. Five. Three.

'You show them, Ania, you show them what a woman like you can do,' Gosia whispered next to me. 'I told you to stick with old Gosia, didn't I?'

Before I could count down to one, it was upon us. At first,

nothing happened. The nail bed I had placed down had embedded itself in the front left tyre that was still trying to turn. Then, as the wood hit the wheel arch, the driver applied the brakes. The nailed wood flew off the tyre as the driver tried to stop the truck as it skirted left, right, left again. The squealing of the brakes became louder and started to smoke.

Then, the truck stopped. I was ready, almost over the edge of the ditch when I saw Aleksi raise a hand for me to wait. He crept through the few trees that lined the other side of the road, nipping in and out, but getting a little closer to the truck.

There were shouts, screams from those in the back. Some had fallen and I watched as others tried to help them to stand. Then, there they were. The two soldiers, both looking confusedly about them, both with rifles in their hands, scanning left and right.

They saw no one. The driver lowered his gun and went to the wheel. I heard him shout, 'What the hell?' and knew it was time.

Within seconds, I was out of the ditch, through the thin hedge, and running full pelt towards them. Aleksi was already there, had the second soldier on his knees and had relieved him of his gun.

The driver looked up, saw me, and lifted his own gun.

He shot. I heard it. But I did not feel anything so assumed he had missed. I kept on at him, another shot. Then another, but it didn't come from my gun. The driver went down. By the time I reached him, there was a neat bullet hole in his head.

I turned behind me. 'Ania!' Wanda screamed.

'Wanda?' I ran to her but she was still standing. She couldn't be that badly hurt?

Then I saw that she was looking at something on the

ground. I got closer. One step. Then stopped. I did not want to go further.

'Gosia!' Wanda screamed. She sat down, held Gosia's hand.

Wanda yelled some more. Told Gosia to wake up. But I could see that her eyes were wide, unseeing, like Basia's had been.

*Red apple.*

*Red door.*

*Red dress.*

*Red coat.*

*Red. Red. Red. Red.*

I left Wanda with Gosia, ran to Aleksi and the passenger. He looked at me, and I at him. Then I placed my pistol against the soldier's head as he cried and begged for his life, for his family. I pulled the trigger, his blood spattering my face.

MEMORANDUM
Date: 4 February 1943

Urgent notice
Internal communication to Kriminalpolizei, Schutzpolizei,
Bahnschutzpolizei, Forstschutzkommando, Grenzschutz and
Polnische Polizei im Generalgouvernement

All police officers in all districts to be offered an award of half
a year's salary for the capture of the partisans who carried
out the attack and killed two officers at Konzentrationslager
Lublin.

Descriptions are of:

A young girl, approximately 14 years of age, five feet tall,
and is linked to the death of a police officer in the Czerniejów
district and has been seen in the vicinity of the camp.

A male, approximately six feet in height, blond hair.

A woman with waist length black hair, approximately five
feet five inches tall and linked to the deaths of two guards in
an apartment in Lublin.

## 23

## THE AFTERMATH

*4 February 1943*
*Czerniejów, Lublin Voivodeship, Poland*
*Ania*

The wind continued to torment me. It rattled at the loose window frames, blew through cracks in the walls and brought nothing but whispers of the danger that we were in.

I could not sleep; the bed was now too big with just Benj and me in it. I got up, placed my feet in my boots and went outside to face the wind and the terrible truths that it brought us.

The trees, their skeletal limbs lit by a moon that was half obscured by clouds that scuttered across the not quite black sky, bowed to the wind, knocked against each other and creaked with a cry of wanting to be snapped in two.

I watched them for a while. Waiting to see if one would break, but they didn't. They just cried out and the wind kept tormenting them as it did me.

The barn, to my left, had some light coming from inside. I knew who would be in there – Aleksi. He had not slept in the house since we had returned, saying that he needed to be alone. I understood. It was how he dealt with things. I just hoped that he would find himself again and come back to us.

I would go to him, in a moment, I knew. Just to check, to see him sat amongst all the debris of my uncle's life, staring aimlessly at the flame that flickered in the gas lamp. But I needed a moment alone first too. A moment to see it all again in my mind and figure out how it all went so terribly wrong.

Gosia had made a mistake, I was sure. Wanda said that Gosia had fired to protect me, had screamed out something about not hurting her daughter. But I couldn't have that thought in my mind, it made me feel all strange again, just like after I had found Tata and Basia – nothing made sense. Instead, I told myself a narrative that worked, and allowed me to still think, to still feel somewhat in control. I decided, then, that Gosia had made a mistake. Fired accidently. It had been a mistake. If she hadn't have done it, I was sure I could have somehow wrangled that gun from the driver; no one would have been shot. We could have given them the hemlock and that would have been that.

Instead, we had two shot soldiers causing those people in the rear of the truck to scream and wail in fear of us. It was only when one man, who introduced himself as Levi, a small suitcase in his hands that he told us contained a camera, had managed to calm everyone, take the map from Aleksi, and make the others follow him into the countryside to the Russian partisans who Aleksi said would either care for them or at least point them in the direction of the other groups.

'We don't have long,' Aleksi said. 'They will be wondering where this truck is.'

Wanda still sat with Gosia, stroking her hair, whispering to her in a language that I did not know.

'We have to move her. To the ditch.'

I did not like the idea of leaving Gosia in a ditch, but Aleksi said he would come back for her body, even though we all knew he was lying.

We did not have time to mourn her in that moment. We had to keep moving.

Between us, we carried her and then let her roll into the drainage ditch, her body floating, her eyes looking at us as if in surprise.

Aleksi crossed himself, muttered a prayer. Then told us to get into the truck.

This, once more, had never been part of the plan. But we had to leave, quickly, and the motorcycle was over a mile away.

'Can we drive with the tyre like that?' I asked him.

He did not answer. He turned the key, brought the engine to life and drove as fast as he could; the smell of burning rubber, the loud flap as the tyre fell apart filled the cab.

He drove down a lane, then through a field, anywhere but near to the camp, which lay to the west of us. I watched the needle of my compass, telling him where to change direction and when.

After fifteen minutes, the wheel gave in and the truck stopped.

'You can get home from here,' Aleksi said.

He took the rifle from Wanda, told me to put the pistol that I hadn't realised I was still holding into my coat pocket.

'Wipe your face. Stay off the roads. I'm going to get the motorcycle.'

'Leave it,' Wanda begged, then began to cry.

'We need it. We still need it,' he said. He did not kiss her goodbye like he normally did, and he raced off.

We too did not wait around. Keeping to farm tracks, to

bushes, trees, anything, we made our way back to my uncle's, arriving just before midnight to Benj's lopsided and relieved face.

He looked at me, then to Wanda, and realised something was wrong. His smile fell away.

'Gosia first,' he said. 'That's what you said. Aleksi and Gosia would come back first.'

I nodded but could not speak.

'Oh, Benjamin!' Wanda wailed. She went to him, held him to her. Benj started to cry too. Wrapped his arms around her. I watched them both. I watched them, waiting for my thoughts to catch up to me.

When they did not, I went to the mattress and lay down. Closing my eyes but not sleeping. I had stayed there, like that for almost a day, only getting up to see that Aleksi was in the barn, Wanda and Benj crying in the kitchen as they had made supper, then had gone back to the mattress again.

Stood here now, I felt as though I had some bearings on my thoughts. But I felt strange – detached. Cold. It was like when Tata and Basia died, but different – worse, somehow. I needed it to go away.

The orange flicker of light from the barn called to me. I went to it, to Aleksi, seeking something that I wasn't sure of.

I stood in front of Aleksi. The light from the lamp cast soft shadows on the walls. I stood there and waited. He did not look up.

'Aleksi,' I said.

'Ania,' he replied sadly. 'Go to bed. You don't need to be here.'

'I do,' I said.

He did not answer.

I sat next to him, leaned my body into his.

'Don't, Ania.'

'Don't what?'

'You know.' Suddenly he was angry. He turned to me, his eyes red. 'I can't understand you. You're so clever, so clever, and yet there are things you do, looks you give me, and I think to myself, surely she cannot not know what she is doing?'

'What am I doing?' I thought of the looks. Of Basia. Of love. Of sex. In that moment, I realised what I had been doing. I was complicit but I wanted him to say it. To tell me.

'When you wore that dress,' he started.

'The red one.'

'Before, I had looked at you like a little girl. Like a sister. I don't know – something. But then you stood there, and you looked at me, the same way you are looking at me now.'

'Gosia,' I said. 'I can't...'

He wrapped an arm around my shoulders. 'You can cry.'

'I can't,' I said. 'I need something else. I can't cry.'

I lifted my head and found that his face was close to mine. Gently, ever so gently, our lips met, for a few seconds, gentle, perfect.

Aleksi pulled away but I tried to move back to him, get him to kiss me again.

'Please,' I begged.

'I can't, Ania. You know I can't.'

'Wanda,' I said.

'Wanda. I love her.'

I nodded. I knew he did.

I stood, went back to the house, and all the while, the burning in my chest had gone. Now my eyes burned, a lump in my throat. I let the tears fall silently.

## 24

### BARTOK'S OFFER

*12 February 1943*
*Czerniejów, Lublin Voivodeship, Poland*
*Ania*

I had been out most of the days since I'd spoken to Aleksi in the barn, since Gosia. I walked for hours, not caring if I got lost, for once allowing my mind to be quiet. And it stayed quiet in such a way that the walking became the hunger that drove my days. I needed the air, the trees, the quiet of the countryside.

As I returned home one evening, quite late, hoping that everyone would be asleep, I found that there was something amiss. A smell first: cigarette smoke but thick – new. Aleksi had no cigarettes, hadn't gone to get any. I hadn't either.

'Ania.' The voice was not Benj's but it was familiar to me. In the kitchen sat Bartok, his red hair wilder than ever, his beard bushier, his face almost completely obscured by all the hair.

Benj sat by his side and grinned at me. 'He's come to help us, Ania. I told him about Gosia. How it all went wrong. And now he's come to help.'

'Ania,' Bartok said again with his gravelly voice. 'You've changed.'

'Have I?' I sat down, unsure of the situation. Bartok I knew, but his sudden presence here, in our home, our world that we had created for ourselves, felt bewildering.

'You've made a fucking mess, Ania,' he said, then drew out a cigarette, lit it and took a deep drag.

'Can I have one?' I asked.

'You smoke now too? What would your father say, eh?' He drew out another and rolled it on the tabletop in my direction.

He scratched a match and lit it for me, watching me as I took a pull of the nicotine.

'How did I make a mess?' I asked.

'You know, when I first heard the rumours, I thought to myself, you know, that could be Ania. A woman who looks like a girl being seen with soldiers, and said soldiers being found dead the next day. Then again, releasing people from a truck, and a few got to us – sent on by some Russian commander – and told us what had happened. One said something about *szalony*. Some small girl screamed it at a soldier.'

*Had I? Had I yelled that at that soldier?*

'I thought it was you, then I thought, no, surely not,' he continued. 'Then I actually meet this commander, Russian, leading his own group who tells me of Aleksi, and then mentions you. Word gets around up there in those woods, you know.' He stopped, took a deeper lungful, then blew it out in a neat stream.

'And then, who do I see but Wojtek, and he says he met you! Mentions Benjamin here too. So then I knew. I knew it was you and I thought to myself, damn, I knew she was clever, and I knew she was a bit mad, but this – this is something else!'

'Is that a compliment?' I asked coolly.

'You have changed. Listen to you. Don't sound like a girl any more, how you used to ramble on and on.'

'We all change,' I said and drew on my own cigarette again.

'So we do. But you still made a fucking mess, Ania. Too visible. I mean, that heist, getting all of those people out of that truck! Genius! But the thing is, things like that do not go unnoticed. Everyone knows who you are now, and mark my words, they'll be looking for you.'

'Let them come,' I said. 'I'm not afraid.'

Bartok laughed, then, unsure of himself, he abruptly stopped, stubbed his cigarette out on the tabletop and shook his head at me.

'I know what happened to your father, to Basia. I heard Krzysztof was there. I know it was difficult for you to see that—'

'It wasn't difficult,' I said, cutting him off. 'I saw what they had done and now I am simply doing the same kinds of things to them.'

'I know, Ania, but—'

'Logic. That's all it is. Even in the Bible it says an eye for an eye.'

'Look, Ania, I didn't come her to get drawn into some religious discussion with you.'

'So why are you here?'

He rubbed at his eye with a closed fist. 'To help you. If you want to fight, then come with me. Now. I have to leave tonight.'

'I've already tried that; they didn't want me.'

'That was Wojtek's group. He's merged now with another. There are many groups, Ania, all changing, merging each day.'

'What about Benj? About the others?'

'The *Ruski*, and who is the other one?' he asked.

'Wanda,' I said. 'And they're not here. They're in the barn.

They stay in there most of the time now. I'd have to speak to them.'

'Look. We'll sort it out. I've written the directions down for you. It's tricky to find us up there but we'll be at this location for the next few days, God willing – it's about forty miles give or take, near a lake. If we're found, we move on, but I'll find a way to make sure you know where we are, leave a mark on a tree, compass points, or I'll come back each day and check.'

I looked to Benj, who nodded at me. He wanted to go.

'I have to talk to the others,' I said. 'But I like it here, Bartok. This suits us. We're getting on just fine.'

'I don't feel safe, Ania,' Benj said.

Bartok rubbed Benj's arm briefly. 'Ania, you've lost one person of this merry band of yours. Are you really willing to lose any more through stubbornness?'

I opened my mouth to argue with him that this wasn't about stubbornness, it was about community, about feeling like you belonged. We had found it and I did not want to give it up, nor did I want someone else telling me what to do.

'I know you, Ania.' He scraped back his chair. 'I know how stubborn you were – are,' he said, correcting himself. 'You may be clever, perhaps a genius. You may be brave, not feel fear. But that stubborn streak of yours puts other people in danger. Think on it.'

He kissed the top of my head. 'Your father was a good man. He loved you very much. And despite the mess you're making, I know he would be proud.'

Bartok left Benj and me at the table, grey and white cigarette ash scattered on the wood. I placed my finger in it and began to swirl it about.

'Ania,' Benj said. 'Please.'

'I'll think about it,' I replied. Knowing all the while that I had already made my decision. We were staying put. This was my purpose, my life. I was in charge, and I wasn't going to have anyone else, ever, tell me what to do. Nor was I going to have anyone reject me again either.

'I'll think about it,' I told Benj again, then flicked the cigarette to the floor, where it smouldered away into nothingness.

# 25

## OLD MAN KAMINSKI

*14 February 1943*
*Czerniejów, Lublin Voivodeship, Poland*
*Ania*

Wanda and Aleksi had moved into the barn, only coming inside for meals where Wanda would cry for Gosia, and Aleksi would not meet my gaze. I knew – in spite of my resolution to keep us together – our family was falling apart. Benj spent his days sleeping, then at night would listen to the house creak and moan, waking me often to tell me that Gosia was trying to speak to him.

'There're no ghosts,' I would tell him over and over again. 'People cannot talk to you from beyond the grave.'

No matter how many times I told him this, he did the same thing every night, driving me to yell at him as I had done to Basia and Tata.

The creature in my chest was quiet. I was sure it was still there, but no matter how many times I tried to chivvy it, it ignored me and instead I was left feeling heavy and empty all at the same time.

After a few days, we had run out of food. I went to the barn to ask if Aleksi should go, or if Wanda and I should hunt for pigeons, pheasants – anything.

They looked at me from the mattress they had dragged in there, a multitude of blankets around them, a small fire that they had built smouldering far too close to the damp and mouldy bale of straw.

'It might catch fire.' I nodded at it.

'Too damp,' Aleksi replied.

'So. Anyone?'

'I can go with you,' Wanda said. She went to stand and wobbled a bit.

'No. You stay.' Aleksi made her sit back down, and she immediately began to cry again.

'Can you go alone?' Aleksi asked, looking at Wanda, his brow creased.

'I can go,' I said.

I left them, went back to the house and looked for my gun. As I did, I saw one of the silver flasks. I picked it up, turned it over.

I placed it in my pocket, the gun next to it, and set off alone.

* * *

I was not sure about going back into the village, worried that I would see the woman from the bakery again, so I set off in the opposite direction, hoping to come across a farm, a house where I could ask for food, or try to be like Wanda and Gosia and simply take what I needed.

My feet soon led me away from the road, into the bushes. I

knew then where I was going – to the river; the river that I had avoided as I did not want to spoil the memory of the summers spent on those banks as a child.

Today though, I needed to go. I needed to walk along the banks, remember Basia and Tata. Look at the water and imagine that it was a summer's day and I would jump in, fully clothed and Tata would smoke, fish and talk with Uncle. I needed to feel that memory – that good memory.

I reached the river. It was full and if there was any more rain or snow, it would soon burst over the banks. On the other side of the water, an open field stretched for about a mile without a hedgerow, a tree, in sight. I knew where that field led to. It led straight into Old Man Kaminski's dairy farm, a farm we had gone to collect milk a few times – I was sure that he was long gone by now.

As I walked, I tried to imagine Basia's voice – how she would laugh – but for some reason, I could not remember how she sounded. I tried to think of Tata, how he looked, but his face was a shadow in my mind.

Ahead of me was a wooden bridge that led to the other side of the bank. I knew that bridge; I had crossed it before to Old Man Kaminski's farm with Basia. Perhaps if I went to the farm, perhaps if I retraced my steps into my past, the memories of my father and sister would resurface.

The bridge was missing a few planks so I had to jump over the gaps, the wood creaking with my weight when I landed. On the other side, I looked back and tried to imagine that I could see myself and Basia as children. She would be holding my hand, my hair long, plaited down to my waist. She would crease her face up in concentration as we crossed the bridge, always scared that it would give way. I would be trying to release myself from her grip, trying to run ahead to the middle of the bridge where I would jump up and down, as Basia screamed at me to stop.

I shook my head. I could see how cruel I had been to Basia sometimes. How I knew that she was scared but I would do it anyway just because I felt no fear.

I thought of what Bartok had said, how I was stubborn and how just because I was not scared, it did not mean that the others weren't. The truth was, I wasn't being stubborn, I was being selfish.

My thoughts and reimaginings of my past kept my mind so busy that I did not notice how far I had walked. It was only when I looked up and saw Kaminski's farm appearing that I realised how I was still being somewhat selfish. Instead of looking for food, for supplies, I had let myself swim in my own thoughts into a past that I could not recreate. I had only the present, and I had to focus.

I made to turn back then looked to the farm again. Old Man Kaminski might be gone, but there might be a new farmer – perhaps his son, that blue-eyed boy. His name eluded me. But yes, perhaps his son would be there and I could get food from him – one way or another.

The farm was unusually quiet. The cow-shed empty of its inhabitants that should still be inside as it was still winter, still too boggy in the fields to let them out.

I looked inside and saw straw with dried cow pats – pats I was sure had been there for some time. A rat scuttled over the straw, then another.

The farmyard was empty of tools, bales of hay. But the house, Kaminski's house, which he shared with his wife with her wiry hair that would never be tamed to stay within the pins that desperately clung onto it, had smoke coming from the chimney. It was either Kaminski or that son of his. That's how farms worked – passed down. Unless…

I stopped. What if he had had the farm taken from him – like the Germans had promised to do to us?

'Can I help you?' a voice asked in German.

I turned to see a man in the doorway, chewing on a chicken leg, the leg itself in his hand halfway to his mouth as if he were going to take another bite. He wore a white shirt that was half unbuttoned, a napkin tucked into his vest. His trousers were grey, his feet bare.

His face was not Kaminski's. He was young; no, not young – perhaps thirty or forty. It was hard to tell. A day's stubble covered his jaw. He was not the son either. I remembered the son – blue eyes. This man's eyes were brown.

'Kaminski. Is Kaminski here?' I asked, knowing that I should leave. That there was something wrong with this man. Yet I didn't want to be selfish; I wanted to get food, take it back to the others and tell them that we should go and find Bartok in the forests and stay there where it was safer.

He blinked, once, twice, then called over his shoulder. 'Is there a Kaminski here?'

It was met with deep laughter. Guttural. Two more men.

'Come in, come in,' he said and stepped to the side. He gave me a smile I had seen on the Blue Policeman when he had unbuttoned my coat. The same smile that Christoph had given me.

I went inside.

In the sitting room, a fire roared in the grate, making the room too warm. Two men sat on a lumpy cream sofa, horsehair escaping from holes in the armrests. The man with the chicken leg went to the only other chair, a rocking chair next to the fire, and sat.

'See here, we have a visitor.'

The two men, both similarly dressed, turned around, their faces as unremarkable as the one who had opened the door. It was then that I saw their jackets, light grey, black lapel, and shining boots dumped on the floor. Their belts and guns lay haphazardly on top of the jackets. Sitting there. Just sitting there, I thought.

'You want some food?' one of the sofa men asked, waving about another chicken leg. 'Come sit next to me and I'll share.' He grinned.

'She doesn't want to sit with you,' rocking chair man said.

'Fuck you. I'm sure she'd rather sit with me than you, Rolf.'

Rolf. I knew the name. Same name. But the voice was wrong. It wasn't him.

A sudden gust of smoke billowed into the room from the fireplace, causing them to wave their hands about in front of their faces and cough. 'There's no wind?' someone said.

The creature woke.

*Red apple.*

*Red door.*

*Red coat.*

*Red dress.*

*Gosia.*

*Tata. Basia.*

As the smoke dispersed, Rolf told me to come sit with them again.

'Can I use the bathroom, please? Get a glass of water?'

He rocked back on the chair. 'How old are you? You lost? What do you want with Kaminski?'

'Nineteen,' I said, not even bothering trying to be a child this time to get away. I didn't want to get away.

'Is that so?' He rocked back and forth again. 'And what did you want with the old man?'

'He was a friend. I came to see him, that's all.'

'A friend, eh? Bit old. We're not old. Want us to be your friends?'

The other two on the sofa laughed.

'You a Jew?' he asked. Then he shook his head. 'You'd be pretty fucking stupid to say yes. Mad even!'

*Mad.*

*Szalony.*

*Red. Red. Red. Red. Red.*

'Can I please get a glass of water?'

He waved a hand vaguely in the direction of the kitchen. He didn't care. He wasn't scared of me, thought I was scared of him, here in the lion's den.

In the kitchen I saw dried blood on the grey slate floor. Recent.

I found a glass, then took out the flask and filled it to the brim.

Then I took out the gun and checked it. Three bullets. I shrugged. It could be done.

I walked back into the room, the glass in one hand, the gun in the other.

The first shot was quick, one of the sofa men who did not even have time to turn around in surprise. It ripped through the side of his face, causing him to slump. The next shot was for his friend beside him, who was half stood and quickly keeled over.

Rolf had managed to get out of the rocking chair, leaving it to rock backwards and forwards on its own. He held his hands up.

'Now, now!' he said and took a step closer. 'I don't know who you are, or what you think you're doing, but if you pull that trigger you will be essentially signing your own death certificate. No one will stand for this.'

He took one more step. I aimed the gun first at his head, then quickly moved it to his left thigh and pulled.

Immediately, he fell and blood spilled out. So much blood.

I bent down as he cradled his leg, placing his hands over the wound to try to stop the blood that gushed out.

'It's no good,' I said. 'Femoral artery. You'll bleed out if a tourniquet isn't used to stop the bleeding. And the thing is, I don't have one.'

He screamed. Yelled at me to save him. 'The belt, my belt, please!'

His face was turning white. Not much time. 'I tell you what. I'll help you, I'll let you live, if you tell me what you did to Kaminski and his wife.'

'Deal! Deal!' he yelled.

I placed the glass on the floor, got a belt, tied it tight just above the bullet wound, causing him to howl with pain, then pulled it again just to hear him scream. The blood soon became a trickle. He looked at it, lay back on the floor and breathed heavily.

'Here. Drink this,' I said.

I placed my hand under his head, put the lip of the glass on his lips and poured it in. He tried to spit it out but he was too weak to struggle much. Once it was all gone, I sat in the rocking chair, placing my hands on the armrests and rocked back and forwards, back and forwards.

'What did you give me?' he asked.

'Water,' I said. 'Just water. The water here always tastes that way. Bitter.'

'Who are you?'

'Ania,' I said.

I rocked again. Back and forth, back and forth.

'Why?' he croaked.

'Why not?'

Back and forth. Back and forth.

'I always wanted a rocking chair, you know. I asked Tata for one. He got one and then in a fit of rage I broke it. It's funny, but I can't even remember what I was so angry about to do that to a chair. I mean, the anger now is so big, so powerful. The anger before must have been quite pathetic in comparison.'

'I don't understand,' he wheezed now.

'Tell me about Kaminski,' I said.

'You need to go for help,' he said. 'Please. I don't feel well. Please.'

'Kaminski first,' I demanded.

'Okay, all right. We just came here months ago, took his cattle. He wasn't happy. Then we came back last week, told him that his farm was to be given to a German family and he had to pack up. He pulled a gun on us. We had no choice.'

'And his wife?'

'She – I mean, she saw it and screamed. She tried to run away – yes, she tried to run away, so we had no choice. Can you get help now? I feel... I feel...' He didn't finish his sentence. The nausea started.

As he writhed on the floor, cried for his mother, I creaked back and forth on that rocking chair and simply waited.

When it was quiet, I stood. His eyes were open.

'That was for Basia. Gosia, too,' I told the corpse. Surprisingly, I felt a tear trickle its way down my face. Just one. That was enough. Just one tear would suffice.

\* \* \*

I made my way back with the food they had in the kitchen – another raw chicken, bread, cheese, milk. I took it all, apart from the chicken they had been eating that still sat on their plates, covered in blood.

Before I left, I washed my hands and face and wiped down my coat in the rainwater bucket, not wanting Wanda, Benj and Aleksi to see me in this state and ask questions, the answers to which would undoubtedly make them worse than they already were.

At the riverbank, I said a last goodbye to the water, wondering if I would one day come back here again. I did not take any more hemlock with me. I would find some if needed.

As I emerged from the trees, I could see the house in the distance – the pond, the barn, the side of the house where the outhouse sat. I wanted to run to it, to those inside. I needed to make this better.

A figure stood by the outhouse. Not Benj. Not Wanda or Aleksi. The man wore a uniform: Blue Police.

Shit.

I reversed back into the trees and waited. Another man appeared, then another. They walked around the back of the barn, down to the pond, then pointed at the trees.

I turned and ran. Bartok had been right. They had found us. My escapades had put us in danger.

The river appeared in front of me. I followed the bank away from the house, the bridge, having to scramble through bushes and thorns that scraped at my legs, hands and face.

As I ran past the trunk of an old oak, I felt a hand grab me, roughly pulling me backwards until I fell.

On the ground, I tried to find my gun, forgetting for a moment that it had no bullets.

'Ania!' It was Aleksi. Wanda behind him.

'Get up. We have to move.'

'The house.' I looked behind me.

'I know. We ran. Benj too. But we got split up. I don't know where he is.'

'Polish, please,' Wanda said. 'I don't understand.'

'He just said that Benj is not with you.'

Aleksi was looking through the trees. 'Talk later. Move now.'

I tried to ask about Benj again. Tried to explain to them that we had to go back and look for him; that he did not like to be on his own.

'We'll go back in a few days,' Aleksi said. 'We'll find him. Now we move.'

Twice I stopped and turned, ready to go back for Benj. 'If they shoot you, Ania, you have no way of finding him. We told him to run. He ran. We told him to hide too.'

'He's good at hiding,' I said to myself. 'In the barn at my house. It was clever what he did.'

'Come on, Ania. We have to stick together now.' Wanda pulled at my hand, and I let her. I needed her to take charge now. I needed to not be the one with a plan. I needed to not think, because I knew if I did, Benj's lopsided smile would appear to me, and I was sure that if I saw that, I would never be the same again.

# 26

---

Benjamin placed his hand on the soil and felt the coldness. 'You left me,' he said. 'Then the men with the guns came, and Wanda and Aleksi, they ran, and I tried to run but I couldn't, so I hid. I stayed a while. They didn't find me. I was good at hiding. I had already chosen a spot before.'

'The hay?' she asked him.

'That was one place. But not the first. My first place was through those trees that were at the side of the barn. I'd dug a hole, that day you and the others – you know, that day with Gosia. I dug a hole deep so I could lie down. I got the wood from the barn, put dirt on it, leaves. Just like that one in the forest. Only I knew where it was, squeezed between two trees, not a place you would really walk through, I thought. Too narrow. You'd go a different way, I thought.'

'You're smarter than you think, Benj,' she told him.

He sighed. Shook his head. 'I didn't like the dark. The cold. But I stayed there and waited. I don't know how long I waited for, but I came out only when there had been no noise for a long time.'

'They were gone, Benj, so why didn't you stay at the house? Wait for me? We were looking for you. We came back to the house three days later but you had gone.'

'I know,' he said. 'I should have waited. But I couldn't stay in that house any more. Not with all those shadows, all those ghosts whispering at me all the time.'

'I've told you that there is no such thing as ghosts, Benj.'

'There are,' he said. 'They made me have nightmares, Ania, whispering all sorts of bad things. And Gosia too. Gosia was there but when I was awake.'

'No, Benj. Gosia was dead.'

'Gosia was dead, but she came back. She was in that house, Ania, with me. As I waited, and then I got up the next morning and I couldn't wait any more and Gosia, she told me to run. Just like my parents had told me to run. She said it the same way – she used the same words.'

'So you ran,' she said.

'I did. But I am not quick – not like you. You know I am slow. It took me time to get away. I went to the woods, Ania. I thought maybe I could find my way back to those people again and maybe they would help me. But I got lost, Ania, and then I thought that maybe I didn't want to find those people after all – maybe it was better I just sit in the woods and wait.'

'Wait for what, Benj? Me?'

'No. Not you, Ania,' Benjamin said. 'Wait for death to find me. I knew I could sit and wait. I knew the cold would get me, the hunger, the thirst. I just had to wait. So I did.'

She did not speak to him for a while, but he knew that she

would eventually talk. As he waited for her, he played with the ribbon in his hands, threading it between his fingers.

'I'm sorry, Benj. I'm sorry that this happened to you. I'm sorry that you thought you had to sit and wait for death.'

'It's all right. You found me,' he said.

'I did. But what happened before I found you, Benj? What was it like? Tell me. You never told me – you were going to, and then, well, it happened, didn't it. Death came and I never got to know.'

## 27

## BENJAMIN AND GOSIA'S GHOST

*16 February 1943*
*Czerniejów, Lublin Voivodeship, Poland*
*Benjamin*

Benjamin was alone. For the first time in his life, he was completely alone. The house whispered to him when he entered it, the whistling of the wind as it snuck through the cracks in the windowpanes, each creak of the floorboards making Benjamin wince with fear.

He was cold and wet. But he wrapped his damp coat around him tightly even though he knew it would not provide him with any warmth.

He checked the three rooms downstairs and did not find Wanda or Aleksi. He was glad he didn't. His biggest fear had been finding their bodies sprawled on the floor like Ania's father and sister.

He sat in front of the fireplace, grey ashes heaped on top of each other, a small sliver of wood poking out from underneath that had avoided being burned. He reached out and took that sliver and held it to his nostrils. He breathed in the charred scent, then lowered it and, between his hands, crushed it.

He shoved his hands under his armpits and began to rock backwards and forwards and hummed a tune to himself that he had made up, and he waited.

As shadows lengthened, as the ghostly whisperings became louder and louder, Benjamin still sat, rocking, humming a tune, and waited for someone – anyone – to come home and find him.

An owl hooted from outside and made him jump. He wiped his face where tears had fallen. No one was coming.

He lay down on the flag-stoned floor and pulled his knees tightly into his chest.

'Benjamin,' the house whispered to him.

He began to hum once more, and more tears fell.

'Benjamin,' the house whispered again.

'Go away!' he yelled, then placed his hands over his ears and scrunched up his eyes. 'Leave me alone.'

'It's me, Benjamin,' the house said. 'It's me.'

Suddenly, Benjamin knew the voice that spoke. Gosia. But Gosia was dead.

He opened his eyes and lowered his hands from his ears. She sat in front of him, wearing her fur coat.

'I told you there were ghosts in this house.' She laughed, her gold tooth shining in the dark.

'Ania said there was no such things as ghosts,' he said. She wasn't real. This wasn't real.

'Pah! Ania doesn't know. She's not old enough to know about ghosts. I didn't used to believe in them, you know. I didn't. But when I was in the hospital, I heard about some of the things that had happened there – how patients had killed themselves or even sometimes had been beaten by the staff. They died there and then I started to see them, hear them.'

'That's not true,' Benjamin said.

'It is. Where terrible things happen, the ground itself, the buildings even, they remember and they hold a part of it within them forever. Trust me, Benjamin, ghosts, death, it's all around us and we walk amongst it all the time without realising the pain that is just beneath our feet, or within the very walls that are meant to protect us.'

'But you didn't die here,' Benjamin said. 'You died on that road and then Aleksi said he would find you but he didn't.'

Suddenly, Benjamin had an idea. He sat up quickly and reached out to Gosia, his hands trying to feel her skin. Surely she hadn't died. Surely Ania was wrong and Gosia had found her way back here. No one had come and taken her body – the soldiers wouldn't have taken the body with them. No. Gosia was alive, real.

His hands felt about in the cold, damp air and not once did they find Gosia's face.

'Are you done?' Gosia asked him. 'I'm dead, Benjamin. I just came back here to keep you company. You know how you don't like to be on your own, how you don't like the dark, so I'm here for you, Benjamin. I'm here just for you.'

Sometime later, Benjamin slept. Nightmares filled his mind. Soldiers and guns, a woman who was not Gosia in a fur coat on the side of the road, half of her head gone, but she was laughing and talking. Ania running down a street and he's following her – trying to catch up with her, but his legs would not move quickly enough. Wanda and Aleksi, who were in a truck that Benjamin drove, begging him to let them out, to set them free, but he couldn't stop the truck and they screamed and screamed at him until, at last, he woke.

His head hurt from sleeping on the floor. His body ached.

He sat up and looked about him, shaking his head now and

again to rid himself of the nightmares. 'Gosia?' he yelled out, his voice bouncing off the bare walls.

There was no response.

He stood and went to the cracked, grimy window and looked out onto a distorted view of a field. The snow had stopped and now a freezing rain pelted the ground. Although he was inside, he knew how cold that water would feel, how it would make him shiver as it found a way to sneak down behind his collar and drip down his back.

'Benjamin.' Gosia was behind him, but he did not turn. He would ignore her and eventually she would go away. She wasn't real. She was dead, he told himself over and over again.

'Benjamin, look at me, please. I have to tell you something.'

He turned. There she was. But different this time. Paler, sadder, somehow.

'You have to run, Benjamin. You can't stay here – not with these voices, not with these ghosts.'

'But Ania will come, I know she will.'

'She won't, Benjamin. No one will come for you. No one ever does. You have to go now. You have to leave. That map, look there at that map – the one that Bartok gave Ania, it's still here.'

He looked to the tabletop. There it sat. 'I'm no good at these kinds of things,' he said. 'Will you come with me?'

'I have to stay here, Benjamin. It's time for you to be brave.'

\* \* \*

Outside, the air was biting. The rain pummelled his skin, finding its way down his collar as he knew it would. His coat was still damp and, within minutes, soaked through. He shivered uncontrollably as he trudged through the open fields. With each step away from the farmhouse, his head became clearer. He breathed in the cold air and held it in his lungs for a moment before letting it out.

He told himself to move quicker, to run, and he started to, his feet slipping in the slushed mud, turning his ankles a few times, but he did not stop trying to run. Soon, his body warmed from the exercise, and he welcomed it.

Benjamin followed the crudely drawn map and tried to make out the written directions that Bartok had added in a rough hand. He followed the fields until he reached a fence, then climbed over it and continued on. The road, a few miles to his left, he kept an eye on. Every now and then throwing himself into the dirt as he imagined cars, trucks, soldiers on the road. He tried not to think about the fact that he was probably not going to find Bartok. He tried not to think about how scared he was.

He knew he needed to stay away from towns, from villages, from roads, so as soon as he saw any types of woods, of forests, he immediately went inside.

He had not told Ania this – nor the others – why he had been so upset in those woods the first time around; why he had cried, had shook and had made a scene in front of all those people with their guns. But now, standing in the woods, the trees closing in on him, he remembered being a child – an eight- or nine-year-old boy, with a scarred and puckered face who had been led into the woods and left there alone.

* * *

Benjamin had had no friends as a child. No one wanted to play with him. The other children were either afraid of his scars, or else they poked fun at him, pretended that their own faces were lopsided and taunted him.

But one day his mother had had enough of him being in the house and sent him on an errand to the butcher.

He had walked the mile into the village, the money tight in his balled-up fist, the spring sun warming his back.

'Look who it is!' He heard the voice before he saw them.

'Over here!' the voice yelled.

Benjamin turned and saw it was Casimir, a boy from his school, standing behind a wooden fence in a corn field. 'Where are you going?'

'To the butcher,' Benjamin said, his voice still slurred from the injury years before, his speech improving, his mother said, but he wasn't so sure that it was.

'Come over here.'

Benjamin clutched tighter at the money in his palm, the coins biting into his skin. 'I have to go to the butcher,' he mumbled again.

'You can go in a minute. Come here, let me show you something.'

Benjamin went to Casimir, his feet scuffling the dirt.

'I'm playing a game,' Casimir said. 'With some others. They're hiding. Want to help me find them?'

Benjamin looked at Casimir, his blond hair flopping over his forehead, his smile inviting this time, not his usual taunting grin.

'I can help find them,' Benjamin said, losing his grip a little on the money.

'Good. Come with me.'

Casimir helped Benjamin over the fence and together they walked through the field.

'You know Filip and Borys?' Casimir asked. 'They're hiding now, in the woods, so we find them and when we do, we go hide and they have to find us.'

Benjamin nodded.

'You ever play it before?' Casimir asked.

'No,' he answered.

'It's a good game. You'll like it,' Casimir said.

It did not take long to reach the woods, and it took even less time to find both boys, who had seemingly been bored waiting for Casimir and sat in the long grass, each of them holding a thin blade of green between their thumbs and forefingers, trying to blow on them to make them whistle. Benjamin had tried this before too and could not do it. But his father was good at it and could make a whole song from blowing on that grass.

The boys looked up and raised their eyebrows in question at Casimir.

'You know Benjamin,' Casimir said. 'He's come to play with us.'

The boys grinned and threw their blades of grass on the ground, stood and dusted the back of their trousers.

'Good!' Filip said. 'That's good, Benjamin. Tell you what. You go hide, run into the woods and wait. We'll count and we'll come and find you. We'll count to one hundred, okay? Give you lots of time to find a good place to hide.'

'What if you can't find me?' Benjamin asked, looking at the dense, dark woods in front of him.

'We'll find you!' Casimir smacked Benjamin on the back a little too hard. 'We've been playing this game for years, so we will definitely find you.'

Benjamin looked at his shoes. He could feel the coins in his palm. He was meant to be going to the butcher.

'How long will it take?' he asked.

'I don't know.' Filip sighed, seemingly getting bored now. 'Not long. We'll find you. If you don't want to play, then that's fine. But don't ask to play with us again. This is your chance.'

Benjamin nodded. This was his chance to have some friends. He wanted them to like him, he wanted to race around the village with them in the summer, he wanted to throw snowballs and go sledding with them in the winter.

'Okay,' he said and walked into the woods, telling himself that even though he would be late home, his mother would be so proud of him for finally making friends.

The woods were not a place that Benjamin had investigated before. The trees seemed to be packed tightly together, their roots all intertwined so that he found it hard to navigate the dank ground.

Rustling of leaves, both above and below, made him shiver. What was running around on that ground? What was up there in the branches?

He kept walking; not far, not too far, he told himself, and he found a spiky bush that he did not know the name of, but he knew if he touched it the sharp leaves would prick at his skin.

He sat behind the bush, leaving one leg straight out so that they were able to see his brown shoe, at least – it would certainly make them find him more quickly.

He tried, as he waited, to count to 100, but he soon lost his place at forty-five and started again. By the third time he had tried to count that high, he was sure that 100 seconds had passed, but no one came. They would come, though. Filip had said that they would.

He tried maybe three or four more times to count to 100 and decided that perhaps he had hidden too well and that he should walk back a little to see if they were nearby.

He left the prickly bush and retraced his steps; at least, he thought he did, but after a few minutes, the woods were not getting thinner. If anything, they were getting darker. Where was the field?

Benjamin started to panic. He had been gone too long. His mother would be wondering where he was and soon it would get dark, and he wouldn't be able to find his way home in the dark.

'Casimir?' Benjamin shouted into the woods. 'Filip? Borys?'

His voice came back to him. 'Please. I'm here!' Benjamin shouted, crying now. 'Please. You said you'll find me! I'm here! I'm here!'

He didn't know how much time was passing, and he was sure he was getting himself more and more lost the more that he walked. He decided to sit on a log and wait. They would find him if he stayed in one spot.

It was then he realised that his hand was empty. Somewhere along the way he had dropped the coins. His tears came quicker now. His mother would be so angry. His father would have no meat with his dinner. He would be in so much trouble.

He wiped at his face and nose with the back of his hand and tried to stop crying. Only girls cried – that's what his father had said. He needed to stop crying about everything. But the more he tried to stop the tears, the faster they came until soon he was hiccupping with sorrow.

Strands of light that had once shone on small patches of the forest floor started to wane. He looked up to try to see the sky through the branches of trees that met and almost touched each other. The day was ending – night would soon settle in, and yet still he waited.

* * *

Now, in the forest, alone again, no longer a boy but a man, Benjamin felt the fear, the anxiety, the worry he had felt all those years ago, sitting on that log simply waiting for someone to find him.

No one had come for him – not until the next morning, when his mother and father found him, curled up on the forest floor, shivering and crying still.

'Matka.' Benjamin had let her take him into her arms, hold him tight. 'I lost the money,' he had sobbed into her chest.

'There's no need for tears,' his father had said, standing behind his mother. 'There's no need to cry.'

Benjamin found out later that Casimir and the other boys had admitted to his mother, and to the policeman, where Benjamin could possibly be found when he had not returned home. They had said that they had searched for him but could not find him and assumed that he had gone home or to the butcher.

Benjamin was sure that they had not looked for him, but he so wanted to be friends with those boys that he had not told his parents his fears. Instead, he had said it had been his fault – he had hidden too well, gone too far into the woods.

His father believed him. His mother, not so much. Night after night, Benjamin would scream himself awake, still thinking that he was in the woods, the night too close around him so that he could not even see his hand in front of his face. After that, his mother would have to leave a candle burning so that when he woke from his nightmares, he would see a light and know that all was well.

There was no light in these woods now though. He knew, as he walked into the darkened depths of the trees, that this time, no one would find him. There was no point waiting. No one was looking for him this time.

## 28

*Autumn, 1969*
*Parczew Forest, Lublin Voivodeship, Poland*
*Benjamin*

Benjamin wiped a tear away. 'I kept walking, trying to follow the map that Bartok gave us. But I went wrong somehow. And I found the stream, this stream, and drank from it and sat down and just waited then for death because I knew I wouldn't be able to find Bartok. I didn't think you would find me. So I just sat and waited. And you know, Ania, when I made that decision, I wasn't scared any more. It was fine. It was over so I didn't need to be scared any more.'

'I'm so glad I found you, Benj,' she said. 'You were so close to Bartok. So close. If you'd carried on, you would have found him.'

'Sometimes, I wish you hadn't found me though, Ania. Not now we know what came next. If you hadn't found me, I would have died, probably. And maybe you would have found a new family to help.'

'But you are my family,' she said. 'Remember that I always told you, you are my family, Benj.'

'And you mine,' Benjamin told her.

A wind blew as if from nowhere, making some of the dried leaves dance. He watched them for a moment, recalling another wind that came. A fresh wind that should have been the sign of the beginning of the change in the season, of freshness, of rebirth. Instead, it brought something else.

'The wind came that day,' Ania said. 'It came for me.'

Benjamin nodded and let her tell the rest of the story – the story that was nearly over now. It was almost complete.

## 29

## THE FOUR ARE REUNITED

*25 February 1943*
*Parczew Forest*
*Ania*

We'd spent over a week searching for Benj near the house. As soon as it was safe to do so, we'd gone back, looked for him and found him gone.

Wanda cried. Blamed herself.

'He's gone to Bartok,' I said.

'How do you know that?' Aleksi asked.

'I knew he wanted to go. He really did. I caught him, that night after Bartok left, looking at the map, trying to memorise it, talking to himself about how he could do it alone, that he wanted to be safe. I didn't let him know that I had heard him. I didn't think that he would ever try to do it alone. But then, if he had no choice, that's where I think he went.'

'Unless they found him? The police? Unless they have him,' Wanda said.

I shook my head. I did not want to think about that. 'Even if that happened, even if it has happened, we still need Bartok. He will be able to help us. He will know – or at least find out.' I swallowed. My mouth was suddenly dry.

We set out, walking back to the Parczew forests. I knew the way. I had memorised Bartok's directions just in case.

We reached Bartok, tired, blistered. My hand throbbed where a thorn had ripped through the skin a week ago, and it would not heal. Now it oozed and made the hand twice the size of the other.

'Who goes there?' an invisible voice yelled out suddenly. Aleksi looked about, trying to find the owner.

'Ania,' I said. 'I'm here to see Bartok Nowak.'

A face appeared out of the trees, streaked with dirt so that I could not tell how young or old the man was.

His body came next. He wore, oddly, leather brown shoes – brogues – a pair of grey trousers, a shirt, even a tie, and a matching jacket, as if he had been studying something in the library. His hands were as dirty as his face.

He sniffed, and kept a large rifle pointed at us.

'You. Drop it,' he told Aleksi, who had his own gun in his hands.

Aleksi placed it on the ground.

'Hands up,' he said.

We did as he asked.

Then he made us walk in file, with him stood behind us, me at the rear, the muzzle of the gun digging into my back.

Soon, there were more faces, women and children, more men, more guns.

'Ania.' Bartok walked up to us. 'Drop the gun, Jakub,' Bartok said. 'Go back to your post.'

Jakub complied and disappeared back through the forest.

Bartok smiled. 'I honestly didn't think you would come. You, you must be the *Ruski*, and you – sorry, I forget your name?'

'Wanda,' she replied.

Bartok looked behind us. 'Where's Benjamin? Oh God.' He rubbed his palm over his face. 'Don't tell me. Please.'

'We had hoped he would be here, that he was coming here,' I said. I was back to talking like a child. Words spilled out. I gave a rambling account of what had happened, desperate for Bartok to fix this – to know where Benj could be.

'You sure he would have tried to come here?' he asked when I had finished.

'I think so,' I said.

'All right.' Bartok turned to the faces that had gotten closer and closer to us as I had recounted our sorry tale. 'Levi, Marcin, Adam,' Bartok barked. One man stepped forward, glasses sliding down his nose, flanked by two younger men, or even boys. But I knew the man's face.

'You're the girl from Majdanek?' Then he laughed. 'This is her. This is the girl from Majdanek. These two too – these are the ones that saved us!'

A cheer of sorts erupted from a few people. Then, 'Thank you, thank you.' Hands grabbed mine, shaking them; a woman gave me a hug.

'Time for that later. Levi, go west, Marcin and Adam east. Me and the *Ruski*—'

'Aleksi,' Aleksi said.

'Right. Yes. Aleksi and I will go north. Małgośka and Ryszard south.'

'And who will Wanda and I go with?' I asked.

'I think you should stay here. You' – he pointed at me – 'do not look well. Pale. Too pale.'

I felt the throb of my hand. 'I want to go,' I said, not breaking eye contact.

'Fine. You want to come too?'

Wanda looked at me, at Aleksi. 'Can I stay? I need to sit.'

Wanda did not look well either. She had lost weight; her cheekbones were too sharp and her eyes were bigger, yet sunk back in her skull.

'Here, you come here with me.' A woman stepped forward, her dark hair shorn close to her scalp. 'You come with me. By the fire. Get you warm, get you fed.'

Wanda kissed Aleksi on his cheek, then did the same to me. 'Be safe,' she said, her voice tired.

'I'm coming with you,' I told Bartok and stepped out to walk in front of him.

'Do you know where you're going?' Bartok asked.

'No. But I'll find my way.'

'Ania. I know the way. Let me help you; let me lead for a moment. You and Aleksi stick behind. Aleksi, keep an eye out.'

Bartok led us down a steep slope, where at the bottom was a narrow lake. The afternoon sun shone, making the rays dance on the water as it rippled under a light breeze that blew. On the other side of the lake, a deer drank from the shallows, its antlers proud and strong.

If it had been any other time in life, this scene would have been beautiful. I would have wanted to stare at it – a new place I had never been. I would have wanted to name all the plants, telling anyone who would listen their Latin names.

'We're growing,' Bartok said as we walked. 'Every day, new people. Some of those that you set free came to us. Some stayed a few days then went on to another group – a mostly Jewish group.'

'What is your group?' Aleksi asked.

'Ours – well, we don't have a name. It's a mix. Jews, Poles, couple of *Ruskis* too,' he said.

Thankfully, Aleksi laughed.

'It's getting harder though. There's fighting amongst groups; all of us looking for food to survive causes tensions to flare. That and some of the Poles don't like the Jews and vice versa. It's a minefield. Russians are all right, as long as we stay away. Not so good at sharing.'

I listened as Bartok outlined the complicated relationships between the groups – some notifying the police and SS where to find other groups, some stealing from each other.

I stopped walking. 'What's the point?' I asked. My hand throbbed. My head too. I felt hot. 'I mean, you're all fighting against the same enemy so why turn on each other?'

Bartok looked at me and shrugged. 'Life goes on. People forget. People are desperate. It's like at first, we are all in it together, but then human nature prevails. Power grabs, relationships change, past hatred resurfaces – it's just the way it is.'

'Are you all right?' Aleksi took my arm. 'Walk with me.'

I carried on walking, for how long I do not know. Every step felt painful, all over my body; even my eyes ached. Infection. I knew what it was. I knew as soon as the cut did not heal what could happen. Infection. Gets into the blood. Can cause sepsis. Death.

It was in the blood. I knew it.

'There!' Bartok ran ahead, and Aleksi followed. I willed my legs to carry on, to run, to see if it was Benj, but it was as though they were filled with lead.

'Ania!' I heard his voice.

'Benj!' I shouted back.

Finally, my legs moved a bit quicker, then a bit more. And

there was Benj. Stood next to Aleksi and Bartok, a lopsided grin on his face.

'You found me.'

I knew I smiled. I knew I fell into his arms. But after that, blackness enveloped me.

\* \* \*

I woke to the wind. An easterly wind that brought with it the promise of spring. It woke me, whispering in my ear, lifting strands of hair from my face and playing with them.

I lay where I was and looked above me at the canopy of trees, light streaming through the branches, and let the wind in. I could not control it – not with all the will in the world. I knew it was bringing a change – I just didn't know what.

The rustle of leaves, the coo of a pigeon, the flap of wings. I watched and waited. The wind tickled at my toes, then my legs. Soon, it found my hand that still throbbed, but there was something covering the skin so that the breeze could not get to it.

Suddenly, from nowhere, a dog barked. I heard it, I knew I did.

'Ania!'

Benj's voice was in my ear. I was being lifted, carried. Benj breathed heavily, wheezing with my weight. We were going downhill.

'Let me help!' Aleksi said.

'No,' Benj huffed.

I continued to watch the sky, watch the powder puff clouds scuttle across the blue. I watched the branches bow and scrape to the wind, giving in to it.

I exhaled heavily. I was ready to give in too.

More voices, yelling. I could hear them. The pop, pop of gun fire. Bartok telling everyone to keep going.

Benj carried me and never once stopped.

Time stopped having any meaning. All I knew was that I was being carried and I was safe.

* * *

'Ania.' I opened my eyes. The sky was still blue; the wind was worse now, whipping the trees as if it no longer wanted them to be there.

'What happened?' I croaked and tried to sit up, but I found that I could not.

I felt a hand under my head, gently, ever so gently, sitting me up, leaning me against a tree trunk.

'Benj,' I said and smiled. I held out my hand to him and he placed it on his cheek. 'I found you, Benj.'

'You did,' he said, then wiped at his eyes.

'Why are you crying, Benj? What's wrong?'

'You're not well, Ania. You fainted and I carried you back to the camp. And then you slept and we looked at your hand and Wanda tried to wrap it in something. Then, the next morning, some police came with dogs and we had to run. You slept again. I thought you wouldn't wake up. But you have,' he said and wiped his face again. 'You woke up.'

Wanda and Aleksi came into view, both of them smiling at me in a strange way. I was too tired to try to understand their expressions, so I just smiled back.

'Where are we now?' I tried to turn my head left and right, but the pain was too much.

'A new place, but only for a few hours. Bartok is making us move on again.'

'Good,' I said, 'that's good,' even though I wasn't sure what was good or not.

Wanda gave me water to drink and tried to feed me a soup, but it would not settle in my stomach and came straight back up.

'I don't feel well, Wanda,' I told her.

'I know, darling.' She sat next to me, stroked my hair. 'It's all right. I'm here, we're here.'

I was in and out of consciousness all morning. The next time I was fully awake, it was just me and Benj. He sat crying, big ugly sobs that made his whole body shake.

'Benj,' I said. 'I'll be fine, Benj. We'll be fine.' I raised my hand to try to touch him, when the wind caught the red ribbon, making it flutter. 'See, Benj, it kept me safe.'

He looked at the ribbon. 'I think I lost mine,' he whimpered.

With slow fingers, I untied the ribbon. 'Here, take this.'

'No, Ania. No. You need it,' he said.

'No, I don't. I don't need it any more. I have you, Benj. You'll wear it and you'll keep me safe.'

It took some cajoling, but eventually he took it and tied it around his own wrist.

'It's time.' Bartok appeared and grinned at me. 'You're a fighter, aren't you?'

'I hope so.'

'It's 10.45. We need to move on, get to the next spot by two, give us enough time to set up something for the night and for the scouts to go out and see what they can find in the villages.'

Benj started to lift me from my spot on the leaf-strewn ground when gun fire echoed through the trees. In surprise, Benj dropped me.

'Ania!'

'Move!' Bartok yelled.

Feet rushed past me, then Aleksi was there, trying to sit me up, but the pain in my head was worse, my back. I cried out for him to stop.

'We have to pick you up!' he yelled. 'We have to.'

'Please stop!' The pain – God, it was everywhere.

Benj picked me up and began to walk. Each step he took I felt pain shoot its way through my body.

I could hear Wanda and Aleksi. 'They're close! We need to be quicker. Benj, give her to me!'

'I can do it,' he grunted.

'Benjamin! Come on!' Aleksi screamed at him, then stopped and more gun fire rang out.

'I can't keep them back for much longer!' Aleksi yelled.

I could hear the yells from the police, telling them to stop, that we had no chance.

We did.

I rolled out of Benj's arms and hit the ground with a thud.

'Give me the gun,' I told Aleksi. 'Give it to me. I'll lie here, look dead. When they get close, I'll shoot them. It will give you time to get away.'

'We can't leave you, Ania!' Benj cried.

'You'll come back for me. I'll still be here.'

Wanda bent down, looked at my hand, then looked into my eyes. 'Aleksi, give her the gun,' she said.

'Wanda, no!'

'Do it,' she commanded. 'She's right. She'll still be here.'

Aleksi handed me the gun. I wasn't sure if I had enough strength to pull the trigger, but I would try.

I lay on my back, the gun next to me, and stared at the sky, the trees, let the wind whip up its stories.

'Ania.' Benj's face was in front of me.

'Go now. Come back later.'

'I love you, Ania.'

'I love you too, Benj.'

Aleksi kissed my forehead, then he was gone. Then it was Wanda. 'Sleep now, sweet girl. Go and find your mother. She's waiting now.'

She stroked my hair, then disappeared too.

I was alone.

I waited. Stayed still and watched the sky shift from blue to white clouds, then back to blue. Blue. I'd always liked blue, I thought. And green. Green was good.

*Red apple.*

*Red door.*

*Red coat.*

*Red dress.*

*Gosia.*

*Basia.*

*Tata.*

*Benj.*

*Aleksi.*

*Wanda.*

'Another dead one – where the fuck did the others go? Over there! Look – down near those trees!' The voice was above me; I could not see them.

I reached for the gun, then with one last burst of energy, I shot at the air around me, hearing the scream, the thud. I fired and fired until there was one bullet left.

Then I smelled him. Pigs' fat. Krzysztof. He stood above me, blood dripping from his face where one of my bullets had nicked his ear. I smiled at him.

I raised the gun. Smiled again. He mirrored me. My gun on him, his on me.

It took one last shot. Into my heart. I had a second before my brain stopped. One second. And I heard just one word before the scream from Krzysztof's lips.

*Szalony.*

# 30

## THE FINAL GOODBYE

*26 February 1943*
*Parczew Forest*
*Ania*

I died at 11.05. Isn't that strange. That same time that was on the grandfather clock in my uncle's barn. The clock that had once been my mother's.

I stayed around a while before I left. I saw Benj come back for me, Aleksi, Wanda, Bartok. Others came, all of them looking at me.

Benj wept, then picked me up and carried me.

Others told him that I should just be buried there, where I had died. But Benj was having none of it. He wanted to take me somewhere he would always remember, he said.

I think he made them all walk for a whole day. No one complained. He wanted it near a village, somewhere he could easily find.

Bartok said he knew just the place – said that below, in the valley, you could hear church bells call out. They thought I would like that – the bells.

Levi was there with his camera, and he let Benj take the photograph of me.

Benj had found his ribbon in his pocket and gave me mine back. Then he howled with pain, sobbing on the ground that it was all his fault, that he should not have taken my red ribbon from me.

Wanda was strong, held on to Benj, gulped back tears. I knew she was sad, but she had seen this coming from the day she'd first looked into the fire, I was sure.

Bartok cried too. He tried not to. Gulped a lot, making his Adam's apple bob. His jaw was set hard and when people talked to him, he could not answer, only grunt.

I wished I could tell them not to cry for me, not to mourn. Perhaps one day Benj would hear my voice, just as he had Gosia's. Maybe one day I could speak to my friends again.

People said nice things. I was brave. Fearless. *Szalony*, Bartok said, but he said it with laughter in his voice, so I did not mind too much.

Benj tried to speak as they closed this makeshift coffin from foraged pieces of wood. He couldn't though. He couldn't get the words out.

Wanda spoke for him. 'Our dear Ania. Our darling girl. We loved her and we know she loved us. She wanted to make others pay the price for what they are doing to us, for what they have done. And she did it in such a way that sent SS looking for her, the police. She was whispered about, talked of as this woman who had no fear and should be feared. She saved us, more than once. And I don't think we ever said thank you. So thank you, dear Ania. Thank you for being you. Unique. We would not be here without you.'

They left after some time. Leaving me alone, in the dark. It would be a few years until Benj would find me again, find me and hear my voice that whispered through the trees, down into the valley, whipping up the hemlock that grew on the banks of lakes and rivers and returned to the trees, waiting patiently for him to come, to hear me again. To find me and help me rest.

## 31

## LIFE WITHOUT ANIA

*5 March 1943*
*Łąki, Lublin Voivodeship, Poland*
*Benjamin*

He knew where to go, and although he knew it was not the safest of places to stay, it was the only place that he could think of in that moment, and he told himself that it was Ania who was guiding him there.

He left with a bag of food that Bartok had given him, and a map that he knew he could follow. Aleksi had tried to give him a gun, but he had refused. He had seen enough death.

Wanda wanted to go with him, and Aleksi said he could come too. But the dream he had once had of all of them together at the farm would not work without Ania. And for once in his life, he wanted to be alone, not fearing it any more.

Three miles from Ania's farm, Benj slept in a field, close to a hedge that rustled with inhabitants all night. When he woke, he found that his face was wet. He wiped it with his palm and looked above him, expecting to see droplets of water falling. Instead, he was met with a black wet nose and panting tongue.

He scrambled up, resting his back against the hedge as his new friend tilted his head from side to side as he stared at him.

'I'm Benjamin,' he told the dog.

The dog wagged its tail. It was blonde, as blonde as he had ever seen a dog, and its tongue was as pink as he had ever seen pink too.

The dog took a step closer to him and Benjamin held out his hand. The dog sniffed it then licked it, allowing Benjamin to then stroke the dirty wet coat. But the dog's tail did not stop wagging.

He looked for a brief moment underneath and saw that the dog was not a he but a she. He stroked her, felt her ribs, each one a ripple under his hand. She was hungry.

'I don't have any food,' he told her.

She licked his face.

'I'm going home, to a farm. Do you want to come?'

The dog whined.

Benjamin, unsure as to whether the dog would follow him, tied around her neck a strip of his shirt that he had torn away. After a few steps, he soon realised that there was no need to have done this. She walked by his side, eagerly looking up at him, grinning almost, and he knew that she would not leave him.

'I need to give you a name,' he told her. 'What name would you like?'

The dog looked at him, then tilted its head again as it considered the choices that Benjamin gave her. Finally, he said, 'Ania,' and the dog barked. Ania it was.

He truly came to believe that Ania had sent him the dog somehow. He talked to her as he had Ania, and found that not only was he not afraid of being alone, but he wasn't afraid of anything any more.

He would imagine Ania telling him that he was brave, that he was smarter than he thought. He imagined her telling him how he was good at hiding and should make some hiding spots when he reached the farm.

It was inevitable he would have to bury Ania's father and sister after burying Ania herself. They all had to return to the ground; that's what the Rabbi had always said – that everyone must return to the ground. He found them where Ania and he had left them. He did not cry when he looked at them; he did what he needed to do.

He took his time. Digging at the soft earth bit by bit, listening to how the shovel bit into the soil, shearing it away. Eventually, it was time to put the bodies into the holes he had made. There wasn't much left of them. The slippery bodies went into each hole, and he covered them quickly as flies buzzed around.

Each day he spoke to the dog, to Ania, and asked her what he should do. She told him to create a hiding spot in one of the fields – a bunker that he could get to. She told him not to eat raw potatoes as they would send your stomach bad. She told him not to light fires at night, to keep his belongings close to him when he slept in case he had to run.

She told him how to string cans and broken glass on wire and attach it to the doors so he could hear if someone tried to open it. She told him how to steal food from other farms – a chicken, eggs, vegetables. He did it all, and did it well, because he believed that it wasn't really him with these ideas, it was Ania.

When the war ended, Benjamin tried to make a life for himself at the farm, but then a new war came. There was nowhere to go after the Russians came and took the farm from him. There was no one to care for him in those first few years, so he spent them living on the streets, a disfigured man begging for money and food. He would look at faces as they passed him, hoping perhaps to see Aleksi or Wanda. He couldn't imagine that Aleksi was happy with what was happening and wondered if they were still in the forests – maybe they had made a life together, in amongst the trees, away from it all.

But then one day, he came across a man called Isaac. A thin man with a heavy brow, bushy eyebrows and white hair. This man walked past Benjamin on a cool autumn morning, limping with his left leg, his right hand trembling constantly.

'You're hungry,' the man said.

'I am,' Benjamin agreed.

'You're not from here, are you?'

Benjamin shook his head. 'I was at the farm. A friend's farm and then they took it.'

The man nodded. 'Isaac.' He stuck out his tremoring hand for Benjamin to take. 'It's okay, you can take it. It just does this sometimes. I can't stop it.'

Benjamin took Isaac's hand in his, then Isaac did something most unexpected; he sat on the cold dirty ground next to Benjamin and stretched out his legs in front of him.

'Where did you spend it?' Isaac asked.

'Spend what?'

'The war – which camp?'

Benjamin shook his head. 'I wasn't in a camp. I was with friends.'

'And your friends are gone?'

'All of them,' he said.

'But you have a dog, I see.' Isaac patted Ania on the head.

Benjamin half smiled. 'She's a good girl,' he said. Then, 'Where did you spend the war?'

'Auschwitz,' Isaac said. 'Took me, my wife, my daughter...' Then he stopped and shook his head, raised a hand and wiped his eyes. 'There's just me left.'

'You came home,' Benjamin said.

'I did,' Isaac replied. 'There was nowhere else for me to go.'

'I couldn't go home,' Benjamin said. 'I don't know where it is any more.'

Isaac stood and held his shaking hand out to Benjamin once more. Benjamin took it, confused, and shook it again.

'No. No,' Isaac said. 'Stand up. Let me help you.'

Benjamin stood and Ania licked at his hand.

'You can stay with me for a while. There isn't much I can offer but you'll be off the street at least – somewhere warm.'

Benjamin liked this Isaac. He felt he could accept the offer and followed Isaac to his house that sat just outside the village, all alone as if it had appeared by magic one day. It had a green door; the paint was peeling, but it was a green he decided he liked.

Isaac opened the door and gestured for Benjamin to go inside. That was when Benjamin saw it. A flash of red on Isaac's wrist.

He grabbed his arm too roughly, making Isaac jump back.

'No. No,' Benjamin said. 'Look.' He rolled up his sleeve and showed Isaac a matching ribbon.

Isaac did not speak for a moment. Then said, 'I knew a girl once. Ania. A genius, but everyone called her *szalony*. She wore ribbons on her wrist. Red ones. She believed that they warded off evil spirits – an old wives' tale. She left me one. I took it when I went to Warsaw. I wore it. My wife thought I was mad. I didn't care. I liked it. It made me think of her.'

'My friend was Ania too,' Benjamin said.

'You know, this was the only thing I managed to keep in the camp. I hid it under my cap, in a pocket. I even put it under a loose floorboard to keep it safe.'

'Ania,' Benj said.

'Ania.' Isaac grinned.

The dog, Ania, barked at hearing her name.

**32**

---

*Autumn, 1969*
*Parczew Forest, Lublin Voivodeship, Poland*
*Benjamin*

'You told it differently this time,' he said. 'Some things are different,' Benjamin told the ground.

There was no answer from her grave, just as he knew there wouldn't be.

The light was starting to wane; the pigeons cooed their night-time calls from their nests; rustling seemed to come from all around. He needed to leave. Soon, it would be dark and Benjamin recently had started to fear the dark again.

'Did it really happen that way, Ania? Is that what really happened? Did we get revenge? Did it make things better?' he asked as he rose slowly, painfully, then leaned against the tree.

Still there was no answer.

He knew she wouldn't talk again – not today, at least. To him, this time the story had made sense. It suited her, this life. He knew though that he would come back again and listen to her and that things might shift a little here and there. But overall, he thought it was right, he thought it was true.

'I have to go now, Ania,' he told her. 'I have to go but I think we got it right this time. It's better this time – better but not right for you. No. Still not right. You shouldn't have died. It should have been me, but I can't change that part – neither can you, can you?'

Stupidly, he waited, wondering if time, the past, would change itself and Ania would be stood in front of him, alive, and things would have turned out better – turned out the right way.

'I'll go now,' he said. 'I'll see you again next year.'

As he walked away, he wondered whether he should write a few things down himself. His memory was notoriously bad, and it wouldn't hurt, he supposed. He had written things down after the war – Isaac had helped him as he wrote his own story too.

'People have to know about what happened,' Isaac had said. 'We have to leave a piece of us behind.'

But now, Isaac was gone, Benj was alone, and Isaac's story sat an unhappy, dusty pile of papers on top of Benj's wardrobe. Had he, Benjamin, left enough of a piece of himself behind in those scratchings made years ago? Probably not – certainly not a large enough piece of Ania's story.

He would write more, he decided. He would take the bus home and start writing things down this very evening before he forgot. And he would come back next year and read out what he had written and see if she agreed with his version of events – whether she agreed with this picture of her life that he had reimagined.

Perhaps then it would all be over. Perhaps then her story would be complete.

As he walked and planned what he would do, the wind called from the east, whispering secrets and making the red ribbon on his wrist flutter. It was not strong yet, but would get stronger. Soon it would send dogs barking, knock on windows and beg to be let in. The ribbon fluttered again. Benjamin placed his hand over it.

'Not yet,' he whispered to the wind. 'Soon. But not yet.'

# POSTSCRIPT

**Parczew C**

Monday, June 15, 1970

## Appeal for information

On Sunday afternoon the body of an unidentified male was found in the Parczew forest area, Lublin. The male, approximately 80 years old, was found holding a photograph and a red ribbon. Police are asking for anyone who has any information to contact them immediately.

Rep
foll
imp

The
that

# The Oxford

Monday 18 1983

## Record breaking sale of WW

The notes and diaries of Benjamin Herchell sold for a record price of £45,000, at Rosebury's Oxford, today. The notes and diaries were purchased by renowned author, Cilka Shaw Crosby, who has written extensively on the subject of WWII partisans. 'I started this project back in 1968, seeking out hidden voices that were often marginalised during the war. It was a difficult subject to explore – these people sidelined and often shunned by their own communities prior to the war, found themselves once again shunned as war broke out, leaving them with no option but to band together as one,' she said. Herchell's diaries are childlike in nature, and fragmented with one wondering what is true and what is not. 'I believe there are hidden truths in these pages,' Crosby maintained. 'I hope that I am able to piece together his story as well as those he so lovingly wrote about in his diaries.'

Rep
foll
imp

The
that
rela
the
beh
of a
exp
in h
its
beh
con
or v

It m
lots

# Oxford Mai

Monday, May 20, 2024

## Sale of CW Crosby's book

The rights for the fictionalised history of Benjamin Herchell by the author Cilka Shaw Crosby were sold today to Big Three publishing house for a record breaking six figure sum, a bittersweet victory for Shaw who died two days prior to the rights being sold. Whilst historians have debunked the stories of Herchell,

Ania Sobolewska and others documented in Herchell's diaries, Crosby maintained that the voices within the historical novel were still ones that needed to be heard. 'Are we not, all of us, trying to add to the historical record rather than detract from it?' Crosby was once quoted as saying.

Rep
foll
imp

The
that
rela
the
beh
of a
exp
in h
its
beh

# ACKNOWLEDGEMENTS

I would firstly like to thank my agent, Jo Bell, who encouraged me to pitch this idea to my wonderful editor, Isobel Akenhead, even though I wasn't entirely sure what story was going to come from it!

You see, it all began way back (the early nineties) when as a child I would look at photographs at my grandparents' house. It was a morbid tradition of the Polish side of the family to take pictures of the dead in their casket (I have no idea why but there we are). Rather than being scared of these dead relatives, I became a little obsessed with looking at them, and one in particular – a distant cousin who died young, small for her age, and was, and I quote, 'a genius bordering on madness'.

Fast forward some thirty years, and the image of her had still not left me, so on a whim, I mentioned it to my agent, who said, 'Ooh, I love this idea,' and sent me off to think about what a young woman, who was sidelined by society, would, or *could*, do during the war. As she became real to me, I found that she needed friends, but not just any friends – friends who were also outcasts who had their own stories to tell.

And so, here we now are, dear reader, with you finishing this book and probably wondering what is real and what is not. Was that my intention, I hear you ask? Perhaps so. I mean, memories are fragmented, history handed to us in the form of stories as we grow, so I think we need to sit and think a while about what we have read, whether it is true, whether it is false, and I suppose whether it matters in the slightest! At the end of the day, just like Cilka Shaw Crosby said, 'Are we not, all of us, even within fiction, trying to add to the historical record rather than detract from it?'

I shall not ramble much more. I have, after all, just written a book and I am running low on words. So I shall get to the others that I must thank. Michal Rodzynski, who still graciously lets me ask him for translations and Polish traditions that I do not know of (the red ribbons was genius, by the way!). A thank you to my dogs, who put up with going for walks at strange times because I am still awake in the wee hours of the morning. Big thanks to family and friends, who once more have put up with me cancelling plans at the last minute because I decided to delete half a novel and then had to write for twenty hours straight to fix the problem!

And finally, to you, dear reader. You may not have liked this book, you may have loved it, but either way, you picked it up, took it for a spin, and essentially allowed me to continue being an author, which is an absolute honour. So thank you again.

# ABOUT THE AUTHOR

**Carly Schabowski** is a lecturer and the USA Today bestselling author of historical fiction, including The Rainbow. Previously published by Bookouture, The Girl with the Red Ribbon is Carly's new WWII historical novel published by Boldwood Books.

Sign up to Carly Schabowski's mailing list here for news, competitions and updates on future books.

Follow Carly Schabowski on social media:

facebook.com/carly.schabowski
instagram.com/carlyschabowskiauthor

# BIBLIOGRAPHY

Cienciala, A. M., 'Poles and Jews Under German and Soviet Occupation, September 1, 1939–JUNE 22, 1941', *The Polish Review*, 46(4), 391–402, (2001), http://www.jstor.org/stable/25779290

Frankel, Rebecca, *Into the Forest: A Holocaust Story of Survival, Triumph, and Love* (New York, 2021)

Holocaust Encyclopaedia, https://encyclopedia.ushmm.org/content/en/arti cle/lublin-majdanek-concentration-camp-conditions

Jaffe, J., 'Holocaust Resistance: Life of Jewish Partisans in the Forest', Jewish Virtual Library (1951), https://www.jewishvirtuallibrary.org/life-of-jewish-partisans-in-the-forest

Mirsky, M., 'She spent the war in hiding, from a forest bunker to a haystack', The Jewish News of Northern California (2020), https://jweekly.com/2020/03/ 19/she-spent-the-war-in-hiding-from-a-forest-bunker-to-a-haystack/

Sanders, Katie and Truslow, Mara, 'The surprising ways 3 women secretly fought the Nazis in Poland', Business Insider (2021), https://www.businessin sider.com/surprising-ways-3-women-secretly-fought-the-nazis-in-poland-2021-4

State Museum of Majdanek: (1941–1944), https://www.majdanek.eu/en

Tec, Nechama, *Resistance: Jews and Christians Who Defied the Nazi Terror* (Oxford, 2013)

Williamson, David G., *The Polish Underground 1939–1947 (Campaign Chronicles)* (Barnsley, 2012)

Made in the USA
Middletown, DE
07 November 2024

64098979R00175